Hearts On The Wind

Sycamore Wilde

∽ℭ∾

Donna & Steve,
Thank you for
your encouragement.

S. Wilde

(Jerry England)
Silva Cotoff.

Dedication

To my Mother
for her continual encouragement and support
in all that I do.

To Judith
for watering my garden of ideas with inspiration.

Chapter One

❦

LAINA MAKGREGOR BRUSHED BACK a few loose strands of silky dark hair and let out an anxious sigh as she moved quickly down the dirt path, her clear turquoise eyes scanning the ground with the intent focus of a gray spotted falcon. This stretch of the lane was packed hard. The scattering of ruddy pebbles remained undisturbed by the light, purposeful steps of her worn leather shoes, yet her gaze touched every stone. She knew her search would be more difficult in the thick growth of grass ahead.

The sound of angry voices reached her ears even before she rounded the corner of the candlemaker's workshop and entered the small village green. With a quick upward glance, she took in the scene in front of her. Two dozen people stood in the clearing, facing the low stone platform where the bellringer occasionally summoned villagers for important news, although there had been no such summons this day. All eyes were on old Ingram Moffat, the village blacksmith, who faced four men — all strangers. The smithy rubbed his bristly jaw and glared suspiciously through narrowed eyes, as he often did, even with those he knew.

Winding her way slowly through the group of bodies assembled, Laina remained focused on the tangle of grass at her feet. The autumn breeze taunted her, sending tendrils of hair across her eyes, obscuring her vision. She brushed them away impatiently, and held them aside with one hand against her smooth cheek.

From the direction of the platform, a stranger's deep voice sailed strongly against the wind. "I told you, I'm willing to pay you more than the horse is worth. I don't have time to haggle over it."

Laina looked up.

"And I told you," the blacksmith said, pointing a thick, sooty finger at the younger man, "I won't be rushed into selling me horse to a stranger."

A swell of murmuring arose from the crowd of onlookers.

"What difference does it make?" the fair-haired stranger asked, his handsome features contorting with annoyance. He folded his arms across his chest, and stood confidently with his feet apart. His black snug-fitting trousers and knee-high leather boots revealed his lean, muscular legs, while the brilliant blue of his doublet over a white linen shirt set off the blonde hair that fell to his shoulders.

Laina lightly touched the place at her neck where a leather cord usually hung. She visualized the green and brown speckled stone, the last beloved token from her mother. Returning her gaze to the ground, her mind beckoned to any force of nature that might help show her where it lay.

The elderly blacksmith stood motionless, his mouth set in a tight, stubborn line.

The stranger gave a disgusted snort and turned to the crowd. "Does anyone in this village have a horse they will sell to my companions and I without asking a hundred questions?"

"Who ye runnin' from?" a voice in the crowd challenged.

"What's your hurry young man?" another added.

The stranger gave a strained smile, revealing straight white teeth, before hanging his head with a sigh.

Although he believed himself to be a patient man, the last few days had pushed Evan beyond his limit. There were only so many mishaps and delays a man could try to compensate for. He very rarely lost his calm demeanor, but he was dangerously close to losing it now. He raised his head and spoke tightly. "As I have said, perhaps before some of you arrived, my name is Evan Prestwick. My companions and I are musicians with the Westport Musician's Troupe."

Laina had stooped down to investigate an unusual shape in the grass, but found only a stiff, crumpled leaf. She stood up abruptly, frustrated by the commotion and the crowd of people that were making her delicate search all the more difficult. Flipping her long braid behind her shoulder, she took a deep breath and set her hands firmly on her slender hips, eyeing the men on the platform.

Evan continued. "We are to play a very important engagement for Laird Galloway this very eve, but my companion's horse has fallen ill." He gestured to a thin man with wavy brown hair standing next to him. Evan's gaze moved pleadingly across the crowd. "We have lost much time already. We need to get back on the road without further delay."

Laina studied the stranger. He carried himself as someone who could afford fine things, and yet the worn appearance of his clothing suggested a life on the road. The masculine angle of his jaw, along with his handsome features and strong, lean body, surely brought him the attention of many young women, she concluded. His companions were reasonably handsome, as well. It was rare to see a group of such fine men passing through the area.

"Anyone? A horse?" Evan impatiently mocked the lack of response from the crowd, speaking as though he might be addressing half-wits.

Laina narrowed her eyes and twisted the corner of her mouth. He was full of himself all right! What made him think he could come charging into their village and expect someone to sell their horse to him that instant? The villagers had precious few horses among them, as it was.

"Galloway Castle is a half-day's ride from here," someone in the crowd pointed out.

"I know that," Evan snapped, "which is why we don't have time for this."

The blacksmith was pointing his finger again, his eyebrows drawn together and his face puckered up as if he'd just tasted something sour. "So you are wanting to offload your sick horse on us…and take one of our good horses?"

"For God's sake, man," Evan shouted, "I have offered to pay you well for it! What is wrong with you people? Haven't you ever sold a horse before? Hell, I'll even bring the horse back to you afterward. Is that something you can understand?"

Laina curled her lips with disgust. Clearly, he thought he was better than the rest of them, and that his problems were more important than their's. He had no right to yell at these good people whom he didn't even know. They had good reason to be cautious and take their time. Laina turned away to explore another section of grass in the village green, dismissing the stranger with a sniff.

"Here is something for you to understand," the blacksmith said hoarsely, "we won't be doing any trading with ye now or ever!" The old man stepped off the platform and stalked from the clearing. The crowd followed, muttering and casting dark glances back at the musicians.

Evan rubbed his forehead. He had done all he could. The Westport Musicians would not make it to Galloway Castle in time. It would cost them dearly. Not only in coin, but their reputation as well. Surely, some of these very same people had attended the festivals at Galloway Castle. Why were they not more supportive?

As if reading his mind, one of the other musicians spoke. "Some of these small villages are wary of every bird and mouse that crosses their path, Evan. Let it go."

Evan nodded tiredly. His gaze drifted aimlessly across the clearing and fell upon a lass, making sweeping motions in the grass with her outstretched toe as if parting the blades to look between them. The faded green tunic that hung loosely on her slender frame gave her the appearance of a graceful elf wearing a grain sack. She looked to be about sixteen or seventeen summers. A smile came to Evan's lips. With long strides, he crossed the green and stopped in front of her.

Laina looked up, her eyes flickering with suspicion. Her rose-colored lips angled slightly to reveal her unspoken opinion of him. The stranger smiled broadly, evidently thinking he could influence her somehow. She waited, like a cat observing a noisy squirrel.

Evan was briefly stunned by the girl's rare beauty. The contrast of her rich, dark brown hair against her fair, satin-like skin, and her smoothly sculpted features and sparkling blue-green eyes, were a most uncommon sight to see among common villagers, who tended to look a bit dull and worn from their lives of hardship.

Reaching into his pocket, Evan extended his open palm. "Is this what you are looking for, lass?"

With a gasp, Laina snatched the precious stone on the broken cord from his hand. Relief washed over her face as she stared lovingly at the treasure and stroked it. Her voice barely more than a whisper, she asked "How did you…"

Her reaction warmed him.

"I noticed it on the ground when we first arrived," he answered. He watched her for a moment. Her cheeks glowed softly, and when her dark eyelashes finally lifted and she looked up at him, her eyes were deep and clear, like a mountain stream.

Evan explained, "I had intended to hold the necklace up to the crowd, to help find its owner." He paused to roll his eyes and rub the back of his neck, "but the conversation was not going so well." A look of irritation settled onto his handsome face.

Laina gave a small huff of indifference. "You shouldn't have been so rude," she said.

Evan shook his head, frowning. "Lass, my patience has been tested more in the last few days than you can imagine."

The wind stirred, as the pair stood silent, their eyes cool and locked.

"I'm sorry," Evan said at last, "I just expected your village to be more helpful."

He looked tired. Laina almost felt sorry for him. But there was no excuse for him to take out his frustration on her village because of his own bad luck. Perhaps, as a musician, he expected people to fawn over him and cater to his needs. Well, he had come to the wrong village for that. The people of Dounehill didn't fawn over anybody, not even Laird Galloway himself. Nor were they inclined to believe anything they couldn't see for themselves. They worked hard and understood their own worth. They didn't rely on much else.

Closing her fingers around the cool stone in her hand, Laina tipped her chin up slightly and said, "Thank you," and slipped the treasure into the leather pouch hanging from her belt.

"You're welcome, lass" Evan answered, noticing the subtle look of distaste that remained on her otherwise flawless face. She avoided meeting his eyes.

He'd had enough. Turning and walking back to his three companions, he grumbled, "Let's see if we can make it to the next village before Ian's horse dies beneath him."

Ian made a sound of disgust. "I doubt she'll make it another two hundred paces."

"Well, let's at least get her out of sight of this village," Evan urged, "then we'll tie her to a tree and you can ride with Andrew. We don't want to be accused of offloading a sick animal on anyone." He shot an annoyed look toward a cluster of small buildings just beyond the green, then glanced over to see the graceful elf watching him. It was a shame, he thought, that such a spirited beauty was stuck in a village of small minds.

He flashed the girl another smile, despite himself. He couldn't be sure, but he thought he saw her smile in return. Chuckling to himself as he turned away, he entertained a tempting idea: perhaps he would stop back by this god-forsaken village after all, on the return trip home. A chance to see the enchanting lass when he was at his best, while taunting the villagers with his unwelcome presence once more. It sounded like fun.

A smile settled peacefully onto Laina's lips at the thought of having her beloved stone back. She watched the arrogant stranger go and hoped she would never see him again.

Chapter Two

CANDLELIGHT DANCED around the gray stone walls of the small, windowless room, though the day dawned bright outside. Muffled laughter sounded from a shadowy corner, where a giant masculine form towered over a young woman. The man's hands pressed flat on the rough wall's surface on either side of the lass, preventing her escape. Bending down to her neck, he playfully took a generous mouthful of her flesh in his perfect white teeth, and growled.

The girl giggled and tried to squirm away from the handsome, well-muscled man. It was useless. Only her chemise managed to slip free from one pale shoulder. With a chuckle, he slowed his attack, snaking his tongue along the gentle slope of her throat, his breath warm on her skin. A smile slid across her lips and her eyelids floated shut — a throaty moan admitting her surrender.

"I could eat you up, lass," he said, breathing deeply of her then pulling back to meet her eyes.

She looked up at him, her auburn hair tossed loosely about her face and shoulders. Still overwhelmed by his powerful presence, she preferred not to think about who he was. It was much easier to lose herself in his spicy, passionate embrace if she could think of him as a simple, common man. After all, didn't all men speak the same language in bed regardless of their rank outside the bedroom? But, nay, there was nothing common about Laird Gavin Galloway.

He smiled broadly, his green eyes sparkling with mischief and delight. He could read the lass. Despite her fear, her desire burned hot and she wanted the same thing he did. Lord, how he would enjoy giving it to her. Reaching one hand around to firmly grasp her bottom, his other hand deftly pulled aside her low bodice to clutch an ample, round breast.

With a gasp, she averted her eyes and arched toward him.

Laird Galloway's confidence and power were intoxicating. His dark, combed-back hair framed a handsome face, and his well-trimmed mustache and beard surrounded a brilliant, easy smile. His deep emerald eyes could be very inviting if you were in his favor, or most unpleasant if you were not. Standing well over six feet tall, with expansive shoulders, his commanding presence and approachable manner drew the attention of men and women wherever he went. Those who knew him were driven to please him. Those who didn't know him, wanted to. So, it was no surprise that he could have any woman he wanted. And at this moment, he wanted Brigid.

Brigid tipped her head back against the wall. The laird's hands moved skillfully, caressing and exploring. Capturing her mouth aggressively with his, he probed and devoured her as if he owned her. Whatever hesitation might have remained, it completely abandoned Brigid at that moment. It was not that she was concerned about giving herself away — it was too late for her to care about such things. The laird simply had a way of completely disarming and possessing her as no one ever had. Brigid liked to think of herself as in control, giving no more than she wanted to, not to any man. But the truth was, she would give Laird Gavin Galloway anything he wanted. Anything.

Her breath quickened as the laird pressed against her so that she could feel the great hardness of him. Her hands stopped exploring the solid strength of his chest and arms, and moved anxiously to the belt of his bulging breeches.

Across the room, the door to the pantry suddenly burst open and the laird turned from the girl.

A soldier standing in the doorway kept his gaze dutifully fastened on his laird, despite the chambermaid's freely bobbing breast. "M'lord! Here you are."

"What is it?" Gavin asked.

"A visitor, laird," the soldier answered. "Evan Prestwick, of the Westport Musicians. He has just arrived at the front gate and has asked to speak with you."

"He's late," the laird said sourly, "and I'm busy."

Brigid smiled and leaned lazily back against the wall, eager for the laird to return his attentions to her.

"How long shall I tell him to wait?" the soldier asked.

"Until Hell freezes ov..." the laird snapped, then suddenly moved toward the door. "Nevermind, I'll tell him, myself. Tell him to meet me on the west wall."

Covering herself, Brigid stepped forward quickly and whimpered. "M'lord? Cannae ye stay a bit longer?"

"Not now, lass. There's a certain musician I need to set straight." He took a few strides, then over his shoulder he reassured, "I'll call for you later."

Looking from the castle's uppermost west wall, Laird Galloway could see a great distance in all directions. Galloway Castle sat on a large mound amidst gently rolling hills. The wide open territory provided early warning of arrivals, while the bordering forests and river to the southwest provided easy access to fresh game.

To protect the enviable fortress and its location, the castle had been well fortified over the years. The original stone wall surrounding the keep that housed the laird, still stood on the uppermost level of the mound, with guard towers on the four corners. Below that, an immense lower level had been added, fully encircling the upper level and protected by a wall twice as thick and tall as the original. Guard towers stood at the corners and midway along each of the four walls. A wide, deep ditch surrounding the entire castle put invaders to further disadvantage. The only access into the castle was across the drawbridge, which could be raised at the first sign of trouble.

The upper level of the mound contained the laird's three-story keep and great hall, a few out-buildings for the kitchen and brewhouse, as well as a garden, small courtyard, and well-stocked fish pond. The immense lower level housed the servant's quarters, workshops for resident craftsmen, a chapel, animal pens, stable, the main gatehouse with guard rooms, and a huge courtyard for practice maneuvers and festivals. All other goods and services were provided by nearby Galloway Village or through a steady stream of visitors and traders.

The laird turned around just as Evan Prestwick strode up to join him at the wall.

"Where the hell were you?" Gavin roared. "We had an agreement that you were to play for the festival last night!"

Evan kept his voice even and delivered his response with a

smirk. "Well, you see, there was this firey-headed woman in Westport…"

"Bullshit!" the laird retorted.

Evan looked indignant. "Are you saying you don't believe I could have lost track of time in bed with a beautiful woman…"

"I know you," Gavin said. "You would dump a queen on her arse in order not to miss one of your music engagements."

"Well then, you must know I had a very good reason," Evan said coolly, looking out over the landscape.

"What was it?" Gavin demanded, glaring at the musician.

Evan didn't like being put on the spot and explaining himself. He knew his reasons were good; why should he have to explain anything to anyone? He had been unable to make it to the castle as planned despite his best efforts — end of story. But, no, he knew that wouldn't be good enough for the laird. Gavin seemed to expect that everyone had a duty to account to him. The curse of power, Evan thought with annoyance. Well, he certainly wasn't going to give the laird any more information than was necessary, as that would simply give the laird more to dispute. So the musician skipped to the end of the story. "Ian's horse died a half-day's ride from here…"

"He could have shared a horse with one of you," Gavin interrupted.

"He did," Evan said, crossing his arms and facing the laird,"until Andrew turned green and began spewing out of both ends. We had no choice but to stop."

Gavin narrowed his eyes, wanting to disregard any excuse.

"You know I would have been here if I could have," Evan said. "How long have you known me? Have I ever let you down?"

Scowling, the laird shook his head. "We had to listen to that doolie, Horhay, play god-awful noise on his strange collection of instruments…"

Evan burst out laughing.

"It wasn't funny," the laird snapped, recalling the embarrassment of providing such dreadful entertainment for his guests.

Evan tried to sober his expression. "I'm sorry. I did everything I could to be here."

"Nobody could dance to it," the laird continued. "Sounded like a bunch of cats yowling from the bottom of a well. Biggest damned racket I've ever heard."

Evan avoided the temptation to laugh again by quickly

brandishing his own scowl and barking, "Hell, you don't know the half of what I've been through for the last two weeks!"

The tactic worked. The laird studied Evan's face briefly, then slapped his friend on the back.

"Sounds like we both need a drink," Gavin said with a grin. "Can you stay the night? Can I get you a lass?"

"I'm afraid not," Evan said. "We have to be in Dumfries by nightfall, or we'll miss another engagement. I'm meeting the others there. They're moving at a slower pace with Andrew."

"Well, at least stay long enough to have a tankard of ale and fill me in on news from your travels," Gavin urged.

"That I can do," Evan said, and the two men walked back to the keep.

Chapter Three

≈≈

A THIN LINE OF TORCH LIGHTS snaked up a tall, boulder-strewn hill as the full orange moon peeked slyly over the horizon. Accompanied by a soft hiss of whispers fading in and out, the cloaked procession made its way to the top, and to the towering stone pillars that stood dark and silent against the night sky. Like ancient sentries guarding a forbidden doorway, the large circle of stones offered no hint of the mysteries that pulsed through them. Only the ragged lines etched into their gnarled gray surfaces suggested powerful forces of countless ages.

Slender fingers of moonlight probed between the stones, searching the darkness as the twelve figures secured their torches in a larger, outer ring of holes in the ground, then moved into position inside the circle. Chanting softly, their faces remained hidden in the hoods of their gray cloaks.

Nearby, approaching the crest of the hill, a girl followed in the shadows. Sure-footed and aware, no twigs snapped beneath her feet. Her long, unbound hair flowing with her movements as her bright eyes penetrated the darkness. Reaching the summit, the stone pillars towered up into full view in front of her, and she darted through a small patch of moonlight. For an instant, Laina's fair features were illuminated, before she slipped back into shadow behind a boulder. Tightening the brown woolen shawl draped around her shoulders, she decided that she was far enough from the group to remain undetected, but she could still see and hear well enough.

It was forbidden for her to be there — she knew that. The old ones travelled great distances to gather at the sacred site but once a year and it was said that their secrets were not for the eyes and ears of mortal men. Some even said that simply being within sight of the ceremony could cause one's body to melt right down into its shoes! Laina knew that was ridiculous. The stories might succeed in scaring most people away, but growing up in the village nearby, she had spent more time in this stone circle than any of these visitors, and there had never been anything for her to fear here. The time had come, she decided, to find out for herself if the wise elders had any interesting secrets.

One of the cloaked figures turned around suddenly, looking out between the stones in Laina's direction. Laina froze and stilled her thoughts, barely breathing from her hiding place. The figure stood in a thin shaft of moonlight, the hood of his cloak concealing the upper half of his face. A large hump on his shoulders caused his head to jut forward at an odd angle, like a bird craning its neck to see a mouse skittering across the ground. After several long moments, he turned away slowly. There was a flash of white at his mouth. A *smile*. He knew she was there!

Laina tried to ignore the prickling sensation that crept across her skin. Should she leave, she wondered? What if they decided to use her in their ritual? She had heard tales about such things, although she had never put much belief in those either. Surely, she would be able to outrun any of them, she reasoned, noticing their aged postures and movements. Slowly and silently she let out the breath she was holding.

The old ones raised their thin, pale arms to the great expanse of sky above them. Their chanting grew louder, their voices dipping and rising together like a great tide, in a strange language and collection of sounds that were not only odd, but unsettling. Laina had never heard anything like it before. She tried to make sense of it, as her thoughts grew thick.

The moon slipped behind a heavy cloak of clouds, sending a giant shadow crawling across the ground, like some legless creature devouring the landscape. The sudden darkening revealed countless stars overhead, flashing like fiery gems. The voices in the stone circle fell eerily silent.

Laina swayed on her feet.

The hooded figures stood motionless. Laina peered into the stillness around her. Not even a breath of wind whispered or moved. It seemed as if everything were *listening*. Several long moments passed. Unnerved and restless, Laina considered the idea of stepping from her hiding place. What in God's name were they doing, she wondered? It was getting cold too, she noticed, adjusting her thin shawl.

A new sound, deep and gutteral, drew her attention back to the circle. The figures were slowly moving in a circular pattern, their cloaks rippling again in the returning wind. Their voices grew steadily louder, grinding together like a beastly growl. Laina wondered how such a noise could come from the elders. It did not sound human. She narrowed her eyes and cocked her head, her hair prickling. Something didn't feel right. It seemed as though she were no longer on the hilltop that she knew so well, but somewhere very different and far away. Without knowing why, she braced herself — her usual confidence scattering like seeds in a gust of wind.

Suddenly her hair whipped back from her face as all twelve voices merged into a single, bone-chilling scream. Shrinking away from the piercing sound, Laina twisted her shawl tightly in her grip, her fingers turning white. A deep rumble tremored through the ground beneath her, while three stars streaked across the sky together, leaving long white trails. Laina's mouth fell open. As she leaned against the boulder of her hiding place for reassurance, she blinked her eyes several times to be sure of what she was seeing. The giant gray stone pillars of the circle had begun pulsing a deep crimson color.

Urgent whispers flooded into her head, talking over one another. Panic surged through her, like murky, suffocating water, sucking the breath from her chest.

She could no longer feel her legs, but she knew she must leave at once. Turning her back on the stone circle, the hilltop seemed to be spinning. Laina aimed herself toward the bottom of the hill, and began stumbling forward as fast as her numb legs would move. A landscape that had been familiar all of her life, was now distorted and foreign. Her vision, normally sharp, could only detect faint outlines as if peering through a dense fog. A sudden terrifying thought occurred to her: what if the beloved forest that she knew at the bottom of the hill was no longer there? She ran forward blindly, claws of terror swiping at her back like a ravenous dragon. Her throat ached from withholding a scream, but she was not one to waste precious energy nor give herself away for such an expression.

Then, with a strangled gasp, she reached the bottom and staggered into the safety of the trees. Her vision cleared, revealing the familiar colors and shapes of the forest at night. She paused to regain her balance and smooth the tangle of hair away from her face.

From the top of the hill behind her, a loud cracking sound shot through the night. Laina did not look back. With renewed strength, she sprinted through the giant trees, the soles of her shoes barely touching the ground or the surface of the shallow stream she darted across. Birds cried out in the darkness as she ran skillfully through the tangles of vines and prickly bushes that reached out for anything they could grasp onto.

Finally emerging into the moonlight again, she raced across the small meadow that bordered the eastern side of her village. Sheep bells jangled at her sudden intrusion, but she didn't stop to greet her wooly friends this time. Jumping the short stone wall, she cut around the end of the blacksmith's shop and hurried down the wide dirt lane of the small village.

A few people bustling about with lanterns called out in greeting. Laina waved wordlessly as she rushed past, thankful for the roar of song and laughter pouring out of the Droothy Hare Tavern.

At the far end of the lane, sat a tiny cottage of mud and straw, with smoke rising from the vent in its thatched roof. The wood-shuttered windows glowed faintly, hinting at the warmth within. Scurrying inside, Laina closed the door quickly and leaned against it, breathing heavily.

The one-room cottage was sparsely furnished. A thick wooden table sat near the middle of the pounded-earth floor, surrounded by a bench and two fur-covered stools, along with a wall-shelf near the hearth, two candle lanterns, and a large chest up against the wall to the right. Two straw mattresses lay on the floor in the far corners of the room.

"Where ye been, Laina?" her father's deep voice asked, as he sat carving a leather pouch at the table. His giant, broad-shouldered frame belied his gentle nature. He looked up, his smokey blue eyes shining beneath thick gray brows. He gazed at his beautiful wild child. "Has the devil been chasing ye?"

Laina's cheeks glowed brightly. The brown shawl, bunched almost completely around her neck, fell to the floor as she released her grip.

"Father, I..." She swallowed hard. "I was exploring." Avoiding his eyes, she stared into the flames in the hearth.

"No doubt," he chuckled.

The hot coals winked at Laina, like red beastly eyes watching her from the stone circle. She moved stiffly away from the door, plucking leaves from her hair and tunic. Worry lines marred her smooth brow and she pressed her lips together tightly as if vowing never to speak of what she'd seen.

Her father watched her for a moment, then set down his leatherwork and carving knife.

"Come here, Lainee, and let me settle your feet back on the ground." He patted his broad lap.

She crossed the distance between them and slid quickly into his strong embrace, resting her head on his solid shoulder. His soft, bushy beard tickled her face and she giggled. The snapping of the fire and the scent of woodsmoke filled her with relief and comfort, and she closed her eyes.

Zachary Makgregor tightened his arms around his daughter, sensing an unusual vulnerability in her. He wondered what had shaken her so, yet he knew that she would tell him if she wanted his help. He was glad for her courage and strength. Being the only child of a leatherworker, Laina needed those traits for their harsh life in southern Scotland. Especially in the absence of her dear mother who had been taken from them the past winter by the coughing sickness. The thought of those darkest of days still brought tears to Zach's eyes.

"Look at me new leather pouch, Lainee," Zach quickly offered, picking it up for her to see.

Laina reached out and lovingly traced the winged carving engraved on the front flap. The symbol was her father's unique design — three circles joined together at the center, with intricate feathered wings spanning the breadth of the design. Zach said they represented the wings of spirit that would keep Laina, her mother, and himself joined together forever...no matter where they be.

"It's beautiful," Laina cooed. "Even better than your old one that the goat ate."

"That goat was sure hurtin' after that!" Zach recalled with a rumbling chuckle that caused Laina to join his laughter. She remembered how her mother had fed the miserably bloated goat an oil tonic, which kept the poor creature squirting for two days. When the goat's legs finally stopped trembling from the traumatic experience, he ran away, most surely in search of calmer pastures.

Laina kissed her father on the cheek and slipped lightly from his lap. Grabbing a clean wooden bowl from the table, she walked to the big iron pot hanging over the hearth. Steam swirled up as she scooped hot barley and vegetable soup into her bowl.

Zach watched his daughter — his eyes soft with affection. She sat gracefully on a three-legged stool by the fire, cupping the steaming bowl with her delicate hands. Her hair, streaming down to her waist, still carried fragments of leaves from her secret adventure. Blowing on the soup to cool it, her long feathery eyelashes fanned against her soft, flushed cheeks and her smooth skin glowed in the firelight. She was a rare beauty, and Zach was frequently reminded of that fact by those in the village who insisted on giving their advice about how he should raise the girl.

"What are ye thinkin' to let the lass run around the countryside by herself, Zachary?" the cobbler's wife often scolded. "Dunna ye know of the dangers?"

"I know the paths she travels, and I know she is careful," Zach would respond calmly. "Do you think her so much safer in the village, wasting her time with foolish lads who cannot seem to stay out of trouble for even a day? Would ye have her constantly fighting off boys who have yet to learn honor?"

Zach's ability to redirect the focus onto the troublesome behavior of the nosey woman's own nephews would fluster her greatly. Her voice would become shrill as she tried to change the subject and shock the giant man. "Well, she be the age for finding a match, ye know! At some point ye have to let her go!"

Zach would shake his head and laugh, "So am I supposed to lock her up or let her go? Make up yer mind woman."

"Alright then," the cobbler's wife would shake her head vigorously, "I'll not be helpin' ye again, Zachary."

Zach would snicker, knowing the woman wouldn't be able to help herself. He also knew that Laina could take care of herself better than most. She could run like a deer and had the sense of a fox. The girl had learned a great deal from her mother. She could shoot an arrow and throw a knife better than any of the boys. And lord, how the lass could *dance*! Zach smiled at the mental image of Laina dancing circles around the villagers as they clapped and stomped their feet, trying to keep up with her. Aye, she was a treasure…and she would wait for the right mate who deserved her. Someone she would choose for herself. Zach would not press her to do otherwise.

Looking up from her bowl of soup, Laina met her father's eyes and smiled. Her lips curved up slightly at one corner, giving a mischievous look to her otherwise angelic face. With her slender, shapely legs stretched out before her and crossed at the ankles, Laina ate the rest of her soup, and Zach made the finishing touches to his leather pouch.

Chapter Four

෩෪

MORNING SUNLIGHT STREAMED through the open wood shutters over Laina's bed. She stretched and breathed deeply of the fresh air, something she and her father were both fond of. Soon enough, winter would be upon them and the shutters would remain closed until spring. She could hear her father whistling in the garden, and chickens clucking softly just outside the window as they searched their favorite grassy spot for bugs. In the distance, the familiar ring of the blacksmith's hammer echoed.

Jumping up from the mattress, Laina reached for her clothes. An image of the stone circle arose in her mind. In the bright light of day, the past night's events seemed unreal. Although she couldn't explain what she had experienced, the stone circle had always been a safe place and she would not be scared away easily.

Dressing quickly, she pulled on her green woolen tunic over her white linen chemise. A leather belt held a small knife at her waist. She found her shoes and slipped them on, then scrubbed her face and teeth from a small bucket of water by the hearth. After weaving her hair back into a thick braid, she approached the table and smiled upon seeing her beloved stone necklace with a new leather cord. Slipping it over her head, she grabbed a chunk of dark bread from a wooden platter on the table and went outside. Her father was just coming from the garden.

"Tis a fair morning, Father," she observed, flinging her arms around him.

"Aye, tis indeed, my sweet." He hugged her tight, lifting her up and holding her off the ground until she kicked her feet and giggled. "I see ye've got your mother's necklace back on, where it belongs."

"Yes, Father, thank you."

She walked into the shed alongside the garden and emerged with her bow and arrows.

"Where ye be off to, Lainee?" her father asked.

She tipped her chin up playfully as she strapped the quiver on. "How would it be if I caught us a rabbit and collected some wild herbs   for   dinner?"

"Ahh, that would be fine. Me stomach growls at the thought of it." Zach grinned. Then he added, "Be mindful, Lainee, wherever you go."

"I will Father. I'll be back in a few hours." Snatching up a small basket for the herbs, she blew him a kiss and disappeared down the lane.

The village was busy with the usual morning activity. People loading and moving carts of hay and grain, men splitting and stacking wood, and children tending livestock. The people of Dounehill enjoyed the bounty of living in the peaceful, fertile territory.

"A good lot of people," Laina's father always said. "They work hard, but can still stomp their feet to song at the end of the day."

Merriment and dancing often spilled out of the Droothy Hare Tavern, into the lane where the children could join in if they hadn't yet been sent off to bed.

"And what will Zachary Makgregor be having for dinner?"

Laina looked over to see the plump cobbler's wife smiling broadly and nodding at the bow and arrows on Laina's back.

"Hopefully, rabbit," Laina answered.

From across the lane, the old candlemaker's raspy voice chimed in, "How about bringing him a bear this time, Lainee?"

Laina laughed. "Aye! And I shall carry it back on me very own shoulders." Walking bowlegged, she pretended to be carrying such a load on her back, rocking from side to side with a serious grimace on her face. Her demonstration was met with cackles of laughter that continued behind her until she passed the green and reached the edge of the village.

It was an unusually warm day for late autumn, she noted, looking up. Skylarks swirled in spirals before darting down to the cleared fields. Deciding that it made the most sense to collect herbs on the hill first, then catch the rabbit in the tall meadow grasses on the way back, Laina headed into the woods and onto the path that led to the stone circle.

The sun was nearly overhead when Zachary Makgregor stopped chopping wood and went inside. He wiped at the sweat on his brow with his sleeve, and took a few gulps of water from the pigskin bag hanging over the back of the chair. Sitting down tiredly at the table, he picked up his new leather pouch and inspected the design carved on the front. With his finger, he slowly traced the circle that represented Laina's mother. She would be so proud of Laina, he knew. He hoped she would approve of his efforts in raising the girl.

Laina and her mother had been very close, spending many hours exploring the meadows and forests together. In the early days, Zach went along on a few of the adventures. He watched his wife talk continually to their babe, explaining the ways of nature. "Susanna, what makes you think this child can understand what you are telling her?" Zach would ask. "She is barely two summers."

Susanna would smile and assure him, "Oh, she understands," and then she would wink at her daughter, and the wee girl would try to wink back. Winking became a game between the two of them, and it amused Zach greatly.

After Susanna's death, Zach had been unable to accompany his daughter on her woodland adventures, as there was always so much work to be done. But he encouraged Laina to continue her secret explorations on her own. He not only trusted her abilities, he trusted her instincts — and, as a result, there was very little he would deny her.

Zach set down the pouch and reached for his leatherworking tools. Thunder sounded in the distance. He frowned. There had been no clouds in the sky. He started to sharpen his small carving knife when he heard the rumble again...growing closer. *Horses! A large number of them.* Just as alarm seized him, he heard shouts and screams. *What trouble is this? Lainee, hide yourself!*

Rising quickly, Zach crossed the room and opened the large chest where he kept the sword from his younger days as a soldier. Quickly unwrapping it from the beautiful storage cloth his wife had made, he darted out the front door just as two riders on horseback thundered down the lane toward him. The smell of smoke reached his nostrils. Screams came from all directions. Enraged, Zach shouted at the men, "What is the meaning of this?"

One of the riders approached, sneering. "We have need for supplies and coin, old man. This village will serve us well." The tall, dark stranger leapt from his horse, drew his sword, and lunged at Zach.

What Zach's aging body lacked in agility, he made up for in solid strength. His face rigid with rage and determination, Zach's sword slammed against the intruder's, one powerful blow after another.

The rider looked surprised; it was like fighting a solid mountain!

Zach could hear the sounds of terror and destruction all around him. *Laina, stay away!*

The two swords came together in a mighty clash, knocking them completely from the hands of both fighters.

Before Zach could take a single step, the rider stepped forward with a victorious smile, swiftly pulled a gleaming dagger from its sheath and plunged it deeply into Zach's chest.

Laina, my sweet...

Zach's solid body crumpled lifelessly to the ground.

Laina stood near the south stone, her body dwarfed by the giant pillars rising up around her. The circle felt safe and peaceful as it always had. Images of the previous night pricked at her mind, thwarting her desire to ignore what she'd witnessed there. A chill ran through her as she looked down and saw the ring of trampled grass stretching around the inside of the circle. It had all been real.

She recalled her mother's teachings about the energy that existed in all things. Since her earliest memories, she had felt her connection to nature and had been able to sense an energy vibrating within the stones. But last night's experience was more than she could comprehend. Laina's mother had instructed her daughter to be mindful and respectful, and she would not have approved of Laina's intrusion on the ceremony. Laina pressed her hand against the massive pillar next to her and asked for forgiveness. She knew she must not be so foolish and head-strong if she wished to be told more of nature's secrets. Someday, perhaps, she would understand what she had seen. Until then, she would be more disciplined and avoid situations where she didn't belong.

Wandering the sunny hillside, Laina felt comforted by memories of her mother as she filled the basket and picked extra greens and herbs to share with the cobbler's wife. The sun was high in the sky when she finished, and she still had a rabbit to catch. Hurrying toward home, she bounded through the woods like a woodland animal, energized by the earthy smells and chatter of birds.

Stepping out of the trees at the edge of her village, Laina stopped suddenly. Great clouds of dust swirled up into the air — or was it smoke? She stood assessing the scene. A line of riders were riding away in the distance. Eager to find out what all the excitement was about, she sprinted across the meadow. The smell of smoke and an odd silence hung in the air. It was only when she came around the blacksmith's shop at the north end of the village that the horrifying scene spread out in front of her.

The basket of greens fell from her hand and rolled into a puddle of blood. All over the ground, people lay dead in bloodied clothing, some of them missing arms and legs. Buildings were torn apart and burning. Laina stared in wild-eyed confusion. This could not be happening.

A scream ripped from her throat, "Father!" She began running down the lane as fast as her legs could carry her, sickly numb to the horror that lay all around. She dared not look closely at the sprawled bodies of those she had known all her life.

"Father!" Her voice desperate and choked with panic, she approached her home. Moving closer, Laina saw her father's limp form laying in a pool of dark blood in front of their cottage.

"Nooooo!" The sound wrenched from her in a great wail that burned her throat. Sobbing as she reached him, her legs gave way. Her tears rained down upon his upturned face, pooling on his closed eyes. A dark curtain of grief descended around her, and her body shuddered violently until no feelings or thoughts remained. Slumped over her father's body, Laina lost awareness of the passage of time or how long she lay there.

Chapter Five

ର)ଓ

AS NIGHT SETTLED OVER GALLOWAY CASTLE, torches flickered in their holders in the large, open great room of the laird's keep.

Two rows of massive wood posts stretching the length of the room supported the high ceiling beams. A couple of large, heavy wooden chairs and an ornately carved side-table faced an immense stone fireplace, with a large tapestry hung above it. Throughout the hall, several benches had been placed, and weapons and banners adorned the walls.

On the wall opposite the fireplace, three doors opened into small rooms, primarily used for storage, while on the far back wall, an archway opened onto a hallway for two more rooms: a small pantry, used for storing and serving food brought over from the kitchen, and a buttery, where beer and wine were stored. A side door off of the hallway provided outdoor access to the west side of the building, for staff moving between the kitchen and the keep.

In the far left corner of the great room, a staircase ascended to the bedrooms on the next level of the keep, which occupied the backside of the building only.

Between the hearth and the back of the room, a very large table surrounded by heavy chairs was being prepared by serving girls for the evening meal for the laird and his highest ranking men.

The laird was examining a large axe near the fireplace when Lowrens, one of his chief officers, hefted open the heavy door of the keep and hurried down the stairs into the great hall.

"M'lord. We have just received word of an attack on the small village of Dounehill in the southwest territory."

"When did this happen?" Gavin snarled, snatching up his leather fighting vest from a bench nearby.

"As best we can tell, Laird, many hours ago. A rider on

horseback tells us that the village lays in complete ruin."

"Survivors?"

"The rider did not see any."

The laird's handsome face darkened as he scowled at the floor for several moments. "Whoever has done this…they're long gone by now."

"Aye, m'lord." Lowrens scowled along with his laird.

Several of the laird's men entered the hall.

Gavin dropped his vest back onto the bench and crossed the room, then sat down heavily at the large oak table, scraping his chair loudly against the stone floor.

"This is the third attack in as many months," one of the men said with disgust, seating himself near the opposite end.

The truth of the statement hit Gavin like a spear. He could no longer conclude that two earlier attacks in his territory had been random. The implications of this latest revelation were staggering.

"What do we know of it so far?" the laird asked. He leaned back and braced his arms on his muscular thighs, forcing himself to remain calm.

"Not much, m'lord." The man who brought us word of the attack was in a terrible state. Tomas spoke with him, but I dinna think he discovered anything of value."

"Just like the other attacks — no one saw anything," Gavin said, his mouth tightening grimly.

"Word from the rider was that it was a bloody mess," another soldier added. "Bodies everywhere."

Gavin jerked forward and slammed his fist down on the table. "Dammit! How can I fight an enemy I cannot see?"

A serving girl came into the hall with a large jug of ale and filled the tankards of the men. The laird noticed that the blue of her apron matched the blue of her eyes.

"Is m'lord ready for his supper?" she asked shyly.

Gavin gave a short nod, his thoughtful look penetrating her.

"I will tell the kitchen," she said, bowing her head and hurrying away.

The men sat somberly, taking long draws from their tankards. The rest of the laird's high-ranking soldiers wandered into the hall as the food arrived. When all nine were assembled, the one called Tomas recounted the story told to him by the rider. Men, women, and children had been cut down in their tracks as if taken by complete surprise — many of them savagely dismembered. The buildings were ransacked and destroyed, some of them set on fire.

Fearing for his own life, the rider had not stayed to look around, but hurried on to notify Galloway Castle.

"Then there *could be* survivors!" Gavin roared.

"He didna think to check for survivors?" someone challenged angrily. "Coward!"

"He was a pilgrim," Tomas explained. "He had no weapon. Even after riding long to reach us, he was still shaken from what he'd seen in the village."

"I want six men there with a wagon by dawn's first light to look for survivors," Gavin ordered. "I want answers! I need more than the word of random pilgrims to know the state of my lands."

"I'll assemble the men," Lowrens said.

"We will find the bastards, m'lord," one of the soldiers assured.

Gavin signaled the serving girls to bring more ale. It was going to be a long night.

Throughout the course of the meal and long afterward, the group of men at the laird's table revisited details of two previous attacks that they had, until now, thought were unrelated.

A few months earlier, two men from the southern part of the Galloway territory were robbed and beaten to death on their way to the castle. The laird's men had searched extensively for the murderers, but eventually concluded that thieves passing through the area must have been responsible. A few months later, a village to the east was set ablaze while all slept in their beds. The incident started in the hay storage, and was blamed on carelessness. In fact, one boy had been severely disciplined, despite his protests of innocence. The laird had not been certain about the explanation, but there was no other. The latest attack left no further doubt. A focused threat was moving among them and targeting the Galloway territory. But who? And why?

The flames burned low in the massive stone fireplace. Gavin's jaw clenched and flexed as he stared into the coals. Despite the lack of any clues or answers, the laird knew he must make a move to do *something*. Sitting and waiting was not an option. An image arose in his mind of a giant chess board, and from his current position, he could do little more than make desperate sweeping arcs in the dark with his sword, hoping to strike something. He could not see the threats that attacked, nor the direction they approached from.

"What kind of vermin are we dealing with?" one man hissed. "They slaughter whole villages, then skitter away into darkness?"

"Aye," added another man, "they're lower than the worms that crawl from stinking corpses."

"When we find them," someone shouted, "they will pay with the blood of their *own* families."

"We do not kill innocents," Gavin reminded loudly, turning from the fire. "But we *will* drag those responsible down the streets of every village until no flesh remains on their splintered bones!"

The room erupted with angry shouts and hammering from fists and tankards on the table. Knocking his chair over as he lept up, one soldier grabbed a nearby bench and hurled it against the wall with a thunderous crash. Wood fragments flew in all directions across the room. The serving girls retreated through the arched doorway near the back of the hall and hid just out of sight.

"We have little time," Gavin boomed over the noise, "and few options." The men settled and turned their attention to him. "We must arm and train the four remaining villages in the territory to defend themselves. We are faced with a threat we cannot see or predict, so we must do whatever we can to be ready for the next strike anywhere at any time."

The laird's second-in-command, Symon, quickly spoke up. "M'lord, most of the villagers are but simple farmers. Their skill in using weapons is limited to catching their dinner."

Gavin nodded. "Aye, this will not be an easy task. However, until we can uncover our enemy, our skills and strength offer little security to those who depend on our protection. We cannot allow them to be slaughtered while we sit in the dark. So we must enable them to protect themselves." The laird tipped his tankard on edge and scowled into it. "Aside from keeping a small force positioned here at the castle, we'll divide our numbers and send troops to assist the villages in building up their defenses." He looked around the table. "Those of you here will lead those troops. Symon, I leave it to you to oversee and coordinate these operations."

"Aye, m'lord," Symon answered — his short, straw-colored hair sticking out stiffly in all directions. He rubbed the stubble on his chin thoughtfully. Laird Galloway was used to getting what he wanted and he wasn't inclined to sit and wait for it. It was just the kind of challenge that Symon lived for.

The laird stood up and began to pace the floor as he spoke. "Pull all old weapons from the storerooms and teach every male of twelve summers and older to use them unsparingly. The women and children will need hiding places near their homes, should they come under attack. And I want a scout posted near every village to alert us at the first sign of trouble. Until this is resolved, we will remain on alert."

The laird's men sat silent, grasping the weight of the task before them.

"I estimate it will take three months to complete the training." Gavin walked back to the table, drained his tankard, and wiped his mouth with the back of his hand. "After that, we'll continue to monitor the villages closely for as long as it takes. No one will slip past us."

Symon's veins pulsed with excitement. He was trained to fight, after all, and he had seen little of it while in the service of a laird with few enemies. But now he would get a chance to demonstrate what he could do. Crossing his arms, he smiled with the knowledge that he and the other soldiers would act quickly and deliver success for their laird.

"One more thing," Laird Galloway said, walking forward and bracing his muscular arms on the table. "I want two men to travel through neighboring territories to see what they can find out. I need someone who can pull secrets from the darkest corners."

The laird directed his gaze to the grizzled soldier who had thrown the bench earlier. "Fingal, you have a lot of unsavory acquaintances from your past who might be willing to talk to you."

To Fingal's left, Tomas flashed a lopsided grin and retorted, "M'lord, to this day, they are the *only ones* willing to talk to him." Snorts and chuckles arose from around the table.

Honored by his special assignment, Fingal smirked and sat up taller, drawing more laughter from his companions. The light-hearted sound was a welcome relief to the evening.

Unable to share in the laughter with his men, the laird simply nodded at Fingal and said, "Take Tomas with you."

The two men looked at each other with mock disgust, then grinned and clanked their tankards together.

"I want reports from all assignments every three days," Gavin ordered, standing to his full height. "Galloway Castle will no longer wait for answers. We will turn over every stone until we find those responsible. And when we do, they will beg to be released to hell."

The laird turned away and didn't pay attention to the roar of approval that went up from his men. He walked heavily to the stairs and thundered upward. He had been over and over the same details, and still, it simply made no sense. His good reputation was widely known and respected. He prided himself on being honorable, fair, and generous in his dealings. He knew of no major grievances against him. Yet, the Galloway lands were being targeted by a deranged enemy. There had to be someone with some information. Everyone in the south of Scotland knew that he would pay generously for it. How could it be that no one had come forward?

At the top of the stairs, Gavin slammed open the thick door to his bedroom, sending it against the wall with a crash. He stood staring blankly into the room, breathing heavily, his hands fisted. What kind of leader was he if his people couldn't count on his protection? How foolish was he if someone could destroy his lands right out from under his feet? In all his life he had never felt so powerless.

Gavin dropped wearily onto a chair and began tugging at his boots. Lord, how he could use a good distraction. Something compelling enough to ease the torment of endless questions. Something that restored his sense of power and control. A woman. Aye, perhaps Brigid, spread naked across his bed. He could lose himself in the mounds of her large, warm breasts and sink himself fully between her legs. A wicked smile captured his mouth briefly before transforming back into a scowl as he threw a boot across the room. It wouldn't be fair, he knew, to subject the lass to the force that raged through him. The chambermaid was already somewhat afraid of him, and he could not know what he might feel driven to do to ease and entertain his restless mind. Dammit, he could wait until tomorrow.

Chapter Six

℘℃℞

"YOU THERE!" A soldier sat mounted on his horse, no emotion on his face. "Get your things. You need to come with us."

Laina raised her head and stared mutely through the thick gray mist of pre-dawn. She could barely make out the shape of the man on a horse.

The soldier raised his voice. "By order of Laird Galloway, we're taking all survivors from this village to Galloway Castle. Rise and get your things."

Laina looked at her father's lifeless body beneath her — a cold and empty shell. He was gone. She pushed herself up slowly and stood.

The soldier spoke again, more gently, but urgently. "Get your things, lass. We must go now."

Numbly, she moved to obey the soldier. Walking to the open door of her home, she stepped just inside and saw the broken furnishings that littered the floor. She did not need to look any further to know that there was nothing of any value left. What was most important to her — what had given value to all else — was gone. She turned stiffly and walked out of the cottage.

The soldier's horse pranced anxiously. Laina paused by her father's body and placed her hand over her heart, her eyes filling with new tears. Then, quietly, she followed the soldier down the lane to the wagon that was waiting.

The castle was nearly a six-hour ride by wagon. Carrying three stunned survivors, it pitched and swayed over uneven, rocky terrain. Creaking and grinding with every movement, it muffled the voices of the soldiers escorting the small group. The passengers stared blindly toward the horizon.

Laina had not seen much of the land beyond her village. Even now, in the clear light of mid-morning, she did not notice the rolling countryside, rich and vibrant with late autumn colors. Birds glided across the sky, and a breeze swayed long meadow grasses in a graceful dance.

Empty and alone, Laina saw nothing.

When, at last, the castle came into view just over a rise, a soldier shouted and Laina looked up slowly — her eyes dull and her face dirty and streaked from tears.

She had never seen anything so large. The beastly structure of massive gray stones towered up toward the sky. Thick walls, like great monstrous arms, surrounded it. She shivered.

Groups of men dotted the landscape at the base of the castle, thrusting and slinging weapons, and shouting at each other. As the wagon drew nearer, the castle grew ever larger.

The wagon rolled toward a great opening that looked like a mouth, with jaws made from giant chains on either side. Closing her eyes in dread, Laina was sure she was being swallowed up. Gripping the side of the wagon where she sat on rough, woolen blankets, Laina kept her eyes tightly closed and listened to the sounds around her. Horse hooves clopped evenly from the riders nearby. Others raced by, pounding the ground. The voices of men called out, harsh and impatient.

"What a sorry lot you've collected," a grizzled voice laughed.

"Aye. A few old ones and an orphaned girl."

"What are we supposed to do with them?"

"Just what we need. More useless mouths to feed," someone grumbled.

"Get out of the way," a voice demanded.

The wheels of the wagon scraped along a rough wood surface, accompanied by heavy clinking from giant chains, until the wagon moved onto dirt again.

The cries of sheep and clucking of chickens reached Laina's ears. And more voices, all talking over one another.

"Over here!" someone yelled.

The wagon lurched, then jerked to a halt. Sounds of movement surrounded Laina. She held tight to the side of the wagon, her eyes still closed.

"Lass, 'tis time to get out," a male voice said, and something nudged her shoulder.

"Hand her to me!" a female voice ordered.

Large, calloused hands gripped Laina's arms and effortlessly pulled her loose from her last place of refuge.

The beast had won.

The morning had passed slowly for Laird Galloway. He tried to preoccupy his thoughts by watching his men practice their fighting in the lower courtyard. But he was in a miserable mood, and was tired of all the people who kept coming up to speak with him, expecting him to be his normal jovial self. He returned to the keep, finding Lowrens in the great hall. The laird looked sideways at the large, red-bearded man and grumbled, "When will those survivors be here — if there are any?"

"The men left several hours before sunrise, m'lord, but travel will be slow with the wagon. They won't likely be back here for another three hours."

"I'll be in my room." Gavin headed for the stairs.

"M'lord?" Lowrens called out, wondering if the laird was feeling ill.

"Send up the chambermaid, Brigid," Gavin said. "We have some unfinished business."

Lowrens smiled. "Aye, m'lord."

The poor timing couldn't be helped, Gavin told himself. He needed release, and there was only one way to do it. A good romp was one thing, but God help him, he felt like ramming some soft, sweet thing up against a wall until he was numb. He would try to go easy on the lass.

When the chambermaid arrived at the laird's room in response to his summons, he warned her that he wasn't feeling quite himself and that he did not want to overwhelm or frighten her. Dressed only in his breeches, he paced restlessly. His eyes, normally bright and sparkling, were dull and vacant. Brigid smiled at the revelation before her. He needed her. She held the key to the laird's release. She had never felt such power. Indeed, she knew a few tricks that would surely sooth him, she thought to herself. Enjoying her new role, she assured the laird that she was not afraid of him and would be honored to serve him in any way she could.

Upon hearing this, Gavin pulled her fully into the room and kicked the door closed. Hauling her hard up against him, he kissed her roughly and deeply, before tossing her onto the giant bed. A fierce need blackened his eyes. Brigid had never seen the laird in such a state. Her confidence scurried under the bed as he stripped off his breeches in one flashing movement and came toward her. Good lord, he looked like a raging steed.

He took her hard and fast on the bed, then bent her over a finely-carved chair, then drove himself into her up against a wall decorated with colorful tapestries, before returning again to the large, canopied bed. Brigid had long since forgotten her own plans for soothing the laird's mood. Her only focus now was to keep her balance as she held onto an overhead bed railing while Gavin thrust her vigorously up and down on his engorged manhood. Although flattered to have his favor, Brigid couldn't help but wonder when he might grow weary.

A layer of sweat glistened across his broad, bronzed chest. His long muscular legs flexed powerfully, while his strong arms and hands held her hips firmly. With his head tipped back, and his handsome face strained with intensity, the laird seemed almost feverish.

Hot and flushed, Brigid's breasts bounced vigorously and her drenched hair clung to her face. Panting, she wiped the perspiration away from her eyes with one hand.

Gavin gave the chambermaid's hip an affectionate squeeze and moved faster, his eyes wild and unfocused. The man was possessed, she concluded. Brigid felt pride in her ability to keep up with him, a feat that many women had been unable to do. The laird gritted his teeth, thrusting hard a few more times, then let out a roar that shook the walls. Brigid screamed, surprised by his intensity.

The laird's body shuddered and he expelled a heavy sigh. Brigid smiled and collapsed on top of him. Her hips felt bruised from his grip, but they were bruises she would wear proudly.

Gavin moaned contentedly and wrapped his arms around the girl. His breathing slowed while he gently stroked her back. "I believe you have healed what ailed me, lass."

Brigid smiled. Relaxing on top of the laird, she relished her accomplishment, and nearly laughed aloud as she wondered how many days it would take for her to walk normally. She would play these scenes over and over in her head, to lift her out of the boredom of her daily routine. Laird Galloway was the finest man she had ever seen, and she'd had the good fortune of being chosen to please him.

Beneath her, the laird was growing hard again. Brigid's eyes sprung open. *Good God...*

A knock at the door caused the chambermaid to scream again,

more from relief than surprise.

The laird sat up, gently lifting Brigid aside while swinging his legs over the edge of the bed. "What is it?" he called.

"It is Lowrens, m'lord. I have news."

"Enter."

Brigid slipped behind the laird to conceal herself since all of the bed coverings were scattered across the floor.

The door swung open and the red-headed giant stood filling the doorway. "Survivors from Dounehill have just arrived, m'lord."

"Good! How many?"

"Three," Lowrens answered.

"Start questioning them to see what they can tell us about the attack, and I'll meet you at the gatehouse shortly," Gavin ordered.

"Aye, m'lord." Lowrens closed the door, then smiled to himself. The chambermaid seemed to have survived her encounter with the laird, Lowrens noted. A hardy lass, indeed.

Laird Galloway turned to Brigid and flashed a fiesty grin. "Lass, are you sure I wasn't too rough with you?"

"I am sure, m'lord," she said, scrambling off the bed, "I must be returning to my duties now or I'm certain to receive a tongue-lashing."

"That you are, dear Brigid," Gavin laughed, leaning forward and swatting her rosy, bare bottom. "Next time, then — a tongue-lashing for you."

Brigid blushed and pulled on her clothes as quickly as possible. "Thank you, m'lord," she said, hurrying out the door.

Gavin chuckled. "Thank *you*, Brigid." Leaping up, he dressed quickly, feeling a renewed sense of vigor and hope. The survivors would have the information he sought. Now he could find and destroy his enemy. Aye, things were about to take a turn. He was sure of it.

Wearing black fitted trousers and boots, topped by a red velvet tunic, Laird Galloway arrived at the gatehouse just as the soldiers had finished questioning the survivors. Lowrens approached the laird.

"Well?" Gavin asked, looking hopeful.

"We got nothing, m'lord," Lowrens admitted.

"What?" The laird glared at his soldier. "Someone had to have seen something! Even the smallest amount of information could be valuable to us."

Lowrens nodded his head. "Unfortunately, m'lord, they are very traumatized. There is an old woman who crawled into the privy to hide during the entire attack, an old man who is blind and only heard the screams, and a girl...who does not say much." Lowrens turned to look over his shoulder. The laird followed his officer's gaze. A dirty-faced lass with a tangle of long dark hair sat huddled in a blanket — a stoney expression on her face.

"Is she dumb?" Gavin asked.

"No, m'lord. She was away from the village during the attack and returned to find her father dead. She has no other family."

"Did she hear or see anything as she was returning to the village?"

"I do not know, m'lord. We could not get her to speak further. It seems to pain her greatly." Upon seeing the laird's disappointment, Lowrens quickly offered, "I could question her more forcefully."

"No," Gavin said. "Perhaps I'll see if the lass will speak to me." The laird walked past Lowrens and approached the girl. She did not look up.

"Lass?" Gavin spoke gently. "Do you have a name?" He knelt down on one knee in front of her and waited. Slowly, she met his gaze. The sadness he saw in her eyes tore at his heart. "I am Laird Galloway, lass. Do you have a name that I may call you?"

The girl swallowed and briefly closed her eyes. "Laina," she whispered.

When her eyes again focused on him, the laird gave her a reassuring smile. "Laina." He paused for a moment to avoid overwhelming her — the sincerity in his green eyes pleading for her trust. He touched her hand lightly. "I understand that you have been through a terrible experience." He watched her gaze drift to the floor. "I've been told that you survived because you were away from the village during the attack. Can you tell me, Laina, if you heard or saw anyone when you returned?"

To the laird's surprise, Laina slowly nodded.

"What?" he asked sharply, then caught himself and softened his tone. "What did you see, Laina?"

Her forehead creased. "Riders."

"Good," Gavin encouraged. "How many?"

She closed her eyes and when she opened them again, they

were glistening. "At least twenty."

"Do you remember which way they were heading?"

Her voice was barely more than a whisper. "North."

Gavin squeezed her hand. "Did you see any of their faces, or a banner, or anything else?"

She shook her head, then looked up into the laird's face. "Will you..." she asked, her eyes brimming with tears, "will you bury my father...and all of them?"

"Aye, lass. 'Tis already underway."

Gavin became aware of someone standing to his right, and looked up. "Margaret," he said with a grin, and stood. "What drags you out of the kitchen?"

"I've brought the lass something to warm her up." The older woman handed a steaming bowl to Laina.

It was the castle cook, Margaret, who had noticed the traumatized girl in the group of survivors when they arrived on the wagon from Dounehill.

"M'lord," Margaret said firmly, "I'd like for the lass to be assigned to the kitchen so that I can keep an eye on her. I can put her to work and keep her mind off her worries. I understand that the other two survivors will be sent to live with families in Galloway Village. I think the girl will fare better here."

"Certainly, Margaret. The lass has been through a terrible ordeal and I can think of no one better to watch out for her." Gavin turned back to Laina. "Thank you for your help, Laina. Margaret will take good care of you." Then he motioned to a few of his men and left.

Chapter Seven

ℬℭ

"NOW, I'LL NOT HAVE YE PECKING AT HER the way ye peck at each other," Margaret warned the young women in the kitchen who stared back at her with well-practiced looks of innocence.

"I don't think she would notice if we did," one of them said. "She seems rather simple and dull."

"Ye watch yourself missie," the older woman warned. "Ye have no idea what 'tis like to lose everything you've known. And if ye did, I have a fair good idea that ye wouldn't be showin' the courage this one does. So shut it, and get back to work."

Despite her short height, Margaret was a formidable woman. Plump with graying brown hair, the cook's troubled life could be read by the lines on her face. Yet, Margaret had decided long ago that there was no value in lamenting the past. One had to pick up and get on with it while one could. And that's what the lass from Dounehill must do too.

With help from some of the other women who worked around the castle, Margaret made sure that Laina was clothed for the onset of winter. In addition to the thin green tunic and linen chemise the girl had arrived in, she now had use of a thicker, blue wool tunic, a newer linen chemise, a pair of gray wool stockings, and a brown woolen cloak that never seemed to fit Margaret well enough for her liking. Laina appreciated the warmth of the heavier tunic, as well as the thick fur coverlet that Margaret retrieved from her own bed for Laina to sleep under at night.

The cook was careful, however, not to fuss over the girl. It was important that the lass be strong and find her own way if she was to survive.

Margaret had time for little else besides cooking and managing the kitchen operations, considering her staff now consisted of four young women whose minds were often elsewhere, and two males who were only marginally helpful and available. Boyd, a young lad who was too crippled to work almost anywhere else in the castle, could only help with small chores on his good days. Boyd's older brother, Malcolm, was supposed to help with heavy lifting when he wasn't training with the soldiers, but he came by the kitchen only occasionally to impress the girls with displays of his strength, which he emphasized with strained facial expressions and exaggerated grunts.

The long, rectangular kitchen building ran parallel to the keep's west wall, at a distance of about twenty-five paces.

Hearths and ovens lined one long wall of the kitchen. Across the room, dried herbs hung from pegs above baskets on the floor that held vegetables when they were available. Large tables in the center of the kitchen provided the work area, and frequently held assorted sweet treats, a favorite of Laird Galloway's. The back of the kitchen opened onto two small storerooms where barrels, bags, and jars of spices and other goods could be kept close at hand. The cool cellar where meats and larger quantities of goods were stored, was accessed by a set of narrow stairs.

In the weeks following her arrival, Laina stayed close to the kitchen, working quietly alongside Margaret. She kept to herself, doing what was asked of her by day and sleeping on a straw-stuffed mattress on the floor in the larger of the two kitchen storerooms at night. Each morning, she arose to find herself in the same nightmare that she couldn't seem to awake from. Gone were both of her beloved parents, and the familiar comfort of the small cottage she had known as home all of her life. Gone were the familiar faces and voices of those in her village who made her laugh every day. Gone were the chickens who gathered about her feet when she brought them treats. She was alone, intruding where she didn't belong. Not being one to cry or complain, she decided simply not to say much at all. The castle folk began to wonder if she might be daft.

"A pretty little thing with no mind," a woman in the courtyard commented one day, without bothering to lower her voice as the Dounehill lass passed by.

Laina did not care what people thought. She did not want attention or pity. Unfortunately, people could be cruel and insensitive about things they did not understand. And they often seemed intent on striking down those around them before they, themselves, might be struck down. Over the years, Laina had wondered about the reasons for such fearful behavior. Here, at the castle, she saw much more of it. She was grateful for Margaret's efforts to keep the other kitchen girls in line, so that there was at least one place of refuge for Laina amidst so many strangers.

Kitchen gossip provided much of Laina's education about the new world she found herself in — the talk most often revolving around the activities of Laird Galloway, the focus of every female who set eyes on him. The man's reputation was even larger than the territory he ruled. Despite Laina's upbringing among strong-willed people who did not easily bow to anyone, she found herself becoming intrigued, like everyone else, by the man who seemed to have the respect and awe of so many.

"Did you see him this morn', training with his men?" Gillian squealed as she kneaded a lump of bread dough — her boyish face and short mousey hair looking at odds with the enraptured expression on her face. "I was watching from the wall of the upper courtyard. He fought off five of his men at once!" She wiped her forehead with a skinny arm, leaving a smear of flour.

Lucy, the youngest in the kitchen, at only twelve summers, bobbed her head excitedly — two golden curls dangling from her white cap, bounced above her large blue eyes. "I saw him too," she said breathlessly. "Try as they might, his men could not best him."

"Symon tried to sneak up from behind," Gillian recounted, "but our laird spun around with his sword and practically sent Symon's breeches to the ground!"

Lucy and Gillian broke into wild giggling at the thought, Lucy covering her mouth with her hands.

"Aye, Laird Galloway does indeed handle a sword impressively on the field..." Audrey, the oldest, interjected with a tone of maturity, "but 'tis an even more impressive weapon that he uses on the ladies in private." She smiled knowingly. Although the same age as Laina, at seventeen summers, Audrey seemed to fancy herself as knowledgeable in the ways of love.

Margaret snorted and disappeared into one of the storerooms.

"Oh, how would you know?" Gillian retorted.

Audrey narrowed her eyes and put her hands on her hips. The flush of her generously-freckled face matched the unruly bush of wirey curls crammed under her white cap. "Why, from me very own experience," she snapped. "There are things you don't know!"

Lucy and Gillian stopped working to consider the boast, while Laina continued slicing vegetables.

"So, then tell us," Gillian challenged with a smirk.

Audrey looked around the room — although there was clearly no one else there other than the four girls. She lowered her voice secretively. "I was working late in the kitchen one eve last week, when the laird came in, alone. Aye, it was he, himself! Standing there..." she pointed to a place several feet away, "like some god, he was. So handsome and so strong."

Gillian folded her arms and said nothing. Lucy stared, wide-eyed.

"He said he was hungry," Audrey continued. "So, I offered to fetch a roasted drumstick for him, I did. He said *that* was not the kind of hunger he be havin'."

"Did he want some of Margaret's special sugar cakes?" Lucy asked excitedly.

Gillian let out a hearty laugh.

Audrey shot an annoyed look at the young girl. "No, you idiot, listen!" She paused to collect her thoughts, then spoke low, her voice breathy. "He didn't look like himself. There was a madness in his eyes. He said the kitchen was too hot, and before I knew what was happening, he ripped off his shirt."

Lucy gasped. "What did you do?"

"What could I do?" Audrey answered. "It was our laird, himself. I had to see what it was he needed of me. At first, I thought he might be drunk on ale. But, nay, when I looked into his eyes, I knew...he be drunk with *lust!*"

A discreet smile crept onto Laina's lips.

"Then, what happened?" Gillian urged her on.

Audrey stared blindly into the air, the volume of her voice rising. "He came at me all at once, he did. There was no time to think more of it. He wanted me."

Lucy's mouth gaped open, like a baby bird.

"He grabbed me with his large, strong hands," Audrey said in a rush, "and pushed me down on the pile of grain sacks. He towered over me — so wickedly handsome. I heard him breathing, like some sort of bull." Audrey put a hand dramatically over her eyes. "That's...when I saw it."

Lucy swallowed. "What did you see?"

Dropping her hand, Audrey screeched at the younger girl, "His breeches couldn't contain him, that's what! He was as stiff and large as a log, he was. Biggest damned thing I've ever seen. And he said, 'I'm taking you now, lass. I can deny my desire no longer.'"

There was a brief moment of shocked silence in the room, before Gillian and Lucy erupted into howls of laughter.

"You can only wish the laird would notice you and throw you onto the grain sacks," Gillian squawked, snatching up a wet towel and throwing it, hitting Audrey in the face.

Audrey whipped the towel off and stormed past Laina to go outside. "You are still too young to know of such things, Gillian Agnes."

"I'm only a year younger than you," Gillian shouted after her. "And don't use me middle name!"

Gillian and Lucy moved to the door, and resumed giggling as they looked toward the laird's keep and watched Audrey stomp across the courtyard.

Using the knife in her hand to skillfully slice a potato, Laina blew a puff of air upward from her lips to move a wisp of hair hanging over her eyes. She did not have a white cap as the other girls wore.

The memory of Laird Galloway's striking appearance drifted into her mind. She had to admit he was the most handsome man she had ever seen. Aside from Audrey's fantasies, Laina wondered how much truth there was to the rumors about him? Was he, indeed, as people said — did he routinely take women to his bed, or anywhere else he chose, and keep them in his company for many hours? It was said that he never tired.

All that Laina knew was that he had been very gentle and kind to her on the day she arrived, and he had allowed her to live and work at the castle — a great privilege. Still, it was hard to imagine what might lay ahead for her in such a place, but quite simply, she had nowhere else to go.

Chapter Eight

෨)෬

A DARK WALL OF CLOUDS rolled over the gray landscape, bringing with it an icy wind. Four horses galloping just ahead of the storm suddenly slowed, their flared nostrils steaming in the cold air. The group of riders moved forward to get a closer look at the charred remains of buildings, which until recently, had been the village of Dounehill. A few tattered pieces of cloth whipped in the stiff wind, as if signaling surrender too late.

"Good god, what happened here?" Evan yelled over the roar of the wind.

"We were here not two weeks ago," Andrew pointed out.

"A vicious attack, from the looks of it," Ian said, eyeing the large quantity of dark stains on the ground as the group came to a stop in the center of the village.

"Who would do this?" Andrew asked. "These people didn't appear to be any kind of threat...or to have much of value."

John, the quietest of the group, tipped his head toward a large mound of fresh-turned earth. "Looks like Laird Galloway's men have taken care of the remains. The bodies have been buried and all of the animals have been removed."

The men sat in silence, each one lost in his own thoughts, remembering the people they'd seen here only a fortnight ago.

Evan regreted the harshness of his words toward the villagers. The graceful elf had been right — he was rude. He frowned as he imagined someone putting their hands on her. "Damn!"

Ian spoke what everyone was thinking, "Looks like they didn't have any warning. No one likely escaped alive."

The wind gave a mournful howl and Andrew adjusted his heavy cloak, looking at the sky. "We better get going. That storm is coming upon us fast."

In wordless agreement, the men turned their horses and left the village solemnly — except for Evan. He sat rigid, staring at the empty village green. He thought of the fair lass standing there in the blowing grass — the confident tilt of her chin, the turn of her mouth as she assessed him with distaste, and the clarity in her beautiful eyes. His hands fisted around the horse reins, and his face grew darker than the storm overhead.

"Evan?" Ian called out from a short distance away, his voice nearly drowned out by the wind. Bringing his horse to a stop, he sat looking back toward his friend.

With an angry jerk, Evan turned his black stallion and trotted to where Ian waited. The wind whipped their cloaks as the two men faced each other. Andrew and John had already gone on ahead, disappearing into the growing darkness.

"Are you coming?" Ian asked, half-joking, but noting something in Evan's expression that he couldn't define. With a sudden tinge of worry, he reminded Evan, "We have an engagement to play in Portsmouth tomorrow afternoon."

Evan nodded in acknowledgement.

Ian sighed with relief, and began to turn his horse.

"I'll meet you there," Evan said.

Ian spun around. "What?"

"I have to find out what happened here," Evan said. "I'm going back to Galloway Castle."

"That will take hours, and you'll be heading *into* the storm!"

"I know," Evan said. He gazed northeast, to the blackest part of the sky.

"Why do you care about these people, Evan?" Despite knowing that Evan had been eager to return to the village to see the pretty girl he had encountered during their first visit, Ian was at a loss as to why Evan would take the situation so hard. It wasn't like him to become attached to anyone or anything. "There's nothing you can do now."

"I just have to know," Evan answered, meeting Ian's eyes. "I'll meet up with you tomorrow. Don't worry, I'll be there."

Ian nodded. He may not understand Evan's decision, but he knew he could trust his friend to make it back on time for their commitment.

Silently turning in opposite directions, the two men disappeared from each other's view.

Riding at full speed, the wind and rain pelting his face with stinging force for much of the journey, Evan arrived at Galloway castle well after dinner. The downpour had ceased, and he was glad to dismount from his horse, and remove his drenched cloak.

"Evan Prestwick, you're back again," one of the guards at the gate observed.

"I am," Evan acknowledged with a tired grin. Then, his expression turned serious. "Do you know anything about what happened to the small village of Dounehill, to the southwest?"

The guard nodded, "Aye. We've got us a war to fight!"

"Against who?" Evan frowned.

"We don't know," the guard hissed, "but we're going to find out!"

"Were there any survivors in the village?" Evan asked, dreading the answer.

"A few." The guard cracked his knuckles, and yawned. "Two old ones and a girl were brought here a few weeks ago."

"A girl? How old?"

"Mmm, maybe 16 summers or so." The guard eyed Evan. "Why? Do you know her?"

"I might," Evan mumbled, looking around. "Where is she?"

"I think she was assigned to the kitchen, on the upper level near the keep."

"I know where it is," Evan said, heading off quickly in that direction.

Laina was washing cooking pots by the light of a lantern outside of the kitchen as Evan strode up. She did not notice him approaching in the darkness, as she swished dark greasy water around in a large pot.

He could not believe his eyes. There she was, *alive* — wearing the same, baggy green tunic, standing amidst mud puddles from the recent downpour. Yet, in the soft golden light of the lantern, she looked radiant and graceful. Relief and joy flooded through him. He wanted to rush over and hug her, but instead, he called out gently, so as not to alarm her.

"Greetings, lass."

She jumped at the sudden sound, and looked up to see the blonde musician who had visited her village just before the attack. Her quick smile of seeing someone familiar, faded as her memories of him surfaced.

"Hello," she said tentatively, wondering what he was doing there.

Despite being disheartened by her caution toward him, he smiled and stepped forward.

"I am glad to see that you survived the attack on your village," he said. "But I am sorry that so many you knew were lost. Did you lose your family?"

"My Father," she answered softly. "He was all I had left." Her eyes glistened.

Evan felt his face growing hot — a combination of unexpected compassion for the girl, and anger towards those who caused her loss.

"I'm also sorry," he said, "for my impatience towards the people of your village. I was being hot-headed, and it was not their fault."

She studied him, curiously. The light from the kitchen door illuminated his face. He was even more handsome than she remembered. His gentle and genuine manner were surprising, as well.

"Thank you," she said.

"I regret that you met me in such a rare state." He laughed at himself. "I hope you will give me another chance to prove myself. If there's anything I can do for you, lass — anything to help…"

The pair stood silent.

She wanted to trust him. He seemed to be honest, speaking what he truly thought and felt, regardless of his mood. Which was more than Laina had experienced with most people, who changed from moment to moment, and person to person, depending on what they thought they might gain from it.

Evan watched her eyes flicker as she considered him. There was so much more he wanted to ask her — *How did she escape the attack? Had she been hurt?* — but perhaps he could ask her at another time. It was enough for now to see her and to know that she was alive, and to speak with her such that she might be encouraged to trust him. He had no right to bombard her with questions. She would likely see that as more bad behavior and manners on his part.

The light emanating from the kitchen dimmed as Margaret appeared in the doorway.

"Lass, can you help me for a moment?" The cook raised her eyebrow upon seeing Evan.

"Yes, of course," Laina answered.

Setting down the pot, she looked up at Evan. "I must go." Surprised by the sound of reluctance in her own voice, she searched his eyes quickly for an explanation.

At that same moment, approaching from the direction of the keep, Laird Galloway roared cheerfully, "Evan Prestwick, what brings you back to Galloway Castle?" Clearly the laird was warmed by drink at this time of evening.

Evan held Laina's gaze as long as he dare, without seeming too forward. "I'll check in on you again," he promised.

Laina gave him a small smile and disappeared into the kichen, just as the laird reached his side.

Ushering Evan toward the keep, the laird filled the musician's ear with stories, but Evan wasn't listening. He was feeling warmed, not from drink like the laird, but from his interaction with the girl — and he chuckled to himself, musing that he still didn't even know her name.

Within a few short days of Evan's departure, winter clutched the land in a silent, icy grip that did not ease for months. Few travellers braved the open landscape, and villages struggled to conserve their resources.

Even Galloway Castle huddled gloomy and quiet during the long, frigid season. Most of the soldiers were gone, assigned to outlying villages on the laird's orders. The plan to train the villages to defend themselves had not gone as well as hoped. Sickness and bad weather delayed the operations. The soldiers were tired and irritable, and anxious to return to the comforts of the castle. Laird Galloway was deeply frustrated over the lack of answers he'd been able to obtain. Fingal and Tomas thought they were close to getting some useful information until their source turned up dead before they could get to him.

Running the kitchen was harder during the extreme winter, as well. Supplies dwindled as snow drifts grew. The distance between the kitchen and the keep seemed much farther when the girls had to run through snow to prevent the food from getting cold. Clothes frequently hung around the cooking fires to dry them out.

Compared to other buildings around the castle, however, the

kitchen was the warmest and most inviting place to be during the winter. Savory smells of bread and stew continually filled the air.

Laina spent the long, dark hours of winter reorganizing the storerooms and the basement. She found comfort putting order to the things around her. Before long, she knew the location and quantity of every cooking supply on hand — knowledge that Margaret found most useful.

The other girls spent much of their time arguing or fantasizing about Laird Galloway, or playing games on the bottom of a wash tub during their breaks.

One day, having had enough of playing games with bossy Audrey, Lucy decided to join Laina in the basement.

"What are you doing?" the younger girl asked, descending the steps and seeing Laina bent over such that the entire upper half of her body had disappeared into a barrel.

Laina popped out, and upon seeing Lucy's horrified expression, let out a laugh. She could only imagine what she must look like from cleaning out the grimy bottoms of storage barrels. "I'm looking for treasure," she teased.

Lucy grinned cautiously. "What kind of treasure?"

Laina held a soiled finger to her chin thoughtfully. "Well, I'm not really sure," she admitted, "but I suppose I'll know it when I find it."

Lucy wrinkled her nose and looked around. "I don't think there's any treasure down here."

"Oh yes," Laina countered, "there's treasure everywhere." She was surprised to hear herself say such a thing, and to still believe it after all she had lost.

"Show me!" Lucy urged.

Laina considered the girl's bright, eager expression for a moment, then smiled fiendishly. "Sure, come here and stick your head in this barrel."

"No!" Lucy responded, then giggled wildly as Laina moved forward and reached for her with a greasy hand.

"Come on now, you have to be willing..." Laina playfully grasped Lucy's arm, pulling her toward the barrel.

"No! No!" Lucy screamed, laughing hysterically.

"You have to be willing..." Laina repeated, "to look in the...deepest...darkest places." Letting the younger girl sink down to the floor in an effort to escape, Laina bent over and tickled her. Lucy's non-stop giggling was infectious, and Laina giggled along with her.

"What is going on down here?"

Both girls looked up to see Gillian, gaping at them in surprise.

Laina feigned a sober expression. "We're looking for treasure."

Unable to contain her glee, Lucy blurted out, "Do you want us to show you where to look for it?"

"What are you talking about?" Gillian asked tentatively with a smile.

"Come here," Lucy demanded, jumping up and lunging for Gillian. The older girl turned and raced up the stairs, followed by Lucy, both of them screaming and laughing.

Laina followed them up, sure that the commotion might alarm Margaret. She got to the top of the stairs just as Margaret asked, "What are you girls doing down there?" The cook grinned broadly at the glowing faces of the two younger girls.

"We were cleaning the basement," Laina answered.

"Well, from the looks of it," Margaret said, noting the greasy smudges on Laina's arms and clothes, "you got a bit more into it than these two."

Heading for the wash bucket, Laina winked at the two girls who beamed back at her for the first time since she had arrived. She didn't fail to notice the scowl thrown at her like a dagger from Audrey, who sat by the empty game board across the room, with playing pieces scattered around her on the floor.

Chapter Nine

ၷၩ

AT LAST, SPRING RETURNED to Galloway Castle, and the courtyards echoed with the clanging of weapons from restless boys and men eager to be outside testing their skills. Women gathered to gossip and share stories, while children chased each other in the sun. Shouts and laughter rang out along with the demanding cries of newborn animals in the livestock pens.

It had been a long winter, and spring's earliest flowers pushed up from the warmed earth to bask in the sun. Laina, too, ventured outside. Since being told that a stone circle existed not far from the castle, she had begun making trips to the site a few times a week, even before the last patches of crisp snow had disappeared from the ground.

Margaret was relieved to see increasing signs of the girl's spirit returning and did not interfere. The cook was also delighted that the lass was speaking her mind more too.

Such an instance came one day. A group of lads stopped their practice session of sparring in the courtyard to watch Laina pass on her way to fetch water from the well. Remembering the girl's silence upon arriving at the castle prior to winter, one boy snickered and said to his companions, "There's the daftie. She didn't learn how to talk in that village she come from."

Encouraged by the laughter of the group, the tallest boy suggested, "Aye. I could take her behind the wood shed to see what's under that tunic and she wouldn't tell a soul."

Laina spun around so quickly that the lads stepped back in surprise. Pulling her pretty lips back threateningly over her straight white teeth, she said, "If you ever think to take advantage of me in any way, I assure you I will have *plenty* to say." Then, raising her voice to be heard across the courtyard, she shouted, "and I will make sure that everyone hears it! So I hope you are not as foolish as you look!" People around the courtyard stared in surprise to see the daft girl shouting at the lads. Patting the small sheath hanging from her belt, Laina smiled tightly at the boys. "I know how to use my knife well too."

The tall lad who had spoken last, flushed dark red.

Laina turned and strolled away, a smile creeping onto her lips as she thought of the look of surprise on their faces. Bullies! Let any one of them face her one-on-one, and see how brave they really were.

Margaret heard about the incident from a woman who had been in the courtyard and witnessed it. "That poor girl completely lost her senses," the woman said, drawing her brows together and shaking her head. "Threw a flakie, she did! Yelled at the whole group of boys."

"Poor girl, my arse!" Margaret said, giving the woman only half of her attention while she continued stirring the pot that hung over the hearth. "That one's got very good sense, and a far better grip on things than most people I know. Far better."

Surprised by the cook's unexpected response, the woman clicked her tongue and left, further humiliated by the cackle of Margaret's laughter behind her.

Lucy stared wide-eyed at Margaret. "Do you think it's true," the young girl asked, "that Laina yelled at the boys?"

"Well if she did, she had a good reason for it," Margaret said, setting down the wooden spoon and putting the lid back on the pot. It had been clear to Margaret from the start that the Dounehill lass was intelligent and brave. And now, to see that the girl was firey too, it tickled the cook's insides. Proud of the girl, she was, for what she had come through. Truth be told, she had fancied the idea, more than once, of having the hardy lass as her own daughter.

Laina appeared at the kitchen door, rosey-cheeked from the fresh air and sunshine. "I've finished fetching the water," she said, setting down the buckets. "'Tis such a fine day, I'd like to go for a walk. I can be back in a few hours."

Margaret nodded. "Aye, lass. Enjoy yourself."

Gillian watched Laina leave, then said to no one in particular, "I've seen the men eyeing her. I don't think she notices."

"I think she notices quite a bit," Margaret responded. "I don't think she sees it as important."

Lucy wrinkled her nose. "Why do you let her go outside the castle walls and roam around by herself?"

"It's not my place to stop her," Margaret answered. "She is old enough to make her own decisions, and that is what she must do."

"Someday, maybe I'll go to that stone circle with her," Lucy suggested.

Gillian snorted. "She doesn't want you tagging along, yammering in her ear."

Ignoring the comment, Lucy stared toward the door. "I wonder what she does there?"

With a smile, Gillian said, "Probably looks for treasure."

Under a brilliant blue sky dotted with white fluffy clouds, Laina crossed the lower courtyard on her way to the castle gates. Near the livestock pens, she noticed a woman holding a black and white baby goat. The woman nodded and smiled at Laina in greeting, revealing a few missing teeth. Returning the smile, Laina approached and gently scratched the goat's small furry chin. His strange slanted eyes closed half-way in appreciation of the affection.

"He's a sweet little thing, isn't he?" Laina chirped.

"Aye, born last week, he was," the woman answered.

The goat lightly nibbled Laina's fingers and she giggled.

From across the courtyard, loud voices boomed, drawing the attention of Laina and the goat woman. Laird Galloway and a few of his men crossed the yard with long strides, then stopped about fifteen paces away. The laird said something to the men, gesturing with his hands. They all burst out laughing.

Laina slyly watched the handsome laird.

The woman beside her purred, "He's a sweet little thing, isn't he?"

Laina gave an amused sniff. There wasn't anything *little* about Laird Galloway. He towered over his men, standing as tall as his tallest soldier, with a build as muscular as any of them. Her eyes wandered curiously over him. Every inch of him looked rock hard. Remembering Audrey's story about his bulging breeches, Laina suddenly felt embarrassed to be studying him so closely. But it was difficult to look away. He had a most engaging manner about him.

He was dressed simply — a white, tucked-in shirt, opened casually at the neck, and form-fitting black trousers with black boots. Laina's mouth felt dry. Her eyes travelled up his body slowly until she realized that the laird was staring directly at her, smiling broadly. She blushed and turned back to the goat woman, said a quick goodbye, and hurried on toward the castle gates. After several paces across the yard, she dared a brief look in the laird's direction. Her breath caught upon seeing the laird nod, his gaze still locked on her. Heat rushed to her face and she did not look back again.

The soldiers at the gate stopped their conversation to watch the lass approach. They rarely got to see one so fair passing through. The girls from the nearby village were often kept away from the castle, whether because of the laird's reputation or that of his men, the soldiers didn't know. Even in her worn, faded tunic, the kitchen lass was fetching.

Laina smiled politely and stepped onto the drawbridge.

"Would you like someone to accompany you, lass?" one of them offered.

"No, thank you," she said, keeping her head down to conceal the flush still burning on her face.

"You should not be going outside of the castle alone, lass," the second one said.

Laina hurried across the bridge, calling out, "I will be fine."

They watched her, in silence, until she disappeared over the rise of the nearest hill.

"You ask her the same question every time she leaves — do you think her answer will change?" the second soldier challenged the first.

"I can hope, can I not?" the first soldier answered, chuckling. "I could roll in the meadow all day with that one." Then, with a wicked smile, he added, " She has no da'. Perhaps she be needin' a man in her life."

The second soldier shook his head. "I imagine our laird will be going after that one, so don't get your hopes or your pecker up."

It didn't take long for Laina to cross the grassy hills and make her way through the stretch of forest to reach the stone circle just beyond. It wasn't as grand as the circle near Dounehill. The circle of stones were small and reddish-orange in color. Still, their energy was strong and Laina felt comforted during her visits.

The dark winter months had given Laina time for mourning the death of the life she had known. Nothing could replace what she had lost, no matter how much she ached for it. Her father had often said, "We may not have all we want, but there's good sense in wanting what we have." Laina understood it was important to appreciate what she had, for if she spent all her time thinking of what her life lacked, that's all she would notice. She knew she must make a new life with those who surrounded her now, even though Galloway Castle and its people were so starkly different from her beloved village. Serious and competitive with each other, the castle folk rarely looked up from their work. Worst of all, there was no music or song filling the air, and they didn't dance, except, Laina was told, for the festivals. Still, the castle folk had come to her aid and they had good hearts. Perhaps her days in the castle would get easier over time, she reassured herself. She had to admit, that with the return of spring, she felt hope sprouting anew within her, rising gently from the charred ground of her past.

Standing on the fragrant, flowered mound of the stone circle, Laina watched tiny seed pods detach from their stems and fly around her, dancing lightly in the air. A warm breeze gently lifted her hair, pulling loose the long tendrils from her braid until her hair flew freely about her like a great, magic mane. She could hear and feel the gentle humming vibration of the stones. The pulsing sensation tingled her toes.

Laina remembered that night many months ago when she had been terrified by the energy of the giant stones near Dounehill. It seemed to her now, that her fear had been the only real threat to her that night. Nature was always vibrating, whether one noticed it or not. To experience its power being unleashed suddenly could be shocking, indeed. But nature, itself, was not evil. It simply responded naturally to the thoughts one might be holding. Laina had known she was intruding that night where she shouldn't be. It was only natural that the dragons were unleashed upon her.

The small red stones in front of her glowed softly — a sight that most people would be unable to see. The speckled stone hanging at her throat grew warm. Closing her eyes, Laina let her spirit rise on the air, then spiral and dip like one of the tiny seed pods floating on the wind, all around the stones. As her physical body sank down gracefully to the ground, her mind drifted into a dream.

Surrounded by mist, Laina was confused at first and began to panic. But a sense of calm settled over her as a hooded figure in white took shape and joined her. The cloaked being communicated wordlessly, and Laina understood. The figure held up an engraved, silver goblet. Laina took it and slowly raised it to her lips, until she noticed that the goblet contained white powder. Without explanation, Laina blew into the cup, sending the powder spiraling into the air in sparkling swirls of color. Laina and the hooded figure burst into laughter, giggling like small children. The figure reached up and pushed back the hood of the cloak. Laina stood looking at her mother, and the girl's eyes filled with tears as the two embraced and held each other. The mist then disappeared with a whisper: "Remember this."

Laina awoke on a soft blanket of spring grass laced with tiny white flowers. Squinting her eyes against the bright blue sky, she sighed. This was her life now. And, she decided, her task was to find the best in it and give herself wholeheartedly to that.

The guards stood on the castle wall watching her return. The wind whipped her loose mane of hair and molded her clothing against her body. She strolled lightly, her shoes dangling from her left hand. The guards didn't take their eyes from the lass as she bent to slip on her shoes. Her hair fell forward and touched the ground while she bared one leg to mid-calf, and then the other.

A group of villagers from nearby Galloway Village entered the castle gates and were bewildered when they weren't detained and given the usual barrage of excessive questioning.

"We know who you are, move along," one of the soldiers said with an impatient wave of his hand, before anxiously returning his gaze to the fair lass with the long, flowing hair.

Laina seemed oblivious to the attention she was receiving as she approached the castle. Reaching her hands behind her head, she braided her hair and casually walked up to the end of the drawbridge, the material of her tunic tightening across her breasts to reveal their well-shaped fullness.

One guard on the wall pitched forward off-balance, cursing as he jabbed his hand on a sharp stone in the wall.

Laina looked up at the group of dumbfounded men and smiled. "I assure you, I have no weapons," she called out.

One of them retorted, "Ah, but you could slay us all, lass."

The other men chuckled and nodded.

"Then it appears," Laina said, putting her hands on her hips, "that you have gone to ridiculous lengths to suit up and arm yourselves."

The men burst out laughing, and were still grinning foolishly as Laina crossed the drawbridge and disappeared across the lower courtyard.

"So, you have good news for me?" Gavin asked, noticing Symon's relaxed stride as he approached the laird in the great hall.

"I do, Laird," Symon sank into a chair opposite the laird. "Our task to train the villages to fend off attacks is complete. We have conducted several practice sessions with them, and they are doing well in their response. I would say that they are prepared and ready to confront anyone that might try to come down on them."

"And they're skilled enough to claim a few victims of their own?" the laird asked. "That would give us the information we need to locate and destroy our enemy."

"Aye, m'lord." Symon crossed his arms and let his head tip back. The task had been far greater and taken much longer than he or any of the men could have guessed. It was only after the hardships of winter that they were finally able to complete the critical task given to them by the laird. And delivering success to the laird was Symon's greatest satisfaction. He lived for no less.

Gavin leaned over and slapped his second-in-command on the shoulder. "You've done better than I could have hoped." The laird reached for a velvet bag sitting on the table and dropped it heavily in front of Symon. It clinked as it landed.

"Thank you, Laird. All of the men have done an exceptional job."

"Understood," the laird said. "Their pay is ready and waiting for them as well."

"Would you agree, Laird, that we are in a position now to reduce the number of soldiers positioned in the villages? I know a good number of the men would like to return to the castle and attend the upcoming Mayday Faire."

"Aye." Gavin nodded. "Keep a few men at each location for now, and the rest can return here. After the faire, we'll send one third of them back."

"It's going to be a good faire this year, Laird," Symon said, standing. "We still have an enemy to find, but the accomplishments of the men have earned a celebration."

Gavin smiled. "Tell the men we'll have plenty of ale ready for their return."

Chapter Ten

𝔰𝔬𝔠𝔯

FOR TWO SOLID DAYS, preparations for the annual Mayday Faire filled every corner of Galloway Castle. Merchant stalls of wood and canvas lined the perimeter of the giant, lower courtyard, to sell and trade all manner of items: knives, cloth, leather goods, tools, jewelry, and animals. People had already started bartering back and forth, most of them good-naturedly, although there were always those who bickered simply for the sake of claiming the better argument.

In the center of the faire setup, long wood tables held large platters heaped with roasted birds, fish, meat pies, cheese, fruit, bread, and a variety of sweet treats. Laird Galloway spared no expense for his festivals and the guests who travelled from distances near and far to attend.

Musicians tuned their instruments and prepared to play from a platform at the far end of the courtyard, while costumed performers greeted the crowd of guests pouring in through the castle gates. Exuberant shouts sounded as soldiers returned after many months away from the castle. The sounds of the faire echoed up to the kitchen and made it difficult for the girls to stay focused amidst all the excitement.

Gillian, Audrey, and Lucy, along with two serving girls from the castle, scurried to and from the faire delivering the food. Margaret and Laina finished loading the last tray of meat pies just as Avery the brewer arrived with a cart, carrying six large trays loaded with tankards of ale from the brewhouse next door. He walked up to Margaret and stood there grinning. She put her hands on her hips and smirked at the large man with the long beard, knowing what he wanted, but waiting for him to ask. He gave her elbow a playful tweak and said, "I'm sure the faire guests would rather be served by you pretty lasses than by me and my whiskered helpers."

"Of course they would," Margaret retorted.

Avery gave a laugh and turned away. "We're taking the kegs over. Your girls can get the guests started with these trays."

"I think I'll be gettin' meself started," Margaret said, reaching for one of the tankards and taking a big swig of ale. A contented smile spread across her face. The brewer paused in the doorway and watched her.

"Ah, this is a fine batch, Avery," she said.

He nodded with pride. "I thought ye would like it!"

"All right girls," Margaret sang out, "let's get these tankards over to the faire. Where are Audrey and Lucy?"

"I lost sight of them on our last trip to the food tables," Gillian answered.

"Ah. Well they'll show up. You girls bring these trays back when you're finished, then you can attend the faire yourselves." The cook looked around the kitchen to assess their progress and noted what remained to be done. Satisfied, she took another big swig of ale and belched.

Laina laughed and handed a tray to Gillian.

"There's music, girls...do you hear it?" The pitch of Margaret's voice sounded noticeably higher than usual. "Oh, we are going to have us a fine time! And I intend to do some dancing." She turned her feet to inspect her shoes. Then, eyeing Laina, she asked, "How about you, lass?" Just in case the girl needing urging, she added, "Laird Galloway expects everyone in his service to participate in the festivals."

"Oh yes, I will," Laina assured, hoisting a tray of ale onto her shoulder and heading for the door. "I wouldn't want to disappoint the laird," she quipped.

"That, you wouldn't," Margaret said, taking another drink.

To be sure, Laina had no intention of missing out on the music and dancing. It was the most exciting thing to happen since she had arrived at the castle. Making her way down to the lower courtyard, her pulse quickened with each step. Hearty laughter and shouts of revelry rang out from all directions, while overhead, colorful streamers flapped gayly in the light breeze against the clear blue sky. Music at the far end of the courtyard drew her forward — beckoning to her like an old friend.

Weaving through the crowd, Laina took in everything around her as she made her way to the musician's platform. She had never seen such magnificent clothing — beautiful velvets and silks in vibrant blues, reds, golds, and greens. Some trimmed with fur or lace, others adorned with elaborate embroidery or buttons. A wandering juggler dressed in red and green, and wearing a funny little cap with bells on it, paused to show Laina his tricks. She rewarded him with gasps of delight, then laughed when he ended his performance with a flip and pretended to land painfully on his rump.

A dozen people whirled and stomped their feet in time with the music, while those who were watching, clapped or banged on nearby tables.

Fond memories flooded back to Laina. She could visualize the dirt lane in front of the Droothy Hare Tavern, where she had spent many nights as a child, dancing under the stars. In the dry season, the villagers would stir up so much dust with their dancing that little Laina would end up coated with a thin layer of dirt. She could still remember the taste of it. Coated in brown from head to toe, she would smile radiantly at her father and he would laugh.

Looking up at the musicians on the platform, Laina tapped the worn toes of her brown leather shoes to keep pace with the lively tune. For the first time since arriving at the castle, she felt swept up in something joyful and wonderfully familiar. So much so, that she had completely forgotten to hand out any of the ale on her tray.

"Excuse me, lass," a male voice beckoned smoothly from behind her.

Smiling, Laina turned, then gasped. Before her, stood the blonde musician again, tall and handsome, dressed in black breeches, black boots, and a rich brown doublet over a white linen shirt. His shoulder-length hair was tied at the nape of his neck, and a black cap on his head, adorned with a pheasant feather, hung slightly to one side.

He raised an eyebrow and nodded at the full tray of ale she was holding on her shoulder. "Might m'lady have a tankard of ale for a thirsty musician waiting his turn to play?"

"Yes, of course," she said, feeling strangely shy and awkward, all at once. She hurried to hand him a drink, the sudden movement causing ale to slosh over the tops of the tankards. Embarassed, she glanced up at him. Evan offered her a broad, dazzling smile, his bright blue eyes crinkling happily at the corners.

He had been watching her move fluidly through the faire crowd, her long dark braid swinging gently with the sway of her walk. As usual, despite her servant's clothing, and apron spotted with berry juice, she looked as radiant as an angel.

"It is a pleasure to see you again," he said, as she tried to calm herself by rearranging the tankards on her tray. "May I re-introduce myself properly?" he asked. Removing his cap, he bowed dramatically. "Evan Prestwick, of the Westport Musician's Troupe."

A smile played with the corners of her mouth. She had to admit, she was happy to see him. But she didn't necessarily want him to know that. There was more she wanted to learn about him.

Perhaps she had met him at his worst. Laina supposed that someone who was as well-travelled as he, might be a bit cocky, as well as finding it difficult to be patient with the simple ways of common villagers. It was understandable...and yet, he had been humble enough to apologize to her for his earlier behavior. Since that first meeting, he had been kind and genuine. Perhaps he was worth getting to know.

"And your name, lass?"

Suddenly realizing he was waiting for a response from her, Laina gave a short cough. "Oh, my name is Laina. Laina Makgregor." Her free hand moved to smooth her apron. "I've been working in Laird Galloway's kitchen since I was brought here," she added, as if it were her new description in life.

"Laina," Evan repeated, letting it roll slowly off of his tongue, like a tasty morsel he wanted to savor. "Well lass, I am happy to have another chance to talk with you." Nodding toward her stained apron, he added, "and I look forward to sampling some of the tarts you so passionately made for these festivities."

Laina looked down at her terribly stained apron and immediately blushed.

Evan burst out laughing.

She rushed to offer an explanation, "I made three different flavors: blueberry, raspberry, and cherry."

Evan nodded. "Yes, I *see*!"

Her blush increased, as did Evan's laughter. Looking down again, Laina burst out laughing too. She had been so excited to get to the faire, she hadn't realized the condition of her apron. With large red and blue smears, it was a hideous mess.

Their laughter eased and Laina noticed that Evan was smiling fondly at her. He was more handsome every time she saw him. He was strong and masculine, yet his build was lean — not bulky like the soldiers Laina typically saw around the castle. When he smiled, she wanted to smile too. Something inside of her flickered.

Evan cleared his throat and looked off in the distance. "I've heard that Laird Galloway encourages all of his servants to join in and dance at the faire." Evan returned his gaze to her. "Will you be dancing too, Laina?"

"I suppose I might..." she said, "when I'm finished working."

"Well then," Evan said, "I sincerely hope you will dance with me when you finish your work." He gave a quick bow of his head.

Speechless, Laina could only nod and smile. Yes, she had to get back to work, she reminded herself. She moved numbly back into the crowd. Her heart pounding, she barely saw the faces around her as she tried to refocus on her task of handing out ale. Her thoughts swirled around Evan, and the fact that he wanted her to dance with him. She was seeing a different side of him, and she couldn't think straight. She suddenly wanted to talk to Margaret — perhaps the cook could help her sort it out.

With a new sense of urgency, Laina began handing out ale to people who weren't asking for any. She worked her way to the outer edge of the crowd as quickly as possible, then raced up to the upper courtyard and across the lawn. Just before reaching the kitchen, she quickly drank the remaining tankard of ale that was left on her tray. She still had a bit of foam from the ale on her upper lip as she hurried into the kitchen. Seeing that Margaret was there alone, Laina blurted out breathlessly, "One of the Westport musicians has asked me to dance with him."

Margaret looked up from the basket she was filling and considered Laina thoughtfully. "And you're preparing yourself with liquid courage, I see." The cook threw back her head and laughed, then took the tray from Laina's hands and set it down.

Laina wiped her mouth with her hand.

"One of the Wesport musicians, eh?" Margaret cocked her head.

"Yes," Laina answered. "I've met him before. He stopped by my village and was very rude. Although, I must admit, the people of Dounehill were not very friendly or cooperative either. And then he stopped by here briefly a few weeks after I arrived. I think I must have met him at his worst. He has been much nicer since."

"Ah," Margaret said, remembering the man she had seen outside the kitchen.

"He's very handsome," Laina admitted. Embarrassed, she quickly added, "I'm not sure what to do."

"Well," Margaret said, untying and removing Laina's stained apron, "I'd say a little dance with him won't hurt. Just have fun, and if he starts to bother ye, dump him on his arse...which I know ye are capable of doing."

Laina laughed. "All right." Taking a deep breath, she smoothed her hands over her face, willing the heat away, and walked slowly out the kitchen door. "A little dance with him won't hurt," she said to herself.

Approaching the edge of the faire crowd, Laina suddenly felt naked without a platter in her hands or some other work-related task. Observing the finely-dressed people, she began to feel out of place, and wondered if she really belonged at such an event. Her thoughts were interrupted by a soldier who suddenly scooped her up, spun her around, and shouted in a drunken slur, "My kingdom for a beautiful lady!" Laina giggled, and after the soldier set her down, he bowed awkwardly and staggered off.

The playful encounter helped her to relax, but she needed to regain more of her courage before returning to see Evan. His clear, blue eyes and easy smile were so charming when he stood close to her. She would look foolish if she were to go speechless again. It wasn't like her to be thrown off balance. She decided to wander around the large circle of merchant stalls, slowly heading back in the direction of the musician's platform. That would give her time to collect herself.

She caught sight of Lucy and Boyd standing near the food tables, helping themselves to some of the sweets. Lucy chattered on, her golden curls bouncing with each movement of her head. She paused only long enough to stuff bits of cream puff in her mouth. Boyd steadied himself against the table edge, leaning on his crippled legs, and hanging on Lucy's every word.

Laina paused in front of a merchant's stall filled with finely sewn leather shoes. Dyed in different colors, some of them had big bright buckles.

"Try a pair on, lass," the merchant urged.

"Oh no, thank you," Laina said, moving along quickly.

By the musician's platform, Evan finished his ale and wondered if Miss Laina Makgregor would be returning. If she didn't, he might just go looking for her. He knew he wouldn't have much time to spend with her before he had to be back on the road.

The thought frustrated him, which, in turn, amused him. It wasn't like him to be so intrigued with anyone. His life left little time for such involvements — he knew the temporary nature of all indulgences and he didn't have any further expectations. This girl seemed different to him somehow. It was more than the fact that she was beautiful. His head was not turned as easily as that. No, it was something about the way she moved and spoke, and the look on her face. She was genuine. That was it. She did not seek to gain or impress, and he found it remarkably refreshing.

If Evan was anything, he was intuitive about people. It was a necessary skill for living on the road. If he had read Laina right, her contempt for him had eased. So maybe he had a chance to redeem himself. He took another drink and decided that he would wait until the end of the current song being played, and then go in search of her.

Laina had travelled past a large number of the merchant stalls, ending up near the opposite side of the musician's platform. The last stall was filled with crates that had clothing strewn across them.

"Enjoying the music are ye?" A twisted old man with one eye and several missing teeth asked, smiling at Laina. He sat on a stool with fabric draped across his lap and a needle in one hand.

"Aye, 'tis wonderful," she said. "What are you making?"

"Costumes!" he shouted proudly.

Laina was only a few feet from the man, but he yelled as if she couldn't hear him.

"I sew for the theatre company. They will be performing tonight!" He was impressed that this pretty young lass would speak to him. Most people moved away quickly when they saw him. Noticing the condition of the girl's garment, he decided that she wasn't spoiled. Nay, she was a sweet one.

Laina admired a few of the dresses laying on top of a large pile of clothing. Her fingers trailed down the satin trim along the fitted bodice of a bright blue dress.

"Here! Try this one on!" The old man was suddenly right at her side, holding up a dark green velvet dress with light green satin peeking out of the bodice and the long sleeves. An intricate leaf pattern embroidered in gold, highlighted the neckline and bodice.

"Oh, no thank you," Laina said, waving her hand in polite protest.

The old man shouted, "I've never met a lass who didn't like trying on a pretty dress. Won't you do it to please an old tailor?"

His one eye twinkled.

She didn't reach for the dress, but suddenly it was laying in her hands. She felt the luxurious weight of it, and absent-mindedly hugged it to her chest.

"You would be doing me a favor, lass." The old man creased his brow. "The theatre company is thinking of replacing me with a better tailor."

"No!" Laina said.

"'Tis true! The bastards!" the man shouted. "I need someone to try on this dress so I can see where I've made me mistakes before they inspect me work again." The tailor looked pleadingly at Laina. "Please do me this favor, lass. It might help me keep my position." His face darkened and puckered up, as if he were ready to cry. He made a noise like a choked sob.

"All right." Laina put her hand reassuringly on his shoulder.

Brightening immediately, he led her behind a screen where she could change clothes.

Once all of the front lacings were tightened up, Laina emerged from behind the screen. The dress revealed her slender womanly curves in stunning detail, the tightened bodice prominently pushing up the soft, creamy mounds of her breasts just above the low neckline.

"Come here and let me see ye!" the old man shouted.

Laina glided over in front of the tailor and twirled around, then put her hand over her mouth and giggled at herself.

The old man beamed. "Ye look beautiful, lass! Warms my heart, it does! Now let's see if I've made any mistakes."

"From where I stand, it looks to be a perfect fit," a second male voice assured.

Laina's breath caught as she turned to see Evan.

He smiled and bowed his head to her. "Greetings again, Laina. You are breathtaking." He did not try to conceal his appreciative gaze as he took in every inch of her. He noticed the spotted stone necklace — the beloved treasure he had returned to her the first time they had met — hanging at her throat. The earthy quality of it was sweet, in combination with the elegant dress she wore.

Embarrassed to be parading about, Laina hurried to explain, "I was just trying on this dress to help this tailor."

"They're going to replace me with another if I don't improve me work!" the old man yelled at Evan.

"I see!" Evan laughed. "Well, we better test the dress to see if it holds up to dancing." He held out his hand to Laina.

"Good idea!" the old man yelled.

Without giving her a chance to refuse, Evan grasped her hand firmly and quickly led Laina around the musician's platform to join a circle dance that was just beginning. Laina couldn't believe what was happening, but she wasn't sure she wanted to stop it either. She stepped into the inner circle with the ladies, while Evan joined the outer circle with the men. Travelling in opposite directions, they passed each other until the music changed tempo, at which point each man would grab the lady nearest him and spin her around.

Some of the men lifted Laina completely off of the ground, while others were clumsy, stepping on her feet and bumping into her. By the time she made it back to Evan, she was laughing so hard her eyes were bright with joyful tears. Pulling her close as the music slowed, Evan welcomed her into his embrace. He held her gently against his strong, firm body, and moved with grace and confidence, twirling her so that she had to hold onto him tightly.

With her tender, shapely body pressed up against his, Evan began to question his willpower. He had no intention of dishonoring the lass during his visit to Galloway Castle, but lord how she made his blood race. One sweet kiss from her soft lips would warm many a night that lay ahead of him on the road.

Leaning down, he whispered into her ear, "I like having you in my arms."

She smiled up at him, but her courage abandoned her under the directness of his gaze, and she looked away to avoid his eyes.

As the music tempo increased again, the couple spun apart and Evan watched with amazement as Laina instinctively hiked up the beautiful green skirt and began doing the fanciest footwork he'd ever seen. Graceful, yet lightening fast, she kept perfect rhythm with the music. Turning her head from side to side, she flashed a feisty smile, as people gathered around to clap and urge her on.

Where in the hell had she learned to dance like that, Evan wondered? He couldn't pull his gaze away. The lass continued to intrigue him with her every move. It was a most unsettling feeling to want her as he did, and know that he would not be able to have her. His lifestyle had brought him many women along the road, and he had no trouble walking away when the time came. Why should this be any different? Something nagged at him, dangling the answer just out of his reach.

The song ended and Laina's voice interrupted his thoughts. Her face beaming, she said "This dress is holding together well. That dear old tailor should be able to keep his job."

Evan laughed and took Laina's hands. "That dear old tailor is Oswyn Erskyn, the finest tailor in all of Great Britain."

"What? But he said..."

"He said what he needed to say to get you into the dress." Evan smiled wryly as he thought how he, himself, would love to get her out of it.

"But why?" Laina asked.

"Why not? Oswyn has a good eye." Evan snickered at his unintentional joke. "He knew the dress would suit you perfectly. He saw a sweet lass who deserved to have some fun."

Laina opened her mouth to respond, but didn't know what to say. Why not, indeed...she decided. Clearly the old tailor was a very kind man and she would most surely thank him.

Evan squeezed her hands. "Laina, it is with difficultly that I must let you go at this moment. I could dance with you for hours, but it is almost time for my troupe to play. Will you join me again afterward?"

"Yes," Laina answered, "I would like that."

Evan raised her right hand to his lips, and lingered briefly with a gentle kiss, then flashed her a feisty smile of his own, before he strode off.

Laina watched him leave, still feeling the place where his lips had touched her skin. She noticed the confident gait of his tall, firm body, the broadness of his shoulders, and the brightness of the sun's rays on his blonde hair. Two women giggled as he passed. He gave them a courteous nod and disappeared around the side of the musician's platform.

Letting out the breath she didn't know she was holding, Laina headed toward the old tailor's stall. She must thank the dear man and return the dress.

The tailor's stool sat empty, however, and Laina's clothing was no longer hanging over the screen where she had left it. She would have to return later.

Anxious to find Margaret and tell her everything, Laina hurried back to the kitchen but found it empty except for a yellow dog scrounging for scraps.

Returning to the faire, Laina looked for Margaret near the food tables. There she found only drunk and boisterous soldiers wanting to lift her up onto the messy tables in the beautiful dress. She barely escaped their grasp.

Hearing a change in the music, she made her way to the

musician's platform. Evan's group had begun to play. He looked
calm and confident as he skillfully played an intricately carved
stringed instrument. His right foot tapped out the beat of the music,
while his fingers moved quickly on the strings. Laina watched the
muscles in his forearms flex as he played. He looked over and
smiled at her.

As the sun sank toward the horizon, a brilliant blaze of color
settled across the sky. Sounds of laughter and music, along with the
beautiful sights surrounding her, filled Laina with a sense of joy
she hadn't felt in a long time.

Noticing a disturbance to her left, she turned her head. Parting
like a wave, the crowd opened up to reveal Laird Galloway,
strolling toward the platform. Wearing a deep red tunic with gold
trim, his towering presence was even more striking than usual.
Flashing his brilliant white smile, he greeted people as he moved
forward.

Laina stepped aside with the crowd, but the laird stopped right
in front of her. He faced her with his hands clasped behind his
back. A few gasps and murmurs arose from those nearby.

"Greetings lass, I was watching your delightful dancing
earlier."

Stunned, Laina blushed. She inwardly cursed herself because
she had been blushing a great deal lately, and she thought it a sign
of weakness.

"What is your name?" Laird Galloway asked.

"Laina Makgregor, m'lord." She gave a brief curtsey.

"Laina?" he asked, suddenly realizing with astonishment who
this girl in the striking green velvet dress was. The pretty kitchen
waif from Dounehill was actually a very shapely and beautiful
woman.

His green eyes blazed. "You look ravishing Laina."

"Thank you, m'lord." Not sure what else to do, Laina stared at
the gold embroidery on the chest of his tunic. It was very intricate,
with loops and curves and…

Gavin extended his hand and gently tipped her head up to meet
his gaze. "Dance with me."

Her legs felt weak. However, knowing that she and the laird
were the center of attention, she did her best to respond gracefully.
"I would be honored, m'lord."

As the laird led her in front of the musician's platform, people
quickly stepped aside. At first, the laird moved formally, holding
Laina apart from him. It gave him an opportunity to observe her

beauty and movements. He had seen her around the castle a few times, and thought her too young and shy to engage. He'd had no idea just how lovely she really was. What a pleasant surprise, he thought to himself.

Laina's skin glowed with the rosy hues of the setting sun. Wisps of her dark silky hair framed her face. She was fairly successful in concealing her fear of the laird, and this amused and intrigued him greatly. There was no shortage of beautiful women at the faire who longed for the laird's company and favor. But the little kitchen maid had captured his full attention.

Laina glanced up at the musician's platform and saw Evan keeping track of her. He winked.

At that moment, the laird pulled Laina up against his giant and powerful, muscled body and held her in a firm embrace. As he began twirling her around the dance floor, people called out to urge their laird on.

Spotting Margaret with her eyes wide and mouth gaping open, Laina expelled a laugh. No doubt, there would be much talk in the kitchen tomorrow.

Round and round the couple danced, as the musicians increased the tempo. Instead of focusing on how overwhelming her encounter with the laird was, Laina listened to the music. When he released his grip so that she could twirl, she interjected some of her fancy footwork with an impish smile. Delighted, the laird roared with laughter and spun her out again and again.

By the end of the song, Laina was breathing hard. She smiled at the laird and held a hand to her heaving chest to calm herself. Laird Galloway pulled her close again, his gaze piercing. She suddenly felt very aware of how big and powerful his body was, and she nearly stopped breathing all-together. His eyes softened and smiled, touching her more intimately than his embrace.

"Lass, will you join me tomorrow for a midday walk in the garden?"

Laina suppressed a gasp. "M'lord, you honor me."

The laird smiled broadly. "Tomorrow then. Raising her hand to his lips, he kissed it tenderly before walking back into the crowd, people nodding and bowing at his every step.

Laina heard whispering in the crowd around her. Suddenly, Margaret was at Laina's side, beaming. "Ohh, missy, we must talk!" Grabbing Laina's arm, Margaret hurried them out of the crowd, much to Laina's relief, and in the direction of the kitchen. Margaret was unusually aglow from all of the excitement and ale.

As they entered the kitchen, Audrey came rushing forward, a hint of accusation in her voice. "I can't believe you were dancing with the laird!"

Clearly the news had just been delivered by Boyd, who sat nearby on a stool, still trying to catch his own breath.

"Tell us everything!" Gillian squeeled.

"Well," Laina began, uncomfortable with all of the attention.

"Where did you get that dress?" Audrey interrupted.

"Did he hold you against his body?" Gillian urged impatiently.

"Let her tell the story!" Lucy insisted.

Margaret sat down and dabbed at her flushed face with a kitchen towel.

"Did he smell good?" Gillian asked.

"What difference does it make what he smells like?" Audrey screamed.

"Let her tell the story!" Lucy insisted again.

There was a brief moment of silence.

"Well," Laina began, "there isn't much to tell."

"What do you mean by that?" Audrey demanded.

Laina gave a small laugh at Audrey's easy frustration. "It all happened so fast...in truth, my head is still spinning from it."

"You do realize, do you not, that he has been with hundreds of women?" Audrey spat. "Maybe thousands."

"How do you know how many women he has been with?" Gillian shouted in defense.

"Everyone knows!" Audrey screamed. "Don't think he is interested in you, Laina, for anything more than...you know."

"Is that true, Margaret?" Lucy asked.

"I've known the laird for many years, and he is a good man. Yes, he loves the ladies. What virile man doesn't? But he is respectful, as near as I can tell."

"He is a good dancer," Laina offered.

"Did he grab a feel of you while you were dancing?" Audrey pressed.

"No!" Laina laughed.

"Did he kiss you?" Lucy asked.

"He kissed my hand," Laina admitted.

The girls stood stunned.

Margaret added, "He wants Laina to walk with him tomorrow in the garden."

"What?" Gillian yelled. "Laina, do you realize how fortunate you are?"

"That's when he'll grab a feel," Audrey concluded with a smirk.

"Okay, that's enough," Margaret said. "Let's get a bit of cleanup done before you girls go home. The rest can wait 'til tomorrow." Margaret motioned for Audrey and Gillian to clear off the work surfaces, then nodded to Lucy and said, "Run get my special platters from the food tables, lassie."

Lucy ran out the door.

Turning to Laina with a broad grin, Margaret said, "Lass, I pulled you away from the faire and I suspect there is more you would like to do."

"Yes." Laina answered. "I must return this dress, and I promised to meet Evan again."

Margaret nodded. "See you in the morning."

Chapter Eleven

෧෬

AS THE SUN SANK BELOW the horizon, countless stars appeared overhead and the faire grew louder and more boisterous. Torch-lighters circled around the festival area, lighting torches and lanterns. Laina was aware of heads turning as she approached, but she ignored the prying eyes. The sea of people seemed thicker in the dark. There had been plenty for all to drink, as evidenced by the loud laughter and slurred speech all around her. In the distance, a portion of the crowd laughed together every few moments in response to someone on the musician's platform telling jokes.

Picking a path through the swaying mass of bodies, Laina emerged in a less-crowded area by the food tables. Tankards and goblets littered the surfaces. Very little food remained. A few people picked morsels of meat from the bones, while a few dogs searched the ground.

A roar of approval went up from the crowd, and Laina almost didn't hear a nearby scream over the noise. It had sounded like Lucy. Laina ran in the direction of the sound and found Lucy being restrained by three very drunk male guests. The platters that Lucy had come back to retrieve for Margaret were laying on the ground. One man, seated on a bench in a dark corner, held Lucy firmly with one arm wrapped around her, while his free hand twirled her curls around his finger. Her white cap lay on the ground at their feet. Another man, so drunk he could barely keep his balance, was bending down to stroke her cheek and making kissing sounds near her ear. Lucy's terrified eyes peered out of her tear-stained face.

Laina reached for her knife, only to realize that she had left it and her belt with her tunic at the tailor's booth.

A third man staggered toward Laina. "Well, what do we have here?"

"Let the girl go, you drunken clods!" Laina demanded.

"We be havin' a lil' fun, that's all," the man slurred as he approached.

"Take your hands off of her now!" Laina looked around for something to use as a weapon.

The man holding Lucy, suddenly released her and stood up. "Ooo, let's play with the older one," he said eyeing Laina's breasts. "Her's are bigger." Free from his grip, Lucy darted away.

Snatching up a large metal platter from the ground, Laina swung it hard against the side of the man's head nearest her. It made a loud clang, and he screamed in agony. A trickle of blood ran down his face from a cut on his forehead.

"You bitch!" the man screamed.

The man from the bench lunged forward, grabbed Laina, and pulled her back into the corner. Laina kicked and struggled like a wildcat. When she screamed, he clamped a large, rough hand tightly over her mouth. "Aw, c'mon lassie," he pleaded. "We dunna want to hurt you — just show us your diddies."

"Aye," added the drunkest man, opening his eyes wide, "we want to see your di-diddlies," and then he began laughing hysterically.

The bleeding man touched his head and stared furiously at the blood on his fingers. He stormed toward the bench. "For what she did to me, the bitch is going to show us more than that!"

"Oh, I think she went easy on you," a smooth male voice said threateningly. Evan Prestwick stood several feet away, glaring at the men. "Whereas, I…" he said, bending down and slipping a wicked-looking dagger from his boot, "will make sure to leave a *much* bigger scar."

The drunkest man had stopped laughing. He lurched toward the musician. Evan punched him square in the face with a loud smack, and the man fell limply to the ground.

"Next?" Evan challenged darkly, holding his knife ready.

The two remaining men stared at Evan. Laina watched in fascination, her mouth still covered. The bleeding man reached for his own knife, and Evan exerted a swift kick to the man's arm, which sent the knife flying into the dark. Enraged, the man lept at Evan, but stopped short when the tip of Evan's dagger poked at his throat.

"Enough," Evan growled. "You've worn out your welcome at this party." Looking toward the man holding Laina, Evan said, "If you don't release her immediately, I'm going to stop being so nice."

The man on the bench shrugged his shoulders with a nervous grin and let Laina go. She gave him a sharp jab to the ribs with her elbow, causing him to suck in his breath, and then she moved quickly to Evan's side.

Removing the tip of his knife from the bleeding man's throat, Evan shoved the man away hard, and put an arm around Laina, leading her back toward the faire crowd.

"Are you all right?" he asked, gazing down at her and giving her shoulder a squeeze. She did not look like a lass who had just been in a dangerous situation. He saw more anger and strength in her than fear.

"Yes," she answered, looking up at him. "I am so glad you came along."

"Do you mean at that moment, or in general?" Evan teased.

Laina laughed. "I normally carry my own knife, but I left it with my belt in the tailor's stall."

"Ah, yes," Evan replied, his eyes twinkling as they wandered over her. "There aren't many places to hide a knife in the dress you are wearing, are there?"

"Not unless I were still wearing my kitchen apron, which has a pocket," she quipped.

The mental image of Laina's berry-stained apron over the beautiful green dress gave Evan a hearty chuckle.

Laina's face brightened. "Did you get to try one of my berry tarts?"

"Why no, I didn't," Evan said with dismay.

"Let's see if there are any left," she said, hiking up her skirt and running toward the food tables.

Evan followed, smiling broadly.

Littered with dirty dishes and spilled food, the tables were in complete disarray. Laina circled them slowly, grimacing when she had to remove a pair of breeches from one of the tabletops.

"Here they are!" Evan called, standing at a table with a tart in each hand.

Laina joined him excitedly.

"There are only two left," Evan said, holding them out for her to examine.

"A blueberry and a cherry," she determined. "You must try both."

Evan grinned and tipped his head for her to follow him. They walked along the edge of the massive stone wall that enclosed the courtyard, following it around the side of the castle grounds to get away from the faire noise.

Finally spotting a patch of grass near the wall, Evan turned to Laina. "Here?"

"It's perfect." Laina sat down, carefully positioning the beautiful green dress around her so that it wouldn't get dirty. It didn't matter that only her chemise was between her bottom and the earth, she liked the feel of the cool ground.

A roar of cheering from the crowd in the distance signaled the arrival of the theatre group. From nearby, the rhythmic sound of someone snoring reached Laina, and she giggled.

"This is delicious!" Evan said, licking a bit of berry filling off of his finger.

"You have to try some of this one too," Laina urged. She broke off a piece and handed it to him.

He plopped it into his mouth and closed his eyes.

"Mmmm. Did you make these yourself?"

"I did. Were the stains on my apron not proof enough for you?"

Evan laughed. "True, that was most convincing."

Laina gazed up at the crescent moon while licking cherry juice from her lips.

Evan watched her pink tongue glide across her lips, and then he decided that he needed to shift his gaze — the sight of her was doing strange things to him. Lowering his eyes from her lips, he saw the moonlight reflecting off of her breasts, which were pushed even higher by the tight bodice as she sat on the ground. The soft, firm mounds of her milky flesh looked like they might pop free at any moment.

Evan groaned and adjusted the way he was sitting. "The laird is a lucky man," he mumbled.

"What do you mean?" Laina slipped another piece of tart into her mouth and looked at Evan thoughtfully.

Evan was immediately sorry he had spoken aloud.

Laina delicately wiped her mouth with her fingers. "Do you wish you had all of this?"

"Oh, no," Evan shook his head, "this is not the kind of life for me. There are too many political games, too many rules, too much treachery. I value freedom and new experiences over the struggle of protecting wealth and position."

"Then why do you think the laird is lucky?"

Evan sighed. It was his own fault for opening up the subject.

He might as well be honest about what he was thinking. "Because he gets you."

"He does not get me!" Laina shouted.

There was a brief disruption in the snoring nearby. Evan chuckled.

"He has you here at his castle," Evan explained, "and he seems quite taken with you. I might wager that when I return for the next faire, you could be on his arm."

Laina stared at Evan in disbelief. "From what I've heard, he likes *all* the ladies, and the more the better. I'm just a servant, and I imagine I am just of brief interest to him. He might even be feeling sorry for me."

"I doubt that," Evan said. "You do not appear to be the type of person that anyone needs to feel sorry for." He paused to take another bite of the tart. "There are many reasons the laird would be genuinely interested in you, Laina. You're smart and beautiful — and in that dress, you're..."

"Exactly," Laina said. "It's the dress. Tomorrow when I'm back in my old clothes — a simple kitchen maid — I doubt the laird will remember me."

"You are definitely not simple, Laina," Evan said firmly, "and you will never be defined by the work you do." In the silence that followed, his words seemed to echo.

Laina suddenly realized that she had stopped feeling nervous around Evan. In fact, she felt very comfortable with him. She didn't know if it was because of the gentle and protective way he held her while they danced, or the sincerity she saw in his eyes, or the fact that he rescued her from nasty men. At some point she had begun to trust him, and for reasons she couldn't explain, it felt familiar to be with him.

"Here," she said, smiling and holding up a piece of tart to his mouth, "you must have the last bite."

He leaned forward to take the bite gently, but then playfully chomped her fingers and held onto them. She giggled wildly and Evan delighted in her sparkling eyes and the joyful look on her face. He watched her expression as his lips and tongue gently played with her fingertips.

Her laughter gave way to a blissful smile and she fell back onto the grass, in a playful swoon.

"You are a very brave girl, Laina," he said. "To have been through all you have, and yet, you show no fear — not of your new life at Galloway Castle, or the laird's attentions, or of me..."

"Being afraid releases the dragons," Laina said dreamily. "Then you wear yourself out running from them, and you miss the magic."

"Is that so?" Evan said.

Laina propped herself up on one elbow in the grass and looked at him. "You don't seem to be afraid of much either."

Evan smiled. "Hmm. I suppose I'm not."

"And why is that?"

"Well," Evan answered, "there seems to be less to be afraid of when you're not under the restraint or control of someone else. Many people live under the rule of lords, which makes them subject to the mistakes and whims of their lord, as well as any others who might have grievances against their lord. I would imagine that the villages under Laird Galloway's rule are feeling fear from the unseen enemy who is targeting the laird's territory. And yet, there is little they can do but rely on the laird's protection."

Laina nodded, understanding.

"Now, in my case," Evan continued, "when there's trouble, I can move on. I make my own decisions about where to go and how to protect myself. I'm in control, instead of letting someone else be in control over me."

"But don't you miss your family?" Laina asked. "Don't you miss having roots somewhere?"

"My travelling companions are my family."

"What about your ma or da? Do you have brothers or sisters?"

"No," Evan answered. "My mother died when I was born, and my father sailed away on a boat as soon as I was old enough to take care of myself."

"How old was that?" Laina asked.

"Twelve summers. Fortunately," Evan added, "I had musical talent early on, and I was able to play for my food and shelter. Life on the road is what I know." He laughed as memories floated across his face. "I have been some amazing places."

Laina studied him in the moonlight. Like herself, he was on his own. Perhaps that's why he felt familiar to her. They had a similar way of moving through life. She visualized him as a small boy, living on the road. What a brave soul. It made her want to hug him.

"It's a good life," Evan said. "But sometimes I'm impatient with fearful people."

"Like the people of Dounehill?" Laina asked with a smirk.

"Well, no..."

"It's true," Laina said, "we were suspicious of anyone outside of our village. But that's because we didn't want to be lorded over by anyone either. They were strong-willed, but good people."

"I'm sure they were," Evan said softly. "I'm sorry for how I acted toward them."

"Well, you found my necklace," Laina said brightly, touching the stone at her neck. "I wasn't very nice to you either when you returned it to me. I am most grateful to have it back."

Evan flashed a playful grin. "So, what's my reward?"

Laina nodded to the tart crumbs on the ground. "You just ate it."

Evan threw back his head and laughed. "Wait a minute, I saved you from those men too."

Laina fell back on the grass laughing, "Ah, you're right! Oh dear, I'm all out of rewards..."

Without thought, Evan leaned down and pressed his mouth to her's. Lord, he had been wanting to do it all evening. He kissed her with tenderness, and to his surprise, she gently slipped her arms around him and their kiss deepened.

Laina was surprised at herself — but then, the whole day had been one surprise after another. She did not want to fight it. It would be over soon, and she wanted to enjoy every magical moment, fearlessly.

Evan's soft lips and tongue made her head spin. He slipped an arm behind her and pulled her up against him, savoring her sweetness as long as he dare. His body ached for more of her, but he knew he couldn't let things go any further. He pulled away gently after giving her a light, parting kiss on her reddened lips.

Dazed, Laina stared up at him, her eyes soft.

"I'm sorry," he said. "I must go. I must go now."

"Now?" she muttered.

He stood abruptly, then reached out his hand to help her up. She saw a curtain of sadness cross his face.

"You must leave right now?" she repeated with frustration.

He frowned. "Aye, our troupe packed up the equipment earlier and we have a campsite in the forest for tonight. At sunrise, we ride on to our next destination." He tried to smile as he boasted, "We are to play the King's court in two days."

It was over already? Laina searched his eyes for an answer as she stood, her lips still rosy from his kiss. She tried to understand — he had his life on the road, and she had her's at the castle. That wasn't likely to change for either one of them anytime soon. She had chosen not to think about that all evening. It was her own fault if she was disappointed.

He held her hand firmly as they walked back to the faire in silence. His thoughts raged. It was driving him mad to leave her, and to think of the laird having her. But he had to be realistic. He could not settle down in any one place, which meant he couldn't become attached. At least not for awhile. The troupe was at the peak of their popularity. They had gained a good reputation and were well sought after by all the nobles. He had responsibilities. He also did not want to interfere with Laina's chances for a good life. If the laird was interested in her, she would be well cared for. It was the logical choice, whether or not he liked it.

At the edge of the crowd, Evan turned and faced Laina. "I hope that when I come this way again, Laina, I will be able to see you." He seemed to swallow back an emotion and added, "That is, if Laird Galloway will allow me to come near you."

"When will you be back?" Laina asked softly.

"In about six months — for the Harvest Festival," he answered. He pulled her into a strong hug and held her for several long moments. The way her graceful, soft body molded against the firmness of his made him weak. He leaned down to lightly kiss the top of her head, then gave in and captured her lips one last time in a scorching kiss. When he pulled away, Laina stood breathless and unfocused. A small sigh escaped her, and he was gone.

Chapter Twelve

ॐ

THE USUAL PRE-DAWN CLATTER in the kitchen signaled the beginning of the day's food preparations. Awakening on her sleeping pallet in the storage room, Laina rolled over and opened her eyes to see the beautiful green dress laying gently across a wine barrel. A sleepy smile spread across her lips. She would need to return the dress to Oswyn this morning.

"It was all real, lassie!" Margaret announced with a chuckle as she bustled into the room, her arms loaded with small pots of imported spices. "And you've got an invitation to walk with the laird, himself, today!"

Laina groaned and pulled the fur coverlet over her head.

"Not feeling so brave today are ye?" Margaret teased.

"I can't imagine what there is for us to talk about," Laina complained in a muffled voice from beneath the cover.

"Ye let him do the talkin'," Margaret advised, "and you sit there and look interested and pretty."

Laina threw the fur coverlet aside from her naked body. "We come from completely different worlds."

"Well, you're in *his* world now."

"Surely, Laird Galloway's interest in me will not last long," Laina reasoned, reaching for the chemise and oversized blue tunic that Margaret had acquired for her. "Maybe today, once he realizes..."

"Stop yer fussin'," Margaret ordered. "Our laird has taken a liking to you and this is not an opportunity to be wasted. Now hurry and get washed — we're getting a late start in the kitchen this morning."

Laina dressed and then walked behind the building to wash from the rain barrel. The shaded area, still moist with morning dew, smelled earthy and fresh. She inhaled deeply and felt the sting of the cold water against her skin. Drying off quickly with a small cloth, she squinted up into the bright blue of the sky. Evan's eyes were that color.

Her mind wandered over the memories of the night before, pausing indulgently to remember the details of each scene. And then she reached the end. The point where he had left the story completely. He had earned her trust, amused himself with her, and then left. Damn him! He was still an arrogant and selfish man, to think he could stir up her emotions and then just walk away. Was she just someone for him to steal kisses from? As the memory of her own desire and willingness arose, she pushed it aside. The point was, she decided, that he had lured her into trusting him and liking him, and then he walked away without a second thought.

Laina scowled at the ground for several moments. If he thought she would be happy to see him in six months when he returned, he would be sorely disappointed. It would serve him right if she *were* on the laird's arm and Evan couldn't talk to her at all. He had made his choice.

Laina returned to the kitchen just as a messenger was leaving.

Margaret looked stunned.

"What is it?" Laina asked.

"The tailor, Oswyn. He has sent word that the green velvet dress is your's to keep."

Gillian clucked in disbelief. Laina put her hand over her mouth.

"And he returned your green tunic," Margaret said, pointing to where it lay folded on a stool near the door. Laina's belt and knife lay on top.

"I must go thank him," Laina said.

"No lass, he is likely long gone. They were packing up during the night. Don't go running off — you must be ready for your meeting with the laird."

"But when will I be able to thank him?"

"I'm sure he knows how thankful you are," Margaret reassured.

"Why would he be giving you an expensive dress like that?" Audrey challenged. "What did you do?"

Laina gave her an irritated look. "I didn't do anything. I...I don't know why he gave it to me."

"Maybe *he* wants to court you," Lucy cooed.

"He's a little old for me, Lucy," Laina laughed.

"Does that musician want to court you?" Gillian asked.

"I don't know what he wants," Laina answered irritably.

Margaret shook her head with a sigh. "Much excitement there is, girls, but we must get to our work or the laird will be a very hungry and unhappy man."

The morning hours passed quickly. Too quickly for Laina. She would have been quite content to scrub barrels and haul wood for the rest of the day. It didn't make sense for her to go off walking with the laird when there was so much work to be done in the kitchen. What did he want from her? What could they possibly talk about? Gathering another load of wood from the woodpile behind the kitchen, Laina remembered dancing with the laird. He had been respectful and gentle with her, and she liked his easy laughter. Still, he was the largest and most powerful man she had ever seen. Perhaps he would send a messenger with a polite excuse to cancel their garden walk. Laina hoped so.

Margaret's voice called from the kitchen door, "Lainaaa."

Laina appeared around the corner of the building with her arms full. "Here I am."

Margaret stepped aside to let the girl enter. "I sent Boyd to find out what time the laird wants to meet with you. The answer we've just received is that an escort will arrive shortly."

Boyd nodded his head in agreement as he munched on a carrot.

Laina dropped the wood next to one of the hearths and sighed. "All right." Removing her apron, she retrieved her folded green tunic from the chair and headed into the storeroom to change. Her older tunic fit her better, and was cleaner at that moment.

"Isn't this exciting?" Gillian squealed.

Audrey made a face and grunted. She was disgusted by all the fuss. It was ridiculous. Couldn't the laird see how painfully simple Laina was? Then again, maybe that's *why* he was interested — it would be easier for him to have his way with her. Audrey's eyes narrowed with envy.

Lucy nudged the jealous girl, "What's wrong with you?"

"Mind your own business!" Audrey hissed.

Lucy looked across the room at Boyd and shrugged her shoulders. He rolled his eyes.

Laina was brushing her hair with long strokes when Margaret appeared in the storeroom doorway.

"Lass, very few people get a chance to rise out of the situation they are born into. If the laird likes you and you please him, he could make things so much better for you."

"What if I like things the way they are?"

"Things won't stay like this forever," Margaret reasoned. "You will marry and have children like every woman does. Rich or poor, that's your role. Which way would you rather do it?"

"Perhaps I don't want to do it at all."

"Now, what do you mean by that?" Margaret asked.

Laina stared off into space while braiding her hair. "I don't know. I don't know what kind of life is right for me. I might do something quite different."

"A woman does what a woman is supposed to do, and we all do it whether we like it or not," Margaret said. "Eventually, we learn to like it. Don't worry, lass — it will all work out."

Laina finished tying her braid and heaved a sigh, just as Lucy poked her head into the room and announced breathlessly, "The laird's escort is here."

Laird Galloway's morning had been very busy — there were accounts to go over and disputes to resolve, and a review of the ongoing practice maneuvers required for the villages. A group of soldiers who had attended the faire were already on their way back to their posts, hung-over but happy.

When Gavin finally got a moment to himself after breakfast, he stood looking out the window of his bedroom and his thoughts turned to the kitchen lass, Laina. For someone who had been through so much devastation in her young life, she certainly had a strong spirit about her. A slow smile crept across his lips as he remembered the womanly shape of her body. How sweet and pure she must be. He would need to take his time with this one. She could be special to him. He did not want her to be afraid of him.

The messenger led Laina around the keep to the east end of the garden. He motioned to a small stone bench just inside the entrance. "Please wait here," he said, and left.

The garden showed signs of recent tending. Laina remembered the way her father whistled when he worked in the garden next to their cottage. It was such a happy sound. Although she hadn't thought about it at the time, it had been very reassuring and comforting every day to know he was there.

"Good afternoon."

Laina jumped. Gavin towered above her. Dressed all in black except for a white shirt, he looked even larger than he did at the faire.

An invisible lump swelled in Laina's throat. She stood. "Good afternoon, m'lord."

Gavin observed the shapeless tunic she wore and smiled at the thought of the curves that lay so well hidden beneath it. Her hair was pulled back into a shining braid, and her cheeks were glowing pink.

Seeing him survey her clothing, she smiled nervously.

He took her hand. "You look radiant in whatever you wear, Laina."

"Thank you, m'lord."

His green eyes showed a hint of amusement, but were gentle. Laina willed herself to relax.

The laird smoothly hooked her arm with his, and stepped forward into the garden. He shortened his strides to match her's.

"Did you enjoy the faire, Laina?"

"Aye m'lord. It was thrilling beyond words."

Gavin chuckled. "What was it that thrilled you?" His eyes twinkled.

"Everything," she sighed. "The music, the dancing, the beautiful clothing…"

He watched the memories float across her pretty face.

"Oh, and dancing with you, m'lord," she added quickly.

He nodded absent-mindedly, clearly accustomed to people gushing over him. "Your enthusiastic dancing enlivened the evening for everyone, Laina."

"It did?"

"Indeed it did. Where did you learn to dance like that?"

"In my village. We danced often at the tavern."

"Children were allowed in the tavern?" the laird asked, surprised.

"Oh, no," Laina laughed. "We danced outside in the lane. We could hear the music from there."

"Ah." The laird nodded.

"We had contests to see who could dance the fastest or do the most steps," she added brightly.

"Did you enter these contests?"

"Yes, m'lord."

"And?" Gavin prodded. "Did you win any?"

"Aye. I won a good lot of ale over the years for my father."

The laird chuckled.

"He gave most of it away," Laina explained, "as he felt it wasn't right to be getting drunk from my efforts. He never wanted me to regret dancing."

"Good man," Gavin acknowledged. He paused by a mound of fragrant lavender and turned to face her. "I've not seen you much since you arrived. Is Margaret working you too hard?"

"Oh no, m'lord. I like staying in the kitchen. The castle..." she hesitated, worried that she might be saying too much. But the laird was watching her and she had to finish, "...it is so very different from my home."

"I see." Gavin picked a sprig of lavender and slipped it into her hair above her left ear. She smiled shyly, avoiding his eyes. He squeezed her hand. "Margaret is taking good care of you then?"

"Yes, m'lord. She has been very kind to me and has taught me many skills in the kitchen."

"Very good." He nodded.

With a small laugh, Laina offered, "I can stuff pheasants faster than anyone."

Gavin chuckled. "Do you ever go outside in the fresh air...when you are not in the kitchen stuffing pheasants?"

Laina nodded. "I go for walks."

"Where do you go on your walks?"

"To the meadows outside the castle walls...and to the stone circle."

"Are you not afraid to leave the castle unescorted?" Gavin asked with the well-practiced casual tone that usually earned him additional information.

"No, I am not afraid."

"What do you do at the stone circle?"

Laina cast a cautious look at him. There was no sign of judgment on his face. His sparkling eyes were attentively focused on her, his lips curled into a soft smile. Laina thought he looked like he wanted to kiss her.

Laina suddenly forgot the question. "I...uh..."

Holding her hand, Gavin stroked her fingers very lightly, his power overwhelming her. She tried to remember what they'd just been talking about.

"Perhaps you go there to pick flowers," he offered, not wanting to intrude on the small bit of privacy she had in her life.

"Aye, m'lord."

"You are a brave girl, Laina." His eyes followed the gentle

curve of her neck and then returned to her mouth.

Anxious to change the subject and escape his intense gaze, Laina looked out across the garden. "M'lord, may I ask you a question?"

"Of course."

"Why do you walk with me when you could have any of the many fine ladies who pass through the castle?"

Gavin chuckled. "You are very straight-forward, lass."

Laina immediately regretted asking the bold question. "Forgive me, m'lord. I did not mean to be rude. It's just that…well, I am only a servant."

"Well, what I see," Gavin answered, "is a beautiful woman who is a joy to be with. Is that not reason enough for me to want to get to know you better?"

"Yes, I suppose so," Laina answered.

The laird took her small hands firmly in one of his and stroked her hot cheek with his free hand. "I guess it's my choice to make and you'll have to trust my decisions." His penetrating gaze pressed deeper into her eyes. "I will not hurt you, Laina."

Her knees felt weak.

"Will you trust me?" he asked.

"Aye, m'lord."

An approaching guard drew the attention of the laird.

"Excuse me, Laird. Symon has important news to speak with you about in the courtyard."

Gavin nodded. "Tell him I'm on my way."

Laina expelled a small silent sigh of relief.

The laird turned back to her. "Laina, I apologize that I must cut our walk short on such a beautiful day. Hopefully we will have another chance soon to pick up where we left off." He raised her hand to his lips and kissed it gently. His lips were warm and soft.

"Thank you, m'lord." Laina bowed her head, to hide the flush rising to her cheeks. She heard the laird chuckle.

Chapter Thirteen

SYMON WAS FROWNING as he stood waiting for the laird.

"What is it?" Gavin asked as he approached.

"I've just received word that your brother, Reynold, and his men will be arriving in a few days."

"Reynold! Good God, what does he want?" Gavin spat.

Nearly six years had passed since the brothers had seen each other. Reynold had shown no interest in family ties, and according to word that filtered back to Gavin, his older brother often worked on secretive and somewhat questionable missions for the king. It suddenly occurred to Gavin, however, that Reynold's spying skills might be of use to Galloway Castle. This might be good timing, indeed. Although, a disturbing question remained: what was it that Reynold wanted bad enough to bring him to the castle?

Symon smirked. "There's more..."

"Yes?"

"Elinor Cobb of Dunstenshire has just arrived. She is waiting for you in the great hall."

Gavin glared at his commander. "Have you no good news for me this day, Symon?"

With so many other issues demanding his attention, Laird Galloway was in no mood to live up to his end of a bargain he had agreed to more than six months prior. In exchange for several extraordinary pieces of imported furniture from Elinor's uncle, the laird now had to honor an arrangement he seemed sure to regret. He sighed heavily and shook his head. "Symon, the next time I think furnishings are worth any price...remind me of this."

"I will indeed, Laird."

Gavin marched off to the keep and found several of his soldiers standing near the entrance. He addressed one of them,

"Have you seen her?"

"Aye," the man responded.

"And?" he said impatiently.

"She appears to be a fine lady, Laird." The other soldiers nodded in agreement.

Gavin entered the hall and looked around. "Where is she?" he asked one of his men inside.

"I believe she is upstairs putting her things away."

Gavin was ready to start grumbling about the bargain again when he looked up just as the lady began descending the stairs. He walked over and waited for her.

She was an attractive woman and carried herself well. Her glossy black hair, pulled back from her face, set off her high cheekbones and bright blue eyes. She smiled brilliantly upon seeing him.

The laird flashed her a dashing smile of his own. "Welcome to Galloway Castle, m'lady," he said, offering his hand to assist her from the last step.

"I am honored, Laird Galloway. I hope it is not inconvenient that I'm arriving a few weeks early; this was the only time my uncle could spare his men as my escorts for the next two months."

"No, it's no trouble at all," Gavin lied. "We will make the necessary preparations immediately." Gavin led her over to the large table and they sat down. He motioned for a serving girl to pour two goblets of wine. "How was your journey?"

"Much longer than I expected." Elinor let out a musical laugh. "I do believe parts of me have gone numb."

Gavin chuckled and toasted her glass. "I trust you will find the keep comfortable and well-equipped to meet your needs."

"If I may," she said tentatively, "I do have a minor request."

"Of course."

"Would it be possible to acquire a thicker mattress for my bed? I am quite sore and I'm afraid I need a bit more cushioning."

"I'll see to it right away." He nodded to the house steward, Bernard, who stood nearby.

Bernard shuffled away quickly to take care of the matter. The oldest servant in the keep, Bernard was often off napping, except when guests arrived or there was excitement afoot.

Gavin studied Elinor briefly while she sipped her wine. Apparently, some ladies required an unusual amount of comfort — hell, he and his men could sleep on the floor without blankets. Indeed, Elinor seemed much more refined than her uncle, whose dealings were most often made in private corners of small taverns. Her movements were controlled and graceful. Gavin was impressed. Although a few years older than Gavin had expected, she was very fair. Perhaps the laird's part of the bargain would not be so difficult after all.

Elinor noticed a spark of interest and admiration in the laird's eyes and she smiled confidently.

"How is your uncle?" Gavin asked.

"He is well," Elinor said. "Although, I worry about some of the people he makes deals with. They are not all as honorable as you are in keeping their word. I fear he may be putting himself in danger at times."

"He is a smart man," Gavin answered. "Sometimes I think he is much more aware than he lets people believe. It gives him an edge, if people are focused on what they think they're getting away with — then they are not as likely to notice what *he* is getting away with."

Elinor laughed and took another sip of wine. "You have a most impressive castle."

"Thank you. It meets our needs."

Elinor set down her goblet and smiled at the laird.

"You would probably like to rest," Gavin offered. "We can talk more later."

"Yes, thank you," she said, rising. "I will look forward to a tour of your castle later, then?"

"Yes, of course." Gavin watched her go up the stairs, then drank the rest of his wine and went back outside.

Less than a week had passed since Elinor Cobb of Dunstenshire had arrived, and already she seemed to be everywhere the laird turned, making changes without asking him, and sticking her nose into business all around the castle.

"That's the way women are," Symon grunted, as he stood with Gavin in the lower courtyard watching the men practice their maneuvers. "They are always fixing things the way they think they should be."

"She has actually made a few improvements," Gavin confessed. "I suppose I should be patient and give this arrangement a chance to work."

"Aye, we'll see," Symon scoffed.

The laird had been casually watching his men practice their fighting, when he suddenly lept into their midst with an unexpected challenge. Quickly disarming one man with a hard knock that sent the man's practice weapon flying into the air, Gavin caught the weapon and spun around, making a thrust that would have killed the man behind him, had the weapon been real.

Symon howled with delight and grabbed another practice weapon from the ground as he jumped into the middle of the fight to join his laird.

The group engaged in a vigorous struggle as the larger group tried to disarm the two in the middle. After taking down six men between them, Gavin and Symon were finally held in check by the remaining men. They laughed and slapped each other on the back.

"A good practice, men!" Gavin boomed. "Let's refresh ourselves with ale." The laird's suggestion met with hoots of approval. He turned around and almost tripped over the cobbler who had walked up right behind him.

The cobbler, embarrassed, apologized and bowed several times.

"Yes?" Gavin smiled.

"M'lord, I wonder if I may have a word with you?"

"I'm listening."

"It's the lady...Elinor."

"Yes?"

"She has requested that I stop my other work and make her a pair of shoes immediately. But m'lord, as you know, I am trying to finish several pair of new boots for your men. What would you have me do?"

Gavin smirked. "Finish the boots for my men. I will speak with Elinor. She is not to give you orders. You were correct to come to me."

Looking greatly relieved, the cobbler thanked the laird and left.

"Good lord..." Gavin grumbled as he headed after his men who were already on their way into the great hall.

Just as the laird reached the steps of the keep, Bernard, the house steward, appeared, clearly aggitated and anxious to speak with the laird.

"Laird, excuse me. Do I look like a garden lass to you?"

Gavin eyed the hunched, balding man and tried not to laugh.

"No."

"Then please tell me why I have been ordered to wander around picking flowers for the table in the great hall."

Gavin immediately understood, and sighed. "I'll talk with Elinor."

Before Bernard could say any more, the laird strode quickly into the keep. He needed a full tankard without further delay.

Standing outside the kitchen wiping her hands on her apron, Margaret watched the laird head into the keep with his men. He had sent no further word for Laina since that pretentious woman, Elinor Cobb, had arrived nearly a week ago. Margaret wondered what could be done to get the laird's attention back onto Laina. He had shown a keen interest in the girl, and the cook was growing more certain every day that Laina would make a perfect partner for their laird. Truth be told, Margaret had a soft spot in her heart for the both of them. Their union would please her very much — perhaps she could even help raise their beautiful babes.

Stepping back inside the kitchen, Margaret walked over to where Laina was chopping parsnips.

"We'll be feeding extra guests throughout this week," the cook said, "please go ask the house steward when the guests will be arriving and how many we need to be prepared for."

Laina froze. "You want *me* to go inside the keep?"

"Aye, that's where the house steward usually is," Margaret acknowledged, then moved to quickly busy herself with one of the pots over the hearth so that she wouldn't have to meet Laina's questioning gaze. She smiled to herself for having the clever idea to parade Laina in front of the laird.

Slowly, Laina headed out the door on her errand, wondering what she would do if she were to see the laird. She hadn't seen him for several days. Things were just starting to feel normal again without his attention on her, and the girls in the kitchen had finally stopped asking their ridiculous questions. Still, she found herself smoothing back her hair and checking the condition of her apron.

She never made it inside of the keep. A guard at the door informed her that the house steward had just gone and wouldn't be back for awhile. Relieved, Laina trotted down the steps and stood in the upper courtyard feeling the sun on her face. The grass was thick and soft. She was contemplating how good it would feel on her bare feet, when a tall, narrow shadow fell across the ground to her left.

"Laina. Isn't it?" a pleasant voice asked.

Laina turned to see an attractive, well-dressed woman with black hair held perfectly in place by white shell hair combs. The woman's eyebrows were arched in question over striking blue eyes, and a controlled smile held her lips. Before Laina could answer, the woman continued.

"Allow me to introduce myself." Glancing down to smooth the elegant satin skirt of her lavender dress, she appeared to stand taller when she looked up again. "I am Elinor Cobb of Dunstenshire. I am to be the laird's lady."

Laina managed to hide her look of surprise, and quickly curtseyed. "M'lady, I am pleased to meet you. I...I did not know."

Elinor smiled. "It is a private arrangement, and not the business of commoners. You understand."

"Oh, yes, m'lady," Laina answered politely.

Elinor said softly, "I hear that the laird has been showing some special attention to you recently."

Laina lowered her eyes. "Aye, m'lady. We danced at the Mayday Faire and...well, I didn't know that you..."

Elinor waved her hand in casual dismissal. "Do not concern yourself with his actions, child. He is a generous laird who enjoys lavishing his attentions on everyone around him...even the servants." Elinor displayed a playful pout of sympathy. "Unfortunately, his attentions sometimes confuse young girls who mistake his generosity for something more. I hope you were not confused by his gestures." She smiled at Laina reassuringly.

"Nay, m'lady. I did not think the laird could truly be interested in me." Laina felt foolish. He had only been toying with her for his entertainment. This explained why she hadn't heard from him again.

"You appear to be a bright girl, Laina. I just wanted to make sure you understood completely."

"Thank you, m'lady."

Elinor smiled and patted Laina's arm. "All men are weak when it comes to the attention of the ladies, including Laird Galloway. Just remember, if he forgets himself and seems to make some type of meaningful gesture, you have to be smart enough to know that it is a brief lapse of his good judgment."

"I will."

"You're a sweet girl, Laina. It would be best if you stay focused on your duties and avoid crossing the laird's path any further."

"Aye, m'lady."

Elinor nodded. "Good then."

Laina watched Elinor walk regally back toward the keep, her beautiful dress swaying with each step. It was very thoughtful for the lady to show such regard for a servant's feelings and well-being. Of course, that's the type of kindness that Laird Galloway showed to his servants too. Laina almost jumped when Elinor turned around suddenly. Laina hoped they were far enough apart that Elinor couldn't see the embarrassment on Laina's face, upon being caught staring after the lady.

Elinor called out across the yard, "I feel like having pheasant for dinner tonight." Smiling sweetly, she added, "Please see to it." Then she turned and disappeared into the keep.

Laina hurried back to the kitchen. Margaret was adding another log to the fire under a group of pots suspended from iron frames on the hearth.

Laina's words tumbled out excitedly. "The house steward was away, but I did meet the laird's new lady, Elinor. She requests pheasant for dinner."

Margaret snorted. "Then she'll have to go catch and pluck it herself because we have no pheasant and I'm not taking orders from her!"

Laina gasped. "But she's to be the laird's lady."

"No, she is not!" Margaret huffed. "She wants everyone to think she is, but our laird has made no such claim, and has no intention of doing so."

Laina frowned thoughtfully, considering everything the lady had just told her. Was it possible that Margaret didn't know?

"Are you sure?" Laina asked.

"Of course I'm sure! I've known the man for fifteen years and I know he is not going to end up with the likes of her." Margaret poked at the fire.

"She was concerned for me," Laina explained. "She advised

me to avoid the laird so that I won't misinterpret his attentions and be disappointed."

Margaret laughed sourly. "She's more likely concerned for herself and wants all pretty young women to avoid him." The cook shook her finger at Laina. "Listen. If the laird decides to pay attention to you, that's his business, and it would be in your best interest to pay attention right back to him!"

Gillian giggled from where she sat working at a table in the center of the room.

"The truth is," Margaret continued "Laird Galloway has only allowed Elinor to come here because he is trading goods with her uncle. Our laird has agreed to try to find a husband for the woman among his many acquaintances. But he did not intend for it to be himself."

"Does the lady Elinor know this?" Laina asked.

Margaret grunted. "I'm sure she does, but clearly she is trying to direct things her own way. She's no "lady" either, she just calls herself that. It won't work with our laird, and you do not have to listen to what she says."

"All the same," Laina said thoughtfully, "I will stay out of her way and avoid the laird. I do not want to cause trouble."

Holding her retort to herself, Margaret knew it was only a matter of time before Elinor would be gone and the laird would be able to resume his interest in Laina. The girl's beauty blossomed more every day, and Laird Galloway wasn't one to pass up such a treasure.

Chapter Fourteen

෧෨

"ARE YE GOING TO BE TORN-FACED all summer long?" Oswyn shouted across the table at Evan. They sat sharing a bottle of whiskey in the Tavern O' the Raven. The old, one-eyed tailor had met up with the musician at a celebration that the theatre group and the Westport Musicians Troupe were both attending, as was often the case.

"I'm fine," Evan said, contemplating the amber liquid in his cup.

"Nay," Oswyn insisted, watching his friend. "Ye are clearly stewing over the pretty kitchen lass at Galloway Castle." He took a drink then added, "She *was* a sweet one, wasn't she?"

Evan glared at the older man. "We can't have everything we want," he snapped.

"Who says?" Oswyn challenged.

Evan ignored the question. "I have a life I enjoy, a skill that pays me well enough, and commitments I must keep to my fellow musicians and those who hire me. I can't disrupt all of that because a lass catches my eye."

"Are ye tryin' to convince me or yerself?" Oswyn barked.

Evan leaned back in his chair and raked his hands through his uncombed hair, looking more frustrated than he meant to reveal. The blonde stubble on his face added to his haggard appearance.

Oswyn decided to take pitty on the poor bastard by softening his tone. "I've never seen ye so twisted up over a woman. Perhaps ye should go back for a visit."

"I'm not twisted up," Evan said. "Besides, there's no time. Our schedule and travel route take us nowhere near Galloway Castle until Fall." He leaned forward and swallowed a quick shot of whiskey. The fire flowed down his throat, then spread slowly and warmly through his body. He leveled his gaze at Oswyn. "It's not fair to Laina for me to keep popping into her life whenever I'm passing by. She needs to build a stable life with someone she can count on."

"I suppose you're right." Oswyn shrugged and looked around the room. "Surely, there are plenty of men who would love to claim her and keep her busy bearing their squalling babes. Or maybe she'll be lucky enough to become a favorite in Laird Galloway's group of women. I hear he…"

"Dammit, old man!" Evan bellowed.

Oswyn laughed and took a drink.

Evan stared darkly across the room. How had he become so intrigued by a lass he barely knew? Why should he care which direction her path took? He had decided long ago not to tie himself to anyone or anything, other than his own good instincts. Women were rarely what they seemed, anyway. Although pleasing at first, they often had a scheme they wanted to fit him into, and he was a free man.

An image floated into his mind: sitting on the ground with Laina under the night sky, the moon casting its glow across her skin, and the soft, full mounds that pressed so tightly against the dress she wore. He could hear the sound of her laughter and see the sparkle in her eyes. She was smart and sweet. She was aware of the things around her, and her place among them. She was unlike anyone he had known — she was free, like he was.

The image faded and was replaced by Oswyn's scruffy face across from him. Evan stood up abruptly and shoved his chair against the table.

Despite the rosy glow rising to Oswyn's face from the alcohol, he tried to look serious for his friend. "You'll get over it, Evan. Ye've met fair women before, and I bet ye don't remember most of their names or faces by now."

"I'll see you in a few weeks in East Lothian, old man," Evan said, ending the conversation.

Oswyn smiled crookedly. "All right then."

<><><>

"To peace," Laird Galloway said, raising a wine goblet in the air.

Three visitors sitting at the laird's table in the great hall, raised their goblets as well. The laird was glad to have turned his attention away from Elinor and her disruptions, to focus on the good news that the men brought from Greendale. Their village was doing well with the defensive practice sessions and the training they'd received from the laird's men.

"We still have not uncovered any information about the identity of our enemy," Gavin admitted. "We've heard of a group of barbarians to the north, but no one has any knowledge of them travelling this far south. Until we know what we're dealing with, it is vital that you keep strengthening your defenses and that we all remain on alert."

"Thank you for your protection, Laird," said the eldest, white-haired man. "The people of Greendale are most grateful."

The group raised their goblets once more, then headed outside for their departure as the day's light faded. Pausing in the courtyard, the laird entertained the men with one final story.

"And that's how you tell if your goose is cooked," Gavin concluded.

The visitors burst out laughing.

From a narrow, open window overlooking the courtyard, Elinor glared down at the small group. She resented their casual laughter and the way they paraded about with the laird. They did not know what it was like to have to work so hard for every scrap of consideration and attention they could get — a reality that Elinor was painfully aware of every moment of every day. If her father hadn't been a drunk and her mother so cowardly and simple, Elinor could have easily married into a family of higher rank and received the kind of respect she deserved. Now her only hope was to use her own resourcefulness and her uncle's connections and influence.

She was determined to improve her position in life. She believed it was only fitting that she have fine clothes and furnishings from exotic places, a grand castle filled with servants to fulfill her needs, and lavish parties where she would be the envy of other women. Her lips snaked into a smile. She had figured out a brilliant and sensible plan.

She knew that Gavin didn't really want to be married — he liked the ladies too much. But he needed a wife to prove his stability to the king and other nobles. If he were to wed Elinor, she would allow him to continue to share his bed with whomever he wished. Lord, she had heard enough about his appetite to know that she certainly didn't want to share it with him! Meanwhile she would run the household and hand out orders to the servants, as someone of her cleverness was clearly born to do. She would get to enjoy the life she wanted and deserved, and Gavin would continue enjoying his exploits while gaining more respectability. It was the perfect arrangement for them both.

In the courtyard, the group said their goodbyes. Elinor turned and left the window. Now was the opportunity she'd been waiting for, to meet with Gavin and tell him of her idea.

As the laird turned toward the keep, he caught sight of Laina disappearing around the back of the kitchen with a large, black cooking pot. For a moment, he considered following after her, but then thought better of it. Nay, he must have someone share his bed this night. He would save Laina for when he could go more slowly with her. He imagined her young, soft body moving under his, her fresh scent teasing him, and the sweet taste of her on his tongue. The laird felt a sudden jerk between his legs. Chuckling aloud, he sprinted up the steps into the keep.

Elinor was waiting just inside with her hands clasped in front of her. "Gavin, I wish to speak with you about a matter of importance — indeed, an opportunity — for us both." She smiled proudly.

"Not now," Gavin said, as he walked past her. "I have other important business I must attend to."

Her mouth fell open as she watched him walk away.

Without looking back, Gavin called out, "We can talk tomorrow morning after breakfast."

The laird walked over to Lowrens who stood leaning against one of the massive wood posts, smiling. Gavin mischieviously smiled back. "I'd like to take a bath in my room. Then, send up a cheerful lass."

"Brigid or Ursula?" Lowrens asked.

Gavin looked thoughtful, then laughed. "Hell, send them both!"

The laird was in a fine mood the next morning as he ate breakfast with his men in the great hall.

"You look well rested, laird." Symon grinned.

"Do I? I didn't sleep a wink." Gavin smiled broadly and used a chunk of bread to soak up juice in his bowl. "What's that saying about two women in a bed?"

Symon smirked. "I wouldn't know."

"Well," Gavin chewed and then swallowed, "it definitely deserves some sort of saying."

"How about," one of the soldiers shouted, "two women in a bed leave no room for sleep!"

The room erupted with snorts and laughter, which grew louder as the soldiers took turns making more suggestions, each raunchier than the one before. When someone slapped the lower backside of a serving girl, followed by a round of cheering and banging on the table, the serving girls stopped coming into the room.

Gavin took the last drink from his tankard and stood up. "Maybe I'll go see if the lasses have woken up." The laird's men expressed their approval loudly as he strode toward the stairs.

Laird Galloway took the stairs two at a time. Elinor met him at the top.

"Gavin, may we speak now?" Elinor said, blocking his path.

Restraining himself from cursing, the laird grimaced and said tightly, "I suppose so." He followed her to a small alcove that he had intended on making into a library. It contained a few crates, an empty bookcase, and two matching chairs he had bought from Elinor's uncle. He waited for her to take a seat, and then sat down, himself, with a heavy sigh.

"Gavin, I've given this a lot of thought," Elinor said, "and I believe I have an idea that would serve us both well." She looked pleased with herself.

He could hear his men downstairs, still roaring with laughter. "Yes?"

"I am very well aware, Gavin, that you are not interested in marrying."

The stiff way she said his name grated on him. And how the hell did she know what he was or was not interested in?

She leaned toward him and smiled slyly. "I, however, could make it a very appealing arrangement for you."

"I doubt that."

Ignoring his jest, she continued. "I think that we would both agree that if you were married, you would gain more favor with the king and other nobles."

"I have all the favor I need," Gavin said.

Elinor glared at him. He was being arrogant and uncooperative, and she found it most irritating.

"Gavin, at least hear me out," she snapped.

"I don't want to hear you out. This is none of your business!"

Fearing that she was already losing the battle, her voice became shrill. "If you were to wed me, I would allow you to sleep with whomever you wished."

"I already sleep with whomever I wish." Gavin had heard enough. He stood up.

Elinor stood up as well, her hands fisted at her sides. "Anyone else you marry is going to demand much of you, Gavin. I wouldn't."

"You've been demanding things since you got here," the laird bellowed.

Elinor sputtered and blinked her eyes. "How can you talk to me like this? My uncle has entrusted me to your care."

"Your uncle is trying my patience by expecting me to find you a husband among my acquaintances. I have no desire to ruin my hard-won alliances. The way you've been upsetting people around the castle, I'll be lucky if I can place you with one of the old farmers who are indebted to me."

Elinor responded with a high-pitched shriek, but Gavin had already turned his back and was heading for the stairs.

His soldiers fell silent as he descended the steps.

"I need some fresh air," he announced with a scowl as he hurried across the hall and out the door. He strode down the steps and across the courtyard, and then took the stone stairs down to the lower courtyard. *Damn that woman!* She had a way of making him want to escape his own home.

He quickly retrieved his horse and rode out through the gates. The look on his face prevented anyone from trying to engage him in talk. Racing at full speed, Gavin crossed the rolling hills with the wind in his face until he arrived at the river. His mind churned over the way his life had gotten away from him. He had spent months being out of control and on the defensive, and he was damned tired of it.

Dismounting his speckled stallion, Gavin undressed from the waist up and layed down in the sun with his arms behind his head, and his legs crossed at the ankles. He laid there for some time, thinking over the issues he needed to resolve. His bronzed chest soaked up the sun. It was time to regain control of his lands and his castle. Dammit, he would not allow others, seen or unseen, to continue monopolizing his energy and resources. He hadn't even been able to go hunting since the previous autumn. Without any further delay, he would launch a greater offensive to remove all threats and irritations, and take back what he wanted.

A slow smile began to relax his face. One of the things he wanted was to have the pretty little kitchen maid, Laina, wrapped in his arms. The sooner, the better. It had been his intention to go slow with the girl, but dammit, he needed something pleasing amidst all the drudgery. Nothing inspired and envigorated him more than sweeping some soft, sweet thing completely off of her feet. And there was something special about this one. Remembering the fire in the girl's eyes and her fiesty smile when she danced at the Mayday Faire, Gavin knew that passion pumped strongly through her veins.

He stood and dressed quickly, envisioning how he would take her to his bed. She would be afraid, of course. But he would show her...everything. He would watch the fire ignite in her eyes, and feel her clutch at him as her own desire awoke. They would make love for hours. In the morning, her kitchen apron would be hanging from one of his bed posts, and he would take her again. Gavin threw back his head and howled like a wolf.

Laina sat in the stone circle watching two butterflies dance together in the air. Tipping her face up to the sky, she closed her eyes and felt the sun touch her face.

Perhaps Margaret was right. Perhaps the lady Elinor had no claim on the laird — in which case, he might want to see Laina again at some point. Despite Laina's doubts about the laird's interest in her, something about him *did* excite her. Not only was he sinfully handsome, but the size and power of him took her breath away. She thought of the way he had kissed her hand, and she wondered what it might be like to kiss his lips.

She laid back in the grass, enhaling it's earthy sweetness.

And what of Evan, she wondered? He had seemed so sincere. Well, sincere or not, the fact was: he had a different life to pursue. Truly, she could not fault him. They had only just met, and they really did not know each other well enough to have any expectations of each other. Laina waved away a bug hovering near her face.

Still, Evan had left so quickly, as if it were easy for him to do.

So, fine...he could do whatever he damn well pleased. She didn't need him. There were plenty of handsome men who passed through the castle, and the most handsome of all, Laird Galloway, was interested in her. Although she would not have envisioned herself with someone such as the laird, it was not up to her to judge the differences in their positions in life. She was not defined by the work that she did — Evan had said that.

Laird Galloway had told her that he wouldn't hurt her and that she needed to trust him. And he had not given her any reason *not* to trust him. It was only her fear and judgments holding her back. Maybe he would call for her again. Now, she hoped so.

Chapter Fifteen

꙰

LAIRD GALLOWAY RODE UP TO THE CASTLE at a leisurely gallop — a smile comfortably spanning his face. Two guards on the wall looked at each other. "He looks a might better than when he left," one of them said to the other.

Gavin raised his hand in greeting as his horse pranced across the drawbridge. Just inside the gate, the laird lept lightly to the ground and was chuckling when he turned and saw Symon waiting patiently a few paces away. The laird's commander had an annoyed look on his face.

Gavin's smile disappeared. "What is it?"

"Your brother Reynold has arrived and is waiting for you in the great hall," Symon answered.

"Good god. Not even a moment's rest around here. Well, let's see if he can be useful — and if he can't, watch me throw him out on his arse!" Gavin roared, striding off to the keep.

A half-dozen men looked up as the heavy door to the great hall swung open and the laird stood on the threshhold, his towering body backlit from the bright sunlight outside.

"Greetings brother!" one of the men called out loudly, holding a tankard high in salute.

Gavin descended the steps into the dim light of the great hall and came to a stop in front of the man, who was nearly as tall as he. Lord, it had been several years since he had last seen his older brother. The jet black hair was now heavily streaked with gray, and hard lines creased the familiar face that was beginning to sag in places.

"What brings you to Galloway Castle, Reynold?" Gavin asked levelly. "Have you grown tired of your devious missions for the king?"

"You do not seem happy to see me." Reynold smirked and refilled his tankard from a jug on the table.

Gavin glanced at Reynold's companions and determined that they were more intent on drinking and muttering among themselves than in posing any kind of threat.

"Let's just say I am cautious, brother," Gavin answered. "I have never known you to do anything without a sizeable payoff involved. What do you want here?"

Reynold took a long draw of ale and smiled. "A soft bed, a warm meal, and of course, to see my brother."

Gavin laughed coldly and folded his arms across his chest. "Who are you hiding from?"

Reynold scowled and slammed his tankard down on the table. "I told you why I'm here! Can you not extend hospitality to your own brother?" He wiped his mouth and glared at Gavin.

The laird studied his older brother for a moment. Indeed, the man looked beaten and tired, as did his companions. Although Reynold's integrity had been questionable over the years, he was, after all, the laird's only brother. Gavin supposed he should give Reynold a chance to prove himself beyond the stories. And if the two men could get along, there was the possibility that Reynold might prove very valuable in providing assistance to restore peace to the laird's lands.

"Forgive me, brother," Gavid said stiffly, gesturing to a serving girl to bring more ale. "I am not being a good host. Despite the distance that has been between us, you and your men are my guests and may stay for a day or two to rest from your journey. We will put straw mattresses along the far wall there, and you are welcome at my dinner table."

A smile returned to Reynold's face as he walked over and slapped the laird on the back. "Don't worry Gavin, it might not be such a bad thing to spend some time with your brother. I can tell you much from my travels."

Gavin tried to sound sincere. "I look forward to it. Are your horses being tended to?"

"Yes, however, now that I know we are welcome to stay, we will bring in our bags."

Reynold's men, who had appeared not to be paying any attention to the conversation, immediately stood without a word and accompanied Reynold out the door.

Gavin let out a heavy sigh. He certainly hoped that his idea about enlisting Reynold's help would make this visit worthwhile.

The laird's patience was worn thin, but he knew he had to move carefully with Reynold. Having peace restored to the Galloway territory was worth a great deal, and the laird was willing to do just about anything to make it happen. Even if it meant enduring more troublesome guests for a few days, and postponing his romantic notions for a few more nights.

At dinner that night, Reynold and his men ate nearly three times the amount that was normally served, leaving Gavin to wonder if the men hadn't eaten in a week. The serving girls could barely clear the empty platters away fast enough as they brought more food. This was going to be an expensive visit.

Gavin had given up on trying to have a conversation with his brother during dinner, as Reynold and his boisterous group seemed intent on slurping and belching loudly while recounting stories amongst themselves. Gavin's own soldiers had already wandered away from the table after the second round of food was brought. Gavin waited until his guests had stuffed their stomachs and were contentedly leaning back in their chairs. That's when he saw his chance.

"So, tell me, Reynold, some of this news from your travels."

A loud crash sounded as a serving girl dropped a platter, sending bowls and meat bones in all directions. She hurried to clean up the mess, revealing her ample bosom each time she bent over. The display brought a round of cheers and much laughter from Reynold's men.

As Gavin was just about to resume his inquiry, the serving girl walked back into the room and tripped over a bone that she had missed in her cleanup. Her embarrassment sent the men into an uproar again.

"Come sit on me lap, lass, and I'll give ye something to blush about," one of the men yelled.

Another one chimed in, "Part of me is blushing too, lass, would you like to see it?"

The men howled with laughter.

Reynold shouted, "Our pitcher of ale has run dry! What kind of establishment is this?"

Gavin snorted with disgust, "For the love of..."

Another serving girl entered the hall with ale, glaring at the men to indicate that she wouldn't be so easily toyed with. Tall, big-boned, and flat-chested, she looked like she could sober up the most drunk among them. Their behavior quickly settled as they contemplated their tankards with renewed seriousness.

Noting Gavin's irritated expression, Reynold issued an order to his men. "Leave us. My brother and I have business to discuss." The men rose instantly and left, although Gavin heard their laughter resume as the large door to the great hall slammed shut. He grimaced, wondering what trouble they might stir up.

Reynold was studying Gavin. "You have a fine castle, brother. You have done well for yourself."

"It could have been your's, Reynold, you know that," Gavin reminded him. "You could have returned when our father died, and taken over what was his."

"I prefer not to work so hard to maintain one treasure, when I can travel and find many," Reynold responded.

"And what treasures have you acquired?" Gavin asked.

"The best of everything," Reynold said, as he took a long drink of ale.

Gavin decided not to point out the fact that Reynold and his men actually appeared to be lacking some basic necessities. From the looks of their clothes and hungry appetites, they hadn't been finding many treasures of late.

Reynold seemed to read Gavin's thoughts. "We do a lot of trading all throughout Europe and have our wealth stored in many locations. It's safer that way. We do not need to travel with it. Six months ago we traded enough in Portsmouth to keep us going for quite some time," he bragged.

"Do you still go on campaigns for the king?"

"No." Reynold leaned back in his chair. "His expectations were beginning to ruin the fun of it. I work for myself now...and for others when it suits me. I know this land from boundary to boundary, you know. I would venture to say that gives me even more power than the king," he boasted.

Gavin stood and paced slowly to the end of the table before turning around. "Perhaps you could do a job for me."

Reynold showed surprise. "Indeed. What is it you need?"

"I need to find out who has been attacking travellers and villages on my lands. Have you heard of anything in your travels that might point to my enemy?"

Reynold rubbed his jaw thoughtfully. "No, but there must be some who wish to have your lands."

Gavin nodded grimly. "Based on the amount of destruction, and the descriptions from survivors, it appears to be a group of about twenty men. They attack unprotected people, murdering without hesitation, and pillage all that they can. Surely, with so many involved in the attack, the veil of secrecy would have some holes. Do you think you can find out who is responsible?"

"Most likely," Reynold answered confidently. "What can you offer as payment?"

Gavin walked to stand in front of his brother. "Name your price."

Reynold stood and smiled, putting his arm around Gavin. "Now aren't you glad your brother came for a visit?"

It had only been two days, and as far as Gavin and his men were concerned, Reynold's group couldn't leave soon enough. They were loud, rude, and constantly provoking trouble to amuse themselves. Nevertheless, Gavin realized that it would take just such men to sniff out the thieves and murderers who had been wreaking havoc across the Galloway territory. For that, Gavin remained grateful and hopeful.

Reynold's men spent most of their time stocking up on goods and sparring with the laird's soldiers. They didn't fight fairly — seemingly intent on inflicting actual injuries whenever they could. Gavin was receiving angry complaints from his own soldiers. They didn't want Reynold's men continually getting the best of them in practice, so they were ready to start fighting back with no rules.

Gavin realized that the situation had reached a boiling point. To avoid further trouble, he ordered that the sparring matches be ceased and he promised his own men that Reynold's group would be leaving soon. He, too, was very anxious for them to go. He had to keep reminding himself that something useful had been accomplished during the difficult visit. Reynold had agreed to find out all he could about the attacks and report back to Gavin. In exchange, Gavin provided a generous amount of weapons and supplies, as well as a sizeable amount of coin.

While Reynold tracked down the laird's enemy to remove the threat to the Galloway lands, Gavin would take steps to remove the disruptions *within* his castle walls. He would send Elinor back to her uncle within the week and would gladly return the few pieces of furniture he had acquired in the deal. The trouble that the woman caused wasn't worth an entire keep of furniture.

For too long, Laird Galloway had been distracted from the

activities he enjoyed. He could barely remember the last time he had tossed knucklebone dice with his soldiers or taken a swim in the river. By god, it was time to get things around the castle back to the way he liked them.

Laina hummed to herself as she stacked empty crates in a corner of the kitchen. The girls had been busy organizing the storerooms in preparation for the imported goods and harvest of surrounding farms that would be arriving within the coming weeks.

Laird Galloway had not sent word for Laina or shown any further interest, leaving her to wonder, again, if his earlier actions had been simply to satisfy his whims of the moment. There may have been more truth to what Elinor had told her than Margaret was willing to give the woman credit for. It was likely for the best that the laird direct his attentions elsewhere, to someone better suited for him than Laina. She had been foolish to get swept up by him, like so many other women, and to believe that his attentions had any real substance to them. Truly, it had been a relief not having all the fuss focused on her.

The sound of Audrey's angry voice echoed across the courtyard outside and grew louder as it moved closer to the kitchen. Within moments, the wirey-haired girl stormed through the door with Lucy close behind.

Audrey spun around and screamed at the younger girl, "You are a little tart and everyone knows it!"

"Oh, leave her alone," Gillian defended, walking in behind Lucy. "You're just mad because Malcolm doesn't notice *you*."

"I never get a chance," Audrey fumed, pointing at Lucy, "when she's parading around in front of the boys and giggling at everything they say — their simple minds go numb from such antics." She giggled wildly and twirled around in an exaggerated imitation of Lucy.

"She doesn't mean anything by it," Gillian argued. "She just gets excited."

Audrey shook her head vigorously, refusing to accept any explanation. "I told her I like Malcolm. That should be reason enough for her to leave him alone."

"I wasn't trying to get his attention," Lucy said, tipping her small, delicate nose in the air. "I can't help it if the boys like me."

"What happened?" Margaret asked hesitantly.

Gillian answered with a calm tone of maturity. "We were watching some of the boys practice archery. When they finished, Malcolm came over and gave Lucy a feather that had broken loose from one of his arrows."

"Oh, there's much more to the story than that," Audrey hissed. "Every time Malcolm hit the target, Lucy screamed and jumped up and down. For God's sake, he simply shot an arrow through the air and hit a big unmoving target. So what? She acted like he should be Laird Galloway's right-hand man!"

Margaret smiled wryly and was glad when Gillian responded, echoing her own thoughts.

"Maybe you could learn something from her," Gillian said.

Audrey ignored the suggestion and glared at the younger girl. "Why don't you stick with Boyd? He already follows you around like a three-legged dog."

"Audrey, that's mean!" Lucy said. "That's why no boys like you. You're mean and hateful." She stalked off to the other end of the kitchen.

Anxious for the confrontation to be over, and knowing that Audrey would go on as long as they participated, Gillian and Margaret moved to busy themselves elsewhere in the kitchen too.

Audrey's face went dark as she watched everyone turn away. Spotting Laina quietly straightening up a corner of the room, Audrey wandered over casually to pretend that she was going to help. She mindlessly shuffled a few baskets around without doing anything useful. Finally unable to contain her frustration, she complained to Laina.

"It's not right for Lucy to flaunt herself that way. A girl shouldn't act so silly to get attention. It makes her look bad. I won't stoop to that level." Satisfied that there was no disagreement or interruption from Laina, Audrey continued. "I have three brothers. I know a lot about men. I know how they think, I know what they want, and..." she smiled seductively, "I would know how to keep one!"

Laina removed her apron and smiled. "Well, perhaps what's troubling you is what you *don't* know."

Audrey's face went blank. Laina headed out the kitchen door, giving a brief wave to Margaret. Laina heard Audrey bellow behind her, "What the hell does that mean?"

◇ ◇ ◇

Laina approached the stone circle slowly, relishing the peace and comfort of the space. It was the closest feeling of being home that she could find. The red stones stood out vividly. "Hello, my friends," she whispered, slipping off her shoes at the edge of the circle.

She moved among the stones, weaving in and out as if flowing in a gentle current. The carpet of tender grass cushioned her bare feet. The light breeze, scented with flowers, whispered in a language as old as time itself. Laina's eyelids drifted shut. She could hear wings fluttering. Large wings...small wings...thrumming again and again. A delicate sound, yet she could feel the movement of air from them. All around her, hundreds of tiny wisps of air fanning her body.

From the air and the grass, a buzzing sound began to grow. Scores of insects joined the chorus, and Laina's body began to vibrate along with the hum. Filling with the tingling energy, she gave herself up to it. Here, there was no time...no heartache...no boundaries. Only the gentle, certain knowledge of being part of it all.

The buzzing stopped, and Laina opened her eyes. She stood in the center of the stone circle, facing east. The wind blew her hair back with a sudden small howl, *"Beware, little one!"*

A cloud drifted in front of the sun, casting a shadow over Laina and the circle. With a small shiver, she picked up her shoes, and padded through the grass toward the trees. The stones watched as she disappeared into the forest.

Under the canopy of trees, light filtered down through the thick fir limbs like gauze curtains. With her next step, Laina felt something sharp slide into the bottom of her bare foot.

"Yow!" she cried. Limping over to a large tree, she sat down against the trunk and turned her injured foot up to inspect it. A long, dark sliver of wood lay wedged under several layers of tender skin. Laina winced as she tried unsuccessfully to grasp the end of the sliver and pull it out. Poking around the reddened skin, she groaned at the thought of her long walk back to the castle.

Fifteen paces away, from his hiding place, a stranger watched Laina with his yellow, bloodshot eyes. Dirty, matted hair hung in clumps from his head, and his stained clothes smelled of urine and vomit. He couldn't believe his luck. Smiling, he revealed his brown teeth. Licking his lips in anticipation, he pulled out his knife and whispered to himself. "I'll slit her smooth neck first, and then do what I will with her. It will be quieter that way. Pretty little bird. I am going to enjoy plucking you."

He grinned as his demented plans took shape in his mind, and his crotch grew hard. He stared at the gentle shape of her bared leg, as she intently studied her foot. He would move fast. There would be no fight. Sometimes the wicked get lucky. Switching his knife to his strongest hand, he advanced.

Without warning, a giant black shape swooped into the man's face, screeching loudly. The powerful slapping of the beast's wings scratched and stung him. The enormous raven had come out of nowhere. The startled man took a quick step back, wedging the heel of his boot in the crook of a large fallen limb. Helplessly off balance, he fell backward, his head making solid contact with a large rock.

Startled by the raven's commotion, Laina stood slowly and tried to see through the hazy light. She saw nothing, except dust flying up into the air near an area of dense brush. She carefully put her shoes back on, then slowly limped back to the castle.

When the stranger was lucky enough to awaken with only a large lump on his head, the girl was gone.

Reynold's men were just departing Galloway Castle as a large group of travelling merchants arrived, bringing all manner of fine goods to trade with Laird Galloway. A darkening sky and sharp wind rolled in with the merchants, but the change of visitors put Gavin in a better mood. The lower courtyard was a flurry of activity when Laina returned, limping, to the castle. A number of horses and riders hurried about while men unloaded large crates and goods from half-a-dozen carts. Laina stumbled trying to dodge a man who nearly rolled a heavy barrel right over her.

"Out of the way you clumsy girl!" the man snarled.

With the wind whipping at her hair and clothing, and the first few raindrops splattering on her skin, Laina skirted around the commotion and hurried to the kitchen. Margaret stood at the hearth, sprinkling herbs onto a rabbit roasting on the spit. The delicious aroma filled the air.

"What's going on out there?" Laina asked, moving awkwardly to sit down on a stool.

Margaret looked up and came toward her, frowning. "What happened to you?"

Laina slipped off her shoe and held her foot up for Margaret to see. The swollen wound was hot and red. "I was walking barefoot in the forest," Laina admitted.

"Good lord," Margaret huffed. "We've got to get that out of there before it becomes infected. Audrey! Bring me my small antler-handled knife, the kettle of hot water, and a bottle of whiskey."

Still sulking from the earlier argument with Lucy, but anxious to see what mishap had occured, Audrey retrieved the items quickly.

"Where are Gillian and Lucy?" Laina asked, looking around.

"I sent them for water," Margaret answered.

Laina guessed that Margaret was keeping peace by keeping the girls apart. She must surely get tired of dealing with their bickering, Laina thought to herself. Her heart swelled with fondness as she watched the cook bend over her foot. Margaret was one of the toughest women Laina had ever known, but her hands could be most gentle when needed.

While Margaret cleaned the wound with whiskey and began digging for the splinter, Laina listened to Audrey chatter on, grateful for the distraction.

"They're merchants," Audrey said, nodding toward the door, "all the way from Portsmouth. They are a surly lot, they are. Come to barter goods with our laird. They've got no women with them."

"I want you girls to stay close to the kitchen," Margaret said, turning Laina's foot so that she could work from a different angle. "Don't be wandering around alone."

Laina squinted her eyes closed and jerked slightly as Margaret announced, "There!" and held the large sliver of wood up victoriously. "Your foot is going to be tender for a few days. No long walks for you."

Suddenly very tired, Laina thanked Margaret and hobbled to the storeroom, where she sprawled onto her sleeping pallet fully dressed. She was asleep within moments. Margaret came in and covered the girl with a woolen blanket. Laina slept through dinner, as well as the noise of the howling wind and the drunken merchants.

Margaret was pleased with the way Laina was finally settling into her new home. As of late, the girl had become more light-hearted and relaxed. Perhaps it was related to the fading interest of the laird. Truly, such attention had put a lot of pressure on the lass. Perhaps the cook would have to give up her dream of seeing a pairing of the two. But as long as Laina was happy, Margaret decided, that's what mattered most. Some things just weren't meant to be.

Chapter Sixteen

☙❧

"I HAVE A MESSAGE for Miss Laina Makgregor," the young messenger announced, standing in the doorway of the kitchen.

Margaret and the girls stopped what they were doing and looked up.

Laina stood near one of the work tables, with an onion in each hand. Spotting her, the messenger continued, "Laird Galloway requests that you join him for a private dinner, Miss Laina. I can escort you there now."

Audrey made a strangled, choking sound.

"Just give the lass a few moments," Margaret called out excitedly, "and she'll be ready."

The messenger nodded and stepped just outside the door in the late afternoon sun.

Margaret scurried over to Laina, took her arm, and directed her into the storage room. Snatching the neatly folded velvet green dress from its place on a shelf, the cook said, "Quick! Put this on."

Lines formed between Laina's eyebrows. "Why is he…"

Margaret removed Laina's apron. "You must go. Our laird has ordered it."

"It was a *request*," Laina responded dully.

"It's the same thing," Margaret said, pulling Laina's tunic up over her head. "Come on now."

Laina's face turned dark. All of this was happening too fast. Did the laird think he could ignore her for weeks and then suddenly order her to have dinner with him? She was not a plaything for him. And how would the lady Elinor feel about this? The laird was putting Laina in a difficult situation, just to please himself.

Margaret pulled the green velvet dress down over Laina's head. Scowling, Laina lifted her arms mechanically to allow the sleeves to slide on. *Damn him, and all men*, she thought.

"Why is he asking for me now? It doesn't make any sense."

"I don't know. You must go find out." Margaret tugged down hard on the bodice and tightened the lacings, forcing Laina's breasts to heave up prominently. "You must look your best."

Laina looked disgusted. Margaret stepped back with a look of admiration and grinned. Even with a scowl, the lass was breathtaking — her smooth complexion, thick dark eyelashes, and graceful pink lips. Thankfully, the long drape of the dress concealed the girl's ratty shoes.

The cook untied Laina's hair and brushed it out quickly in long strokes. When Laina started to re-braid it, Margaret put a hand on her arm and said, "Leave it unbound." The silky, dark tresses cascaded over Laina's shoulders and down to her waist. The contrast of it against her fair skin and the green of the dress was stunning.

"This is ridiculous," Laina said.

Margaret steered Laina toward the door. "Hurry now." The cook was quietly beaming. Perhaps there was still hope for getting the girl together with their laird.

Laina was aware of everyone staring at her as she crossed the kitchen. She felt like a prized pig being taken to auction. She didn't have time to think or argue about it. She did not want to disappoint Margaret, and apparently it would not be appropriate to refuse the laird's request. So, she decided, she would go along with it for now. Surely the laird would come to his senses and it would be over soon.

She had to hurry to keep up with the messenger as he walked quickly across the lawn and sprinted up the steps to the keep. The jarring motions pained her foot, further irritating her temperment. She was fantasizing how she would like to tell the laird that she was flattered by his attention but she did not really see any point to their meetings, when one of the big wood doors of the keep swung open and Laird Galloway stepped out.

He smiled broadly and held out his hand. "Laina."

He wore a white shirt that matched the brilliant white of his teeth, and black trousers that hugged his muscular legs. His green eyes sparkled as he gently took her hand and wrapped his large fingers around her's.

She had forgotten how commanding his presence was, and how overwhelmed she felt when looking into his handsome face and meeting the directness of his gaze. He gave her hand a reassuring squeeze.

Her lips formed a hesitant smile. "M'lord."

She looked even more beautiful than the last time he'd seen her. And she had dressed in her finest for him, which pleased him greatly. "I have been looking forward to spending time with you again, Laina," he said. "It is unfortunate when matters of business continually get in the way of more enjoyable activities."

His sincerity and manner were disarming. It was true, he was a very busy man, and yet he was choosing to make time for her. Most women would be grateful for such favor.

"I am honored, m'lord," she said quietly.

"Come. I have something to show you," Gavin said. Holding her hand, he led her through the front door and thoughtfully waited for her eyes to adjust to the dim light before descending the steps into the great hall.

Laina had only been inside the keep briefly, twice before, and then she had entered through the side door near the pantry. Her duties were usually restricted to the kitchen — an effort by Margaret, she suspected, that was meant to protect her, since it was widely known that the laird's men could be a randy bunch with young ladies.

Having only peeked into the great hall quickly from the back hallway on previous visits, Laina's eyes widened at the grand size of the room in front of her. The laird's voice interrupted her thoughts.

"I've requested that we be served a light evening meal upstairs in the solar, so that we can talk undisturbed. It's a very special room, Laina. I think you will like it."

Feeling the heat and strength of his hand enclosed around her's, her heartbeat quickened.

Gavin led Laina across the massive room, but stopped when he noticed her uneven, halting step. "Lass, is something troubling you?"

"Oh, it's nothing," she waved her free hand. "My foot is just healing from a splinter."

In one swift movement, the laird scooped Laina into his well-muscled arms. "There's no sense in you walking on it and making it worse," he said.

"No, really," Laina laughed nervously, "it's not that bad."

The laird held her against his solid chest as he strode toward the stairs.

With one arm around his neck, she could feel his hair brushing against her skin. The pleasant, spicy scent of him engulfed her. *Good lord, was this really happening*, she thought?

"Honestly, I'm fine," she insisted.

The laird smiled.

Realizing how intimate her position was, with her face just inches from his, heat rose up her neck and into her cheeks. Gavin sprinted up the stairs and walked along a corridor lit with low-burning torches in metal brackets, before ascending another narrow set of stairs.

Laina willed herself to remain calm, and reminded herself that he was just a person like any other. The people of Dounehill had taught her that. But then, none of them had been this close to him, feeling his strength and enhaling the scent of him.

Gavin stepped up one last step onto a small landing, then pushed open a heavy wooden door in front of them with a kick of his foot. Afternoon sunlight flooded into the hallway from the bright room.

Laina blinked in disbelief. The laird stepped forward into a room filled with colorful tapestries and large pillows piled on the floor. Two massive chairs with velvet cushions sat in the middle of the room at a small table. Most astonishing was the wall directly opposite them — a large pair of windows from floor to ceiling revealed an extraordinary view of the rolling countryside.

Laina gasped. The rich, green landscape stretched out before her, while she floated high above like a bird. After a moment, she realized that she was still in the laird's arms and clutching onto him tightly. Relaxing her grip, she nervously met his eyes.

"Breathtaking, isn't it?" he asked, his generous lips just inches from her face.

Quickly shifting her eyes, she replied, "I have never seen anything so…glorious."

Gavin set her down gently, and stepped back, clasping his hands behind his back.

Laina moved forward and touched one of the windows. "The glass, it's so clear."

"It's imported," he said. "I couldn't let this view be wasted."

Laina looked around the room. A large, ornately carved fireplace decorated one wall. An intricately carved wooden chest sat in a corner. Exotic tapestries with colorful scenes of flowers and animals hung all around the room. In front of the fireplace, large pillows in beautiful fabrics covered the floor.

In awe, Laina held a hand up to cover her gasp.

"I thought you would like it," Gavin said, pleased by her reaction. She was oblivious to his attention as she looked around the room. He studied the curve of her neck and the satin texture of her skin. He was delighted that she had left her hair unbound. And the way the dress showed off the curves of her body and her tiny waist, made his blood boil. God help him to go slow.

Laina turned toward him, her face glowing like a child. "Where did all of these fine things come from?"

"I do a lot of trading," Gavin replied as he stepped to the table and began pouring two glasses of wine.

"With the lady Elinor's uncle?" As soon as the words tumbled from her mouth, Laina wished she could take them back. The laird's business was private.

Gavin stiffened slightly and looked up. "Where did you hear that?"

Laina lowered her eyes with embarrassment. "There was talk in the kitchen, m'lord."

"Ah yes," Gavin said. "Those kitchen women seem to know a lot about what goes on around here."

He held out a glass of wine for her. She looked up slowly and saw that he was smiling. He winked at her. "What else did you hear?" he urged, as he took a sip of his wine.

"That you are anxious to send the lady Elinor home," Laina said softly.

Gavin burst out laughing, and walked over to close the door. "Well, they've got that right too."

"I thought..." Laina hesitated, "Well, the lady Elinor spoke to me in the courtyard and told me that she is to be your lady." Laina nervously took a drink of wine.

"Did she?" Gavin looked mildly annoyed. "Anything else?"

"She told me that I should not misinterpret your attention for affection, and that it would be best if I avoided you." She took another sip of her drink.

The laird was impressed by the girl's honesty.

"Let me set something straight," he said, the intensity of his gaze holding her firmly. "Elinor is not to be my lady now or ever. She came here because I promised her uncle that I would try to find her a husband, while he and I did some trading. She evidently had her own ideas about becoming lady of this castle, but I have never had any interest in her, and I grow weary of her telling everyone otherwise. She will be leaving as soon as I can spare a few men to see her home."

"So..." Laina said, "I do not need to worry about her being angry with me for coming here?"

Gavin smirked. "No. And if she bothers you again, tell me."

Laina took another drink of wine and gave a big sigh.

The laird chuckled. "You most certainly may interpret my attention as affection." He reached up and lightly touched her cheek with the back of his hand.

Laina froze like a rabbit with a hawk circling overhead.

Gavin saw her reaction and realized he was moving too quickly. He did not want her to fear him. A little fear was healthy, even exciting. But too much fear would prevent her desire from igniting, and that was a flame that he was aching to see.

Still feeling the heat from the laird's hand where he had touched her face, Laina's thoughts tumbled over each other as she sipped her wine. What might he expect of her? She had heard much about his reputation, but she hadn't actually considered that he might think of her in such a way. Might he want her to go to his bed? Then what? Would she be forgotten, and labeled badly for the rest of her life?

"You do not need to be afraid of me, Laina," the laird said gently.

She met his gaze. "It's just that I don't know you very well, m'lord."

"That's why I've called you here," Gavin said. "How will we get to know each other if we don't spend time together?"

"Yes, m'lord."

The laird pulled out one of the chairs at the small table for Laina, and then sat down across from her. Sharing the platter of cheese, fruit, and bread on the table, Gavin told Laina about some of the humorous situations and people he had dealt with in his role as laird. His stories made her laugh.

"It's a real problem," the laird was saying as he refilled her glass, "my men continually scare the serving girls. Then their parents take them back to the village and I have to find new servers."

"Maybe there is another way you can go about it," Laina suggested.

The laird raised an eyebrow. "Such as?"

Laina giggled. "Find servers that aren't as attractive."

"Impossible!" Gavin laughed. "Those men will chase anything."

"Oh no." Laina shook her head in mock seriousness, fully

feeling the effects of the wine. "I'm sure if the servers were, say, *older*, and had a few teeth missing...and a few warts, your men would pay more attention to their food."

Gavin's laughter grew as he imagined it.

"Oh, and..." Laina added, giggling with her hand over her mouth. "You could use that old man who cleans out the horse stalls. Most of his nose is missing!"

Gavin threw back his head and roared with laughter. "It would serve them right!"

"You could do it just long enough to teach them a lesson," Laina suggested, wiping tears of laughter from her eyes.

"I'll do it!" Gavin announced triumphantly.

Her face glowing from their shared laughter, Laina looked out the windows. Gavin watched her, thinking how she delighted him.

The setting sun filled the room with a rosy glow, and painted the sky with pink and purple streaks. Gavin stood and lit candles around the room before adding more wood to the fire.

Laina watched him move around the room. His commanding presence made her breath catch in her throat. He was in charge of everything he did, and yet, he was gentle too. It was no wonder that women obsessed over him. Turning from the fire, Gavin beckoned Laina to join him on the pillows. She slipped off her shoes and padded gingerly across the wood floor.

The wine made her feel light and free. She had to admit, she was having a wonderful time.

"M'lord, may I ask you a question," she slurred slightly.

Gavin took her hand as she sat down. "Of course."

"Why did you invite me here?"

"Because," he answered, kissing her hand lightly, "I wanted to know you better and there were too many distractions for us everywhere else."

"Oh," she said, feeling the softness of his lips on the back of her hand and suddenly forgetting why the question had been important to her.

"Laina, I want you to be careful for the next few days while the merchants are here at the castle," he said. "They are a rough bunch, and I do not fully trust them."

She nodded. "Margaret has instructed all of the girls to stay near the kitchen until they leave."

"Good." Gavin looked into the fire for a moment and his expression turned serious. "There's one more thing I want to set straight with you."

Sensing his body stiffen, Laina stiffened too.

"The destruction of your village was a terrible tragedy that I regret I could not prevent. It is my duty to protect the people on my lands. One of the reasons I've been so busy since you arrived is that my men and I are continually broadening our efforts to track down these murderers. I want justice for you Laina. And I want to protect you and everyone else who depends on me. I will find these men."

"Thank you, m'lord. I am grateful for all you have done for me. I am making a new life here, but yes, I miss my home. They were good people."

"Tell me about them," Gavin said, gently squeezing her hand.

Laina's eyes glistened with tears but did not spill over as she recounted dear memories of her parents and her village. When she spoke of the happy times, she laughed out loud. When she described the beautiful leatherwork her father did, she beamed with pride. She recounted how, when she was young, her mother loved to sit with her in the stone circle, telling stories and talking about nature.

Gavin now understood why the lass took walks to the stone circle. It was the one thing she had left that reminded her of her beloved past. He did not press her for any further details surrounding the murderous last day in her village. It was enough to know that she had escaped and was showing the courage to continue living with her delightful spirit in tact.

The fire crackled and sent flickering shapes around the room as the sky grew dark outside. The laird had been holding Laina's hand for quite some time. She didn't remember when she had begun leaning against him, but she was mesmerized by the vibration of his deep voice, booming through his chest where she rested her head.

Laina decided there was much she had not realized about Laird Galloway, or given him credit for. As Margaret had said, he was a good man. He could have easily sent her to the nearby village to live with the other Dounehill survivors, yet he had welcomed her inside the castle walls. And he and his men were working hard to track down the murderers who had destroyed her beloved home. She suddenly felt very foolish, not only for resisting him, but for not offering her indebtedness to him.

As if sensing her thoughts, Gavin slipped his arms around her, enclosing her in the warmth and safety of his solid embrace. Laina tipped her head back to look up at him, a peaceful smile on her lips. Cradling the back of her head with his upper arm, the laird's mouth descended on her's with a gentle, longing kiss.

Laina responded to him and heard him groan.

He left her mouth briefly to blaze a trail of kisses down her neck, then returned, slipping his tongue between her lips. He explored boldly, tasting her sweetness. Holding her protectively, like a delicate bird, his powerful tongue beckoned to her.

With her head reeling, Laina surrendered.

Chapter Seventeen

෨෨ඌ

THE DOWNPOUR OF BLINDING RAIN had been plaguing Evan Prestwick for hours. Returning from a long ride to meet with the king's representative, Evan was most anxious to rejoin his fellow musicians before dark. No doubt, they were enjoying the warmth of the tavern this very minute, the bastards.

He had thought himself lucky to find a rock overhang to take brief refuge under. Little good it did. The rain slanted in from all directions, attacking his small, struggling fire and refusing to give him even a moment's peace. He stabbed angrily at the small amount of squirrel meat roasting on a branch, then watched as the meat slipped off into the fire. He made no effort to retrieve it. He had lost his appetite anyway.

Had the sun been shining, it would have done little to improve Evan's mood. He hated being given orders. One of the benefits of being a musician was that you could choose where you wanted to perform, or simply wander freely and play where you landed. There was always someone willing to pay with coin, ale, or food, and sometimes even a bed for the night. It was a pleasing life when he and his companions could do it on their own terms. Unfortunately, answering to others and following rules was the way of things for most people, and Evan knew that he had to go along with it once in awhile.

He mopped the rain from his face with a wet sleeve and thought about the order he had been given from the king. The Westport Musicians Troupe was being specially commissioned to play at the sudden wedding of the king's brother, Edmund. This would be Edmund's fourth wedding, but the king was sparing no expense for the lavish celebration for his younger brother and the new bride. The Westport Musicians would be paid handsomely.

Not only had Evan never cared much for Edmund, but the king's order came at a very inconvenient time. The Westport Musicians were already scheduled to play at the Harvest Festival at Galloway Castle. Now they would have to withdraw their name. Laird Galloway would not be pleased. Worse still, Evan had been looking forward to the soonest opportunity of seeing Laina Makgregor again. Oswyn had been wrong when he said Evan would forget her. Not only had Evan not forgotten her, he hadn't been able to stop thinking about her. He had mentally retraced the details of their brief encounters more times than he could count, remembering the brightness of her eyes, the softness of her lips, and the way she smelled of fresh herbs.

Frowning, he stood up and kicked the fire until the fragile flames hissed and slithered into wisps of smoke in the rain.

"Laird Galloway has probably claimed her by now anyway," Evan grumbled. "He'd be a damned fool not to." The scowling musician put on his dripping hat, mounted his horse, and disappeared into the gray downpour.

Laina awoke to a dull thudding in her head. Squinting her eyes from the intrusion of light, she propped herself up on the pile of large pillows in Laird Galloway's solar and gazed groggily around the room. She was alone. Memories of the previous evening with the laird trickled slowly back to her. Laughter and stories, holding the laird's hand, leaning against his solid body, and…his hot mouth on her's.

Her hand shot up to her bodice and she closed her eyes in quiet thankfulness that she was still fully dressed. At least she hadn't gone that far. She remembered kissing him, more passionately than she had ever kissed anyone, and then she remembered laying back on the pillows. She must have passed out from all the wine. It had been a wonderful evening. She wondered if the laird would be disappointed in her.

Slowly she stood. Gray early-morning light hung in the room. Through the large windows, Laina could see storm clouds moving swiftly across the sky, darkening the landscape below. At any moment the swollen shapes looked ready to burst open and soak the land.

Laina rubbed her head. Small flames in the fireplace flared on the glowing coals. What time of day was it? Where was the laird? Walking over to the heavy door, Laina pulled it open on its large groaning hinges. She jumped to see a man standing there.

"Yes, m'lady?" the soldier said.

"May I speak with Laird Galloway, please?"

"He is away for a few hours, m'lady. He has asked that you stay here, under my guard, until he returns." The guard gave a tight smile to soften his serious tone. "I will inform one of the servants that you are awake and require assistance." He reached for the large iron handle to pull the door closed.

"The kitchen staff will be worried about me," Laina hurried to add.

"Laird Galloway has taken care of everything, m'lady. He wants you to stay under protection." The guard pulled the door handle again, and the door closed heavily.

Protection? From what, Laina wondered? She turned away from the door. The room felt cold. She went to the hearth and put more wood on the fire. Kneeling in front of the growing blaze, she folded her arms across her chest and held herself.

She envisioned Margaret in the kitchen, bustling about to prepare the day's meals. The kitchen was a wonderful place to be on a day like this. Warmth from all three hearths would be filling the room, and the air would smell of fresh bread and savory stew. Laina's stomach growled.

No doubt, Audrey, Gillian, and Lucy would be gossiping terribly after Laina had spent the night in the laird's keep. What would people around the castle think of her? And, oh lord, the questions the girls would pummel her with when she returned.

Laina looked up at the sound of the door opening. A young girl entered with a tray containing fresh biscuits and a goblet of warmed cider. Laina recognized the girl as a daughter of one of the servants. Embarrassed by the way the situation looked, the girls nodded at each other quietly.

The guard at the door asked the girl to show Laina to the water closet on the floor below. A short while later, Laina returned to the room, and the door closed solidly behind her again.

Approaching the tray, Laina recognized Margaret's special biscuits. She felt comforted as she bit into one of them.

Lightening flashed outside. The dark, heavy clouds tumbled angrily, releasing a curtain of rain that shimmered in the flashes of light. Laina picked up the warm goblet and approached the window.

Longing to smell the fresh, stormy air, she carefully unlatched one of the large windows and pushed it open. A cold blast of wind whipped her hair back. She closed her eyes, and breathed in deeply. The rain-scented air sent tingles through her body. Opening her eyes, she raised the engraved silver goblet to her lips, smelling the spicy sweetness of it. Something nagged at the fringes of her memory. The goblet — she had seen it somewhere before.

Staring into the liquid, Laina puzzled over the flickering images in her mind. It had been a dream or a vision. She had seen a goblet filled with white powder, and she had unexplainably blown the mixture into the air. Her mother had been with her, and they had laughed about it. Laina smiled at the memory. But there had been a warning too.

Laina suddenly held the vessel to the window and poured the liquid outside, just as large drops of rain began slanting into the room. Closing the window, she set the empty goblet on the table and returned to the pillows, curling up in front of the fire. She watched the flames and wondered if she would ever see Evan Prestwick again. Damn him. Their kisses under the stars had been so sweet. Perhaps not as passionate as the kisses she had just shared with the laird, but Evan was a gentleman, and the laird...well, he could do whatever he wanted. It had not seemed wrong though. Both men stirred feelings within her. Wondering if Evan could kiss as passionately as the laird, she drifted off to sleep while the rain pounded against the windows.

Gavin and his riding party came thundering through the front gates as lightening flashed across the sky. The laird rode his horse all the way up to the keep, then dismounted and handed the reins to one of his men. Sprinting up the steps and inside, he shook himself off like a large animal and dropped his soaked cloak on a bench by the door before descending the steps into the hall.

"M'lord, may I have a word with you?" the house steward asked, nervously approaching the laird.

"Why, certainly Bernard. What is it?" The laird nodded encouragingly at the old man.

"In private, please, m'lord." Bernard whispered.

"Of course." Gavin led the way into a small storage room off of the great hall. Bernard quickly followed him into the musty room of gray stone walls. The laird closed the door, then turned to the old man.

"M'lord, please forgive me for interfering..."

"You are free to speak with me anytime, Bernard. You have been a devoted servant in this castle longer than I've been alive."

Gavin casually folded his large arms across his chest and waited for the servant to continue.

"It is your own business, m'lord, to do as you wish with the ladies..." he said nervously, then turned his head and coughed.

"Are you worried about the young lady, Laina, staying in the solar?" Gavin smiled.

"Yes, m'lord," Bernard said with a gravelly voice and coughed again.

"How chivalrous of you, Bernard. I assure you that I am taking good care of her. In fact, there's probably nowhere that she would be safer."

"No, m'lord," the old man rasped. "It is not you that I fear is a threat to her, but the lady Elinor."

The smile vanished from the laird's face. "What do you mean?"

"M'lord, I am sorry to intefere in your personal matters..."

"What is it that you know?" Gavin bellowed, causing Bernard to jump.

"I...I saw the lady Elinor mixing a drink that was taken up to the young lady. That was not long after I heard Elinor fussing to one of the women servants about how the young wench was sticking her nose in where it didn't belong. I do not trust the lady Elinor, although I know she is your guest...."

Gavin jerked open the door and raced from the room. The old man trembled as he heard the laird's heavy footsteps pounding through the great hall and up the stairs.

Gavin was in a panic. His mind raced. "If that witch Elinor had hurt Laina..."

Sprinting along the upper corridor and ascending the smaller staircase, the laird burst through the solar room door with such force that the door slammed against the wall.

"Laina!" His face contorted as he saw her lifeless form in front of the fire. "God, no!"

From her curled position, she slowly raised her head, rubbed her face and smiled.

Gavin blinked and stared at her. Rushing to the empty goblet on the table, he wiped his finger along the inside, and put the residue to his tongue. He frowned and moved swiftly toward her, "Laina, the drink in the goblet..."

"I'm sorry, I poured it out the window," Laina admitted, embarrassed to be wasting what was given to her.

"You what?"

"I don't know how to explain it, m'lord. It was just a strange feeling I had."

In one fluid movement, the laird kneeled and pulled her into his arms, hugging her so tightly she squeaked like a mouse being stepped on. He stroked her hair for several moments, his breath coming fast and heavy, then released her and stood up. "I will be back shortly," he said, anger darkening his face.

Laina stared after him in silence. She was alone in the room again. Thunder rumbled and shook the walls. It did not come from the storm outside, but from within the keep. The roar of the laird's voice boomed throughout the structure, followed by the shrill, indignant screaming of a woman. Laina heard Gavin bellowing, "Out! Out! Get her out of here!" She could not hear the rest of it, as the voices became muted. After some banging, there were several moments of silence and then Gavin reappeared in the doorway to the solar. He stood on the threshold, his face hot and red, his eyes black as night. Laina shrank back against the pillows and remained silent. She had never seen the laird in such a state.

Gradually his fists relaxed from their clenched state, and the expression on his faced eased. He turned to Laina. "Forgive me, I thought you would be safe here."

"What's going on?" she asked in a small voice.

Gavin closed his eyes briefly, trying to compose himself. "I have just discovered that Elinor wished to do you harm."

"Why?" Laina gasped.

The laird's mouth twisted. "Because, lass, you were getting my attention, and she was not."

Laina stood up and walked slowly over to the serving table. "She put something in the drink?"

"Yes. One of the servants saw her, and I could taste a hint of the bitter poison."

Gavin stepped forward and embraced Laina. "This is the second time I've failed to protect you."

Pressed against his massive chest, her voice was muffled. "It is not your fault, m'lord. You have done everything you can."

Easing his hold on her, Gavin shook his head, frowning. "It has not been enough."

Laina tipped her head up to look into his face and saw a torment she wouldn't have expected. It was so important to him to protect those who depended on him. Clearly, he took all of the responsibility on himself. Without thinking, she reached her hand up to gently touch his hot face.

The laird immediately bent and pressed his mouth against her's, forcing her lips apart and kissing her with feverish need. Holding her firmly in his powerful arms, his lips and tongue moved passionately over her's.

Although surprised by his sudden aggressiveness, her body quivered under his absolute control. She had never known anything like it. It sent waves of excitement through her. When at last the laird released her, Laina stood breathless. She watched him turn toward the fire and poke the logs. When he turned back around, his face had gone dark again.

"There's more," he said. " I kept you in this room this morning because I felt that you might be in danger from a completely different source."

"From who?" Laina asked, stunned.

Gavin reached into his pocket and withdrew a brown object. It took Laina a moment to understand what she was seeing, and then the color completely drained from her face. It was her father's leather pouch. The one he had finished the day before he was killed.

Her eyes filling with tears, she choked out the words, "Where...how...?" Reaching out her hand to touch the leather, sobs overtook her.

"Last night after you fell asleep, I went downstairs to join my men for a drink," Gavin explained. "As we shared stories, one of them showed me this pouch he had received in trade for a knife. I recognized the carved design as matching the one you had described to me last night. The pouch came from one of the travelling merchants."

"I want to see him!" Laina demanded, her face reddening.

"We don't know where he is, exactly," Gavin admitted. "The merchants were camping at the edge of the forest, so my men and I went to confront them. I could not know what they might try to do in my absence, so I wanted to make sure that you were held safely while I was gone."

"What happened?" Laina asked, wiping impatiently at her

eyes.

"As we were nearing their camp, they mounted their horses and abandoned their tents. We chased after them for quite some distance, until the storm completely blinded our progress. We know they will return. Most of the goods they were trading are still here, and I don't expect them to give those up." Gavin scowled. "We have men posted all around the territory to alert us when the bastards dare to return. We'll be ready for them, and we'll meet them outside of the castle. We will find them, Laina, and justice will be done."

Laina looked down at the pouch in her hands. "I want to be there."

"I will see to it."

"I would like to return to the kitchen now," she said quietly.

Gavin nodded. It broke his heart to see her so saddened. He walked her down the stairs in silence. The great hall was empty and dark, except for a few candles burning in their holders. The sound of their footsteps echoed hollowly on the stone floor as they crossed the room and ascended the steps to the large doors. Laina stood clutching the leather pouch to her chest with both hands.

Even with her tear-stained face and red nose, Gavin found the lass irresistibly fetching. He wanted to carry her up to his bedroom and make love to her all afternoon while the rain drummed on the windows. With a look of wild hunger on his face, he leaned down toward her.

She stared blindly beyond him, her body stiff.

He paused and stood upright. "Do not worry, lass," he said, opening the door of the keep. "We will find them."

Numbly, Laina stepped outside and let the rain mix with her tears as she slowly walked back to the kitchen.

Chapter Eighteen

ഉ)ര

"HOW DARE YOU lock me in here!" Elinor screamed at the soldier. "My uncle will have your head for this! Do you hear me?"

"Tis a pleasure to see you down there, m'lady. Suits you very well, it does. Now shut up!" the guard retorted before stalking out of the gatehouse to escape her screeching.

On the laird's orders, the guards had escorted Elinor to their gatehouse, moved aside the metal grate from the hole in the floor, and lowered her by rope into the narrow chamber below. She had refused to be cooperative until they threatened to strip her naked before dropping her into the pit.

The heavy grate cover made a horrible scraping sound as it was moved back into place. Elinor sat in a state of disbelief and horror, ten feet below. How could she have ended up in this slimy hole? Somewhere along the way, her clever strategy had gone terribly wrong, and that just didn't make sense. Thank goodness they had allowed her to keep her clothes on. Although, even now, she could feel the wetness from the floor and the walls seaping into her fine garments. She began to sob.

Inside the keep, Gavin paced back and forth as he met with his man, Lowrens. Gavin was furious. He had a mind to strangle Elinor, himself, but it was just a fantasy since he would never kill a woman deliberately.

"Laird, I'll make the ride, myself, and be there by dark," Lowrens assured. He would deliver the message that either Elinor's uncle or his men would need to come collect her immediately.

Gavin nodded his approval and stormed angrily from the keep. He didn't stop until he reached the guardhouse. The guards were squatting on the ground, throwing dice and placing bets. They looked up and stood as the laird approached.

"Is the witch locked up?" Gavin growled.

"Aye, and she has gotten very quiet," one of the guards smirked.

"That's a welcome change." Gavin snorted. He entered the guardhouse and walked over to stand above the pit where Elinor was being held. She was whimpering.

"Gavin, please...," she cried.

"Finally some accomodations you are truly deserving of," he said through clenched teeth.

"I... I have done nothing," she whimpered.

"Do not lie to me Elinor or I shall cut your throat right here," Gavin roared. It was an empty threat, but the intent to scare her worked.

"You have no proof!" she screamed. "That little wench Laina is lying if she told you that I tried to poison her. She just wants to improve her rank in life, Gavin. She is not worthy of you. I am the one who is your equal, Gavin. I am the one who can run your household, and by God, I would not let anyone stand in my way..." Elinor suddenly stopped. A heavy sense of doom settled over her.

The outline of Gavin's dark figure towered above silently. His face was hidden in shadows. Elinor was glad she couldn't see it. She couldn't remember what she had just said, but she had an uneasy feeling that she might have said more than she should have.

"Gavin..." she began.

He cut her off, and his voice was cold and sharp like a blade. "I am finished dealing with you Elinor. I am turning you over to your uncle under the condition that he escort you, accompanied by my soldiers, to the king to receive your punishment. I will not ruin my alliances by having your death on my hands. You will remain locked up until your uncle arrives."

Elinor buried her face in her hands. "Gavin, you must not keep me in this godforsaken pit," she pleaded. "How long will it be until my uncle arrives?" She looked up. "Gavin?"

There was only silence. The laird had left.

"Ready my horse and tell my men to prepare to ride within the hour." Gavin ordered.

"You have received word?" Symon inquired.

"Aye. The merchants have been spotted. They are camped half-a-day's ride to the north." Gavin looked up at the sky — finally clear after two days of rain. "They will not escape us this time."

Audrey had been in the courtyard and noticed the men gathering. She hurried back to the kitchen with the news. Rushing inside, she screamed, "Margaret!" Looking around, she saw only the girls. "Where's Margaret?" she asked them.

"She's down in the cellar. What's going on?" Gillian asked.

Audrey pressed her lips firmly together and shook her head. "I'll wait until Margaret is here."

"What for?" Lucy asked.

Audrey shook her head again. "Something important is happening and I want to tell her."

"Why don't you tell us while you're waiting for her?" Lucy pressed.

"Because," Audrey yelled, "I want to tell her myself!"

"What do you want to tell me?" Margaret asked, stepping up from the last cellar stair.

"I saw the laird and his men in the courtyard," Audrey announced. "They were armed and mounting their horses. There must be two dozen of them!"

"Where are they going?" Gillian asked.

"I don't know," Audrey admitted.

Gillian snorted in disgust.

Boyd had just arrived and beamed with self-importance at knowing the answer. "They are going after the merchants to find out who has been attacking the villages. The laird says he will cut off the heads of those who are responsible, and put them atop poles so the birds can peck out their eyes!"

"Good lord!" Margaret gasped and turned away.

"Oh that will look great for the Harvest Festival next month!" Audrey barked.

"That's disgusting," Lucy squealed.

Margaret looked over at Laina, who seemed deep in thought. "Are you all right, lass?" Margaret asked.

Laina nodded, then added quietly, "I am grateful to the laird for trying to find my father's murderer." Her eyes blurred with tears. "Damn!" she said, wiping at her eyes with her apron.

Margaret moved to put an arm around the girl. "Poor lass, such a terrible tragedy you have endured." Margaret patted Laina's arm. "I think the laird favors you greatly. You can rest assured that he will bring you justice."

"Do you think the laird..." Tears began running down Laina's face faster than she could wipe them away.

"The laird will be safe, lass. Don't you worry." Margaret reassured.

Laina shook her head. "Do you think he will expect something of me when he returns?"

Margaret was surprised by the question. "My goodness lass, any woman would be happy to have the laird's attentions. He can change your life and your future. Would you not be honored to be with him in whatever manner he requests?"

Laina blew her nose into a small, tattered kitchen cloth. "Yes, yes...I would," she said weakly.

"It is natural that you are scared," Margaret reassured. "Especially after all the stories you've heard about him around here." She glared at Audrey, who was smirking and seemed to enjoy Laina's breakdown. "But Laird Galloway is one of the finest men I know," Margaret continued. "He favors you, Laina — and you must not reject this opportunity."

Laina nodded and dabbed at her nose. "I know. I'm being silly."

"Cheer up lass. The Harvest Festival will be here in another month. There will be music and dancing, and you can wear your pretty green dress," Margaret reminded.

Words escaped Laina's lips before she could stop them, "I hope that Evan will return."

"Who?" Margaret asked.

"The musician she met at the Mayday Faire," Audrey spouted. "Seems our laird is not enough for her."

"That's not true," Laina snapped, although she couldn't actually explain why she felt so emotional and mixed up.

"Musicians are an unpredictable lot, Laina," Margaret said. "They are fond of travelling and keeping their options open. They are often quite poor and live a hard life. Constantly surrounded by women too. Truth be told, he has likely forgotten about you, lass." Margaret gave the girl a sympathetic look before walking back to the hearth. "You best be focusing your attention on our handsome laird. You will likely be at his side for the Harvest Festival."

Laina blew her nose again. She knew Margaret was right — and even Audrey too. A girl would have to be daft to be daydreaming about anyone other than such a fine man as their laird. What was wrong with her? She was letting her childish fear get the best of her. Evan Prestwick was a convenient distraction from facing her future. But Evan was gone — he had made his choice. The laird truly cared for her, and she could not deny that she felt drawn to him. The way he made her feel, the things he excited in her, were hard for her to understand. But what *was* certain: her life was at Galloway Castle now and she was no longer a little girl. Perhaps it was time for her to move forward and experience all that she was meant to as a woman. There appeared to be no better man to do that with, than Laird Galloway.

Gavin and his men made good time to the merchant encampment, arriving just before dusk. The laird was surprised that the merchants made no attempt to run again as the laird's men approached. Gavin's stallion stomped to a halt in front of a group of men seated around a fire. "Who is the leader here?" Gavin demanded.

One man stood. "We don't have a leader, but I'm as close as you'll get."

Gavin scowled. "What do you know of the attacks on the villages in this region?"

"Nothing. " The man looked genuinely surprised. "Why would we know anything? We're merchants, not raiders."

Gavin leaned forward, his face darkening. "Then why did one of your men have possession of an item that was taken from one of those villages, and why did your group run from my men two days ago?"

The merchant spoke calmly. "I'll answer your second question first. We ran from ye because we thought you wanted justice for the tanner's daughter."

"What are you talking about?" Gavin snapped.

"One of our men dishonored the lass the first night we arrived. When you came after us, we guessed that she had told someone."

Gavin was stunned. This wasn't the information he had been looking for, but it needed to be dealt with as well. "Where is this man?" Gavin motioned to two of his men to be ready to grab the man.

The merchant shook his head. "He's gone."

"Don't toy with me," Gavin said, "or you will pay for his deed!"

"I'm telling you the truth. The man — Forster, he was called — was not getting on well with several in our group. Seeing as how he had caused a great deal of trouble for us, we gave him a choice." The merchant sneered. "He quickly decided to strike out on his own. That is why we are not running from you now. We have no war with you, and I ask that you not hold us responsible for one man's deeds."

Gavin gave no indication of his decision on the matter. "Now answer my other question. Why did one of your men have possession of a leather pouch that was taken from a ravaged village?"

"That is an even easier answer," the man shrugged. "We are merchants. We come into possession of all manner of things. We do not ask where they come from."

One of the merchants seated by the fire took out a knife to cut off a piece of meat cooking over the flames.

"That's it!" one of the laird's men yelled. "That's the knife I traded for the pouch."

Laird Galloway turned to the merchant. "Explain this."

The bearded man stood up and nodded. "Aye, I traded a carved leather pouch for this knife. Would like to have kept the pouch, but I needed the knife. Lost my last one in the river."

Gavin's voice grated like stone against stone. "*Where* did you get the pouch?"

The man looked thoughtful and rubbed his whiskers. "Let's see, it was about six months ago near Portsmouth. I had quite a few drinks that night, I did!" The man laughed at the memory.

Gavin glared at the man and waited.

Suddenly taking notice of the dangerous level of the laird's impatience, the man continued quickly, "Ah, yes, it was an interesting story about that pouch. The man who sold it to me said that he, himself, had acquired it from the leatherworker who had made it. Said the old man put up quite a fight over it, but couldn't refuse his offer in the end."

"Do you know the man who sold it to you?"

"Nay."

"Would you recognize him if you saw him again?"

"Not likely. No, not likely. It was a long time ago, and my vision was a might bleary from all the drink that night, you know." He chuckled again.

The laird sighed heavily.

Suddenly the man brightened and added, "But I do remember

the man's name because it was the same as me granddad's."

"What was his name?" Gavin asked as levelly as he could manage.

The man wiped his knife on his breeches. "Reynold. That was his name."

The blood drained from Gavin's face. Suddenly he remembered that first night his brother Reynold had arrived at the castle, and how he had been bragging about a trip he had made to Portsmouth six month's earlier. Gavin turned to Symon. "Where were Reynold's men heading when they left the castle?"

"South, to Dubenshire, I believe." Symon had never seen such a look of fury on his laird's face.

"Isn't Greendale on the way to Dubenshire?" Gavin's voice rose sharply.

"Aye, it is." Symon answered, knowing what his laird was thinking. The three visitors from Greendale had just visited Galloway Castle a few weeks prior, speaking of their good alliances, which would benefit the laird. An enticing target.

The laird's next command came out in a rasp. "To Greendale."

The laird's men rode through the night. Laird Galloway gave thanks for the full moon lighting their way, and asked forgiveness for the murder he was about to commit. Worse than the rage at his brother was the rage at himself for not discovering the truth sooner. Good god, he had actually hosted the devil in his home, and given he and his men weapons. It made Gavin sick. And his appearance showed it. The ususal smile and sparkle in his eyes was gone. His gaze was dark and lifeless, his face wrenched in a tortured scowl.

The group stopped only once to water their horses and take a quick break. Then they rode on, every one of them filled with fury and the intent to stain the ground with the blood of their enemies. Overhead, the yellow moon eyed the riders through a lacy curtain of drifting clouds. Shadows moved across the landscape, chasing the group. The moon's glow could not dispel the dark dread of such a night.

An hour from Greendale and two hours before dawn, the laird's group met a rider coming toward them from the south.

"It's terrible," the man babbled. "Greendale...totally devastated...bodies everywhere. Buildings burned to the ground!"

"Did you see who did it?" Gavin's voice was hoarse and strained.

"No," the rider said. "But there are survivors, and I heard that the attackers headed northwest."

"They're headed back to Galloway Castle..." Gavin said slowly, the horrible realization sinking in.

"While we're away," Symon added. "They must know."

"Good god," Gavin said, then addressed the rider again. "When was the attack on Greendale?"

"Yesterday, late."

The laird quickly motioned to four of his men to continue on to Greendale to assist the survivors, then he and the rest of his men turned in unison and left in a dead run. The rider from Greendale shielded his face and waited for the blinding cloud of dust to settle.

Chapter Nineteen

✿❀

REYNOLD'S GROUP ARRIVED at Galloway Castle a few hours after sunset. The guards at the gate had been amusing themselves with bawdy jokes when they spotted the riding party approaching.

"Hail!" Reynold raised a hand in greeting. "Is my brother here?

"No, he is on a mission with some of the men," one of the guards said, exchanging a look with the guard next to him. "Why have you returned?"

"We have important news," Reynold replied.

"Have you found our enemy?" the guard asked.

"I must hold the news for my brother, but if we may wait inside the castle, my men and I can share some of our best scotch with you."

A small group of guards discussed the matter quietly among themselves, while Reynold and his men waited at the end of the drawbridge.

One of the guards grumbled, "It was good to be rid of them, and now they're back?"

"Is it safe to let them in?" asked another. "What if they cause more trouble?"

Reynold yelled impatiently, "For god's sake, this was my home too. Are you going to make us stay out here until my brother returns? I assure you that my men will be on their best behavior."

The most senior guard smirked and turned back to the other guards. "We can't very well make him wait outside. He is on a mission for our laird. Advise our men to drink the scotch slowly and stay alert."

The laird's guards motioned for Reynold and his men to enter. Reynold smiled broadly at the suspicious men. "Did we wear out our welcome with you?" he taunted. "Let us make it up to you." Several of his men pulled out large bottles of scotch and waved them in the air.

The senior guard smiled stiffly.

Reynold had learned to be patient in getting what he wanted. He would watch and wait for the right moment to strike. In the meantime, there was no reason not to enjoy himself a bit as well. There was plenty of time, according to Reynold's informants — Gavin and his men were off chasing merchants and wouldn't be back before dawn. Laying waste to the castle and it's inhabitants would be a delightful task that Reynold would savor slowly after the guards had passed out. Imagining the look of horror on Gavin's face upon returning and seeing the destruction, made Reynold snort with amusement.

There was much drinking and laughing as the night wore on. Reynold's own men seemed to be getting drunker, while the laird's guards remained too sober. Either the guards could hold their scotch better than most, or they were pacing themselves, Reynold decided. Either way, he would wait. He knew his men could take the guards regardless. His group couldn't have pulled off such vicious attacks against greater numbers if they didn't have some tricks up their sleeves. The people of Greendale had put up quite a fight. It proved to be much more entertaining, Reynold thought. But in the end, holding women and children at knifepoint was a very effective way to disarm the men, and then the tender throats could be slashed anyway, and the rest was easy.

While Reynold's men shared drunken stories with the guards, Reynold discovered that Elinor Cobb of Dunstenshire was being held in the castle pit. Having never cared much for the pretentious woman, he decided it would be greatly amusing to go and taunt the wench, so he staggered off in her direction.

Elinor was a wretched mess, from what Reynold could see of her in the light of the lantern as he gazed down into the pit. Her circumstance had done little to decrease her venom.

"Just when I thought things couldn't get any worse," she hissed, upon seeing him.

He laughed. "I see you're letting yourself go, these days. You know, for a woman your age, you really should stay on top of that."

"Get out of here!" Elinor screamed.

"Now, now, that's no way to make friends...and it appears you don't have any." Reynold grinned devilishly. Oh this was fun.

Elinor was sure she was in hell. Maybe if she stopped talking, he would leave.

"I imagine," he continued, "that you've not been getting many visitors. Perhaps I can fill you in on all the news you're missing. What would you like to know? Where the latest parties are that you can't go to? Or which ladies are getting married to wealthy men?"

Reynold chuckled at his cleverness and took a swig from his bottle of scotch. "Surely there is something you're still interested in besides manipulating your way into Laird Galloway's castle." He smiled at her silence, and took another drink. "I guesss," he slurred, "you jus' weren't good enough for Galloway Castle, so the laird put you where he thought you belonged."

Elinor exploded. "He is a damned fool!" she screeched. "He does not consider the necessities for securing his future and his position. All he can think about are his god-awful desires and that simple little kitchen wench, Laina. What can she possibly know about being a proper lady of a castle? She is pretty, that is all. And he, the laird of a castle governing numerous territories, is acting like a damned fool over a kitchen worker!"

"Her family must be very proud," Reynold observed. "They stand to profit richly."

"She's a pathetic little orphan," Elinor groaned. "She even sleeps in the kitchen."

"Gavin always did like the downtrodden," Reynold noted. "I agree with you, he could stand to learn a thing or two about building his wealth."

Elinor felt sick, but she dare not wretch in her confined space. She began weeping softly.

Perceiving that he'd gotten as much fun out of this visit as he was going to get, Reynold stood up. "Well Elinor, do take care of yourself. I'll stop in next time I'm in the area." He snickered. The night was still early and he was just getting warmed up. A tantalizing idea came to him and he grinned darkly. As Reynold's men and the guards continued their merriment near the front gate, Reynold strolled out of the guard tower and headed for the kitchen.

Laina lay curled up warmly under her fur coverlet, sleeping peacefully. Images of a handsome man swam before her eyes in the dream. He held her firmly, his lips and tongue ravaging her mouth.

It was delicious. She wanted all of him, and she wanted to give herself to him completely. His face blurred and she became confused. She could hear a man calling her name.

Awakening with a start, Laina realized that someone was standing near the foot of her mattress.

"Is your name Laina?" the male voice asked in the dark.

Fear prickled her skin. "Yes," she answered evenly. "Who is there?"

"Don't be afraid, lass. I am Laird Galloway's brother."

"Has something happened to the laird?" Laina asked with concern.

"Not yet."

"Excuse me?" Laina asked, confused. "Why are you here?"

There was no response for a few moments as Laina heard footsteps. Then the man reappeared in the doorway, holding one of the kitchen lanterns. It illuminated the small storeroom. Laina slid back on her mattress, clutching the coverlet to her naked body.

The man looked drunk. He smiled at her and licked his lips.

Laina felt terror slice through her.

"Don't worry, lass. I share everything of my brother's."

Laina screamed.

Reynold was on her in a second, jamming his hand hard over her mouth and pinning her down firmly with his body. "Now listen," he said. "It's very simple. You give me what I want, or I will kill everyone in this castle."

Laina whimpered, her eyes darting around for any sign of something she could use against him.

Reynold moved his free hand under the coverlet and grabbed one of her breasts. The firm mound filled his hand. He smiled and groaned.

Her fear dissolving into rage, Laina began thrashing and kicking with unleashed fury, and was lucky enough to bring her knee up hard into his crotch.

Reynold howled and moved to defend himself from the surprising onslaught. First, the naked girl threw her fur coverlet over his head so he couldn't see, then she continually pelted him with heavy jars, bags of potatoes, a few empty crates, and other heavy lumps that he couldn't identify. All he could think was that he wanted to get out of there. When he was finally able to pull the coverlet off of his head and turn toward the door, a chair came crashing down on top of him and everything went black.

Boyd had heard Laina's scream, and hobbled over as fast as he could from his own sleeping quarters in a shed behind the kitchen. However, from what Boyd could see, it was not Laina who needed rescuing. A cloud of flour filled the air, and Laina stood completely naked in the middle of the room, her eyes wild. Boyd looked away politely, although it was one of the most enchanting sights he had ever seen. Reynold was out cold on the floor. Laina dressed quickly, while Boyd ran to the kitchen door and sounded the ram's horn to call the guards.

Returning to the storeroom where Laina stood trembling, Boyd made his way around Reynold and all the debris on the floor to reach her side. He held her until the guards arrived. One look at the room, and the men realized what had happened.

Reynold was locked up in the guard tower while he was still unconscious. Additional guards from around the castle were called to assist in restraining Reynold's men. An easy task, due to their extreme drunkeness. With their weapons removed, they were locked away in one of the guard rooms.

◇◇◇

The laird's party came thundering up to the gates just after sunrise.

"Is Reynold here?" Gavin called out to the first guard he saw on the wall.

"Aye, he is, laird. And locked up!"

"Good god, what has happened?" Gavin galloped across the drawbridge then jumped off his horse and turned to the soldier in charge. He was quickly brought up-to-date. He breathed a prayer of thanks. He had been chasing ghosts for the last 24 hours and he had become convinced that his world was being destroyed every step in front of him.

"Laina…is she alright?" Gavin asked.

"Aye. It is your brother that shows more damage from the encounter with her," the guard grinned.

Gavin's expression remained dark. Before this day was through, his brother would be dead.

"Is Reynold conscious now?" Gavin asked, looking in the direction of the guard's rooms.

"Aye."

The laird took a deep breath and walked to where his brother was being held. Reynold was a bloody mess. He was covered with cuts and bruises, as well as a few good-sized lumps on his head and a blackened eye. The laird stared at his brother in disgust.

Reynold sneered and said, "Everything you've ever had the power to attain, I've had the power to take away."

"Not anymore," Gavin said coldly, pacing away from his brother briefly to gather his composure. "Tell me why, Reynold. Why have you been leading this murderous campaign against me?"

"Because it is more profitable, clever, and exciting than playing the game the rest of you play. I do not answer to anyone. I can take whatever I want. And, therefore, I hold more power than anyone." Reynold chuckled. "Focusing on the destruction of *your* lands has been the cream on top."

Gavin shook his head in disbelief. "But why? What do you have against me? You could have just as easily had all of this. I didn't take it from you."

"Correct, you didn't. But it wasn't given to me."

"What are you saying," Gavin asked. "As the oldest son, you had first choice."

"Our father made it clear to me that I did not have the choice. He did not trust me and he did not want me ruining his precious reputation."

Gavin withheld his surprise. He had never known this. His father had told him that Reynold had no interest in his duty, and therefore, Gavin needed to take responsibility.

"But it doesn't matter," Reynold said, "because I really didn't want it. However, since it wasn't offered to me, it was an entertaining target for me to launch my attacks against. In the process, I have acquired treasures that most men only dream of, by wiping out entire villages!"

"You don't look like a wealthy man to me," Gavin scoffed.

"I get joy from the attainment of things," dear brother, "not from hanging onto them. Hanging onto them is a burden. There's no need to carry things around with me. I am never without for long."

"You only have six men in your group, yet the attacks on the villages were carried out by twenty," Gavin noted.

"It's easy to find men who are desperate for coin. They were allowed to keep much of what they found, and they knew that if they spoke of it, they and their families would die."

Gavin paced the floor, flooded equally with dread and relief. The nightmare was ending, but the duty before him would haunt him forever. He turned back to Reynold, "Do you remember attacking the small village of Dounehill and attaining a leather pouch with a symbol engraved upon it?"

"Aye, that was a bloody treasure hunt!" Reynold smiled broadly.

"Did you meet the man who made the pouch?" Gavin asked steadily.

"Aye, I stuck my own knife in him. The old man fought surprisingly well up until that point," Reynold chuckled.

"Are you aware that the girl you attacked last night is his daughter?"

Reynold threw his head back and laughed. "Well now, isn't that a fine turn of events! I would say that fighting runs in the family."

Gavin waited for Reynold to stop laughing. It was all the laird could do to keep from rushing into the cell and killing his brother right then and there.

"How did you know when the villages were most vulnerable?" Gavin pressed.

Reynold laughed. "Why, brother, it was just as easy to find people willing to talk for payment, as it was to find people willing to kill for it. My connections are my power. Now do you see? This is MY kingdom."

"Strange that you were dethroned by a girl and a crippled boy." Gavin smirked.

Reynold's face twisted into an ugly grimace. "Would you like to see what I could do to them right now?" Reynold threatened.

"You had your chance," Gavin said calmly, "and you lost." With that, he strode out of the room.

"Here comes the laird!" Lucy squealed, just as he strode up to the kitchen door and filled it with his massive frame. Seeing Laina at one of the work tables, he walked directly over to her.

"Laina, are you all right?" he asked, putting his hand on her cheek and searching her eyes for his answer.

"Yes," she said, giving him a small smile. She looked tired.

Everyone in the kitchen had frozen in place to watch the interaction between the two. Even Margaret could not pretend to politely look away. Having the laird, so close and personal, was exciting to them all.

Gavin spoke softly to Laina. "In addition to his attack on you last night, I have learned that it was my brother, Reynold, who killed your father."

Laina gasped. Then as the realization took hold, fury transformed her face.

The laird held her gaze and asked, "Do you want to kill him or shall I?"

She stared down at the floor for several moments, twisting her apron in her hands, her mind racing. She finally met the laird's eyes with tears brimming in her own. "I would like to be there to see it," she said, her lips quivering with an anger she couldn't suppress.

Gavin nodded and extended his hand to her. "Let's take care of this now."

Laina cast a quick look at the others in the kitchen. The girls looked terrified. Margaret nodded reassuringly.

Laina took the laird's hand, her face hardening to stone. They arrived at the lower courtyard to see Reynold being held by two guards outside.

Laina glared at the heavily bruised, bloodied man. Reynold smiled back.

Gavin looked at Laina. "Are you sure you don't want to kill him yourself?"

"He's not worth my energy," Laina hissed. "I want no further memory of him."

Reynold made a face like he was pouting, but stopped as the laird approached him.

"However," Laina added, "I do have something to say to you."

Reynold smiled. The laird leaned over and whispered into his brother's ear, "If you say anything to her, I will cut out your tongue right here and hold it in front of you."

Reynold's smile disappeared.

Laina folded her arms across her chest and looked at Reynold with disgust. "You think yourself clever for victimizing unsuspecting people, but there is no cleverness or courage in hiding your attacks. You are a pathetic coward. Anyone can sneak around in the shadows like a rat. Clearly, you are so weak that you cannot run the risk of facing other people's strengths against your own."

Reynold frowned. It was all he could do to keep quiet.

"You killed my father," Laina continued, tears sparkling in her eyes, "a very good and kind man. He would have given you anything that he had. But you threw away his precious life — that which was of the greatest value, for something that was worth almost nothing to you." Laina sneered. "That makes you as big of a fool as you are a coward."

Despite his fierce scowl, the beaten man in front of her paled. She felt small satisfaction that her words had pierced him. There was nothing she could do that would be enough for her. She nodded to the laird, letting him know she had nothing more to say.

Turning toward Reynold, Gavin smiled tightly and repeated his brother's earlier words back to him. "Now, brother, *this* is a fine turn of events."

Nodding to his guards to let go of Reynold, Gavin drew his sword. Before Reynold took his next breath, Gavin stepped forward and powerfully ran his sword through Reynold's chest. Reynold made a gurgling noise and collapsed to the ground.

Laina turned and walked away.

Chapter Twenty

A WEEK HAD PASSED since Reynold was put to death. His men were systematically put to death as well, after the laird's soldiers extracted as much information as they could to track down other accomplices. The castle was also freed of Elinor. She sat in the pit for 6 days until her uncle finally sent his men to collect her and escort her to the king for judgment.

Laina had not seen or heard from the laird, other than a message delivered to her one morning by a castle messenger. The boy delivered five red roses and a message saying that the laird would call for her soon. The delivery brought cheer to the kitchen.

"You see, lass, he has not forgotten ye!" Margaret exclaimed. "He's just a very busy man — and, like you, he has been through a terrible ordeal."

"Aye, the next time I see him," Laina agreed, "I will express my gratitude for all he has done for me."

Margaret grinned. "You do that, lass."

Boyd hobbled into the kitchen more awkwardly than usual, thrown off balance by the huge sword he was wearing at his side. It was a gift from Laird Galloway for the boy's bravery and assistance in saving Laina and capturing Reynold. Boyd wore it proudly and only took it off to sleep.

As he moved across the room, it banged into a bucket making a loud clang.

Audrey wrinkled her face in disgust. "Why are you wearing that thing? You can barely walk as it is."

"This is me reward," Boyd boasted, "Laird Galloway wants me to guard you women."

Audrey snorted. "Then we're in trouble."

"You were not here when Boyd took Reynold down," Laina

said sharply to Audrey. "If it were not for him, I could be dead or worse. It took great courage." Laina smiled warmly at Boyd. He beamed back at her.

"Boyd carrying a sword," Audrey spouted, " is like a goose wearing a hat. It has no purpose and looks ridiculous."

"Things hold value for people in different ways," Laina said.

Audrey put her hands on her hips. "What does that mean?"

"It's not necessarily *how* you use something, but rather *what it means* to you," Laina explained.

Audrey shook her head impatiently. "No, really, what do you mean?"

Laina snapped, "Just because *you* don't see the purpose of something, doesn't mean there isn't any."

"I don't understand," Audrey complained.

"Exactly," Laina said, walking away.

Audrey's face turned red. "And what the hell do you mean by that?"

Margaret spoke loudly. "Audrey, take this fresh bread over to the keep's pantry for tonight's meal. Gillian and Lucy, come with me to check the traps in the fish pond." Margaret smiled at Laina and nodded, "You can finish the meat pies you're working on."

Boyd cleared his throat and fidgeted with the hilt of his large sword. "Would you ladies like me to escort you to the fish pond?"

Lucy giggled.

"Aye," Margaret said, hiding her grin, "please, do."

Scowling, Audrey loaded her arms with bread loaves and plodded over to the keep, entering through the side door. A large rat scuttled into hiding as she stepped into the dark pantry. Audrey envied the girls who worked in the keep. It was a much easier job than working in the kitchen. Margaret never let anyone rest. There was always something to be done. And the girls who worked in the keep got to be around the laird every day. Audrey imagined what it would be like to wait on the handsome laird who might, at any moment, order her to his bed.

Setting down the loaves of bread on the counter, she closed her eyes and moved her hands across her breasts. Turning her head side-to-side, she imagined the laird touching her, kissing her...his large hands grasping her, his hot breath on her throat. She opened her mouth and imagined him ramming his tongue inside. A strangled moan escaped her.

Audrey's fantasy was interrupted and her eyes popped open at the sound of seductive laughter echoing from the great hall.

Quickly securing the loaves in the large wooden bread box, she stepped back into the narrow hallway and moved quietly to peek through the arched doorway leading into the great hall.

A young woman sat on the laird's lap, playing with his mustache and beard. Laird Galloway leaned to nibble on the girl's neck, and she giggled wildly. Audrey recognized the lass…a tart, that one!

The laird grabbed a handful of the girl's large breast. Audrey's mouth fell open as she watched the scene in front of her. The laird pulled the girl's chemise off of her shoulders and down to her waist. In response, the girl bounced up and down, her large melon breasts jiggling in all directions. How did someone get breasts that large, Audrey wondered?

Gavin leaned forward and took the tip of one of the girl's breasts into his mouth. The girl threw her head back and squealed. The laird was most enthusiastic, sucking and licking and groaning, while squeezing other fleshy parts of the girl's body with his hands.

As much as Audrey wanted to stay and watch, she feared being discovered and she couldn't wait to get back to the kitchen and share what she'd seen. Leaving quickly through the side door, she hurried back to the kitchen. On the way, an interesting idea occurred to her: Laina should see this for herself!

Audrey arrived breathless at the kitchen. Laina sat alone in the room at the center table, molding the crusts of the meat pies. Audrey smiled — this was perfect.

 Sensing someone at the door, Laina looked up.

Using her excitement to her advantage, Audrey announced, "Laina, I just saw the laird and he requests that you come see him at once."

"He did?" Laina asked, her face lighting up.

"Yes." She bobbed her head. "He apologized for being too busy to see you these past weeks, and he said he has time right now."

"Oh my," Laina said, smoothing loose strands of hair back from her face as she stood up.

Audrey tried not to laugh. "You look fine. Use the front entrance."

After Laina left, Audrey smirked and made a small snort of laughter. It was time that Laina's dream come to an end. She would never be good enough for the laird, and Audrey was tired of hearing about it. Laina's humiliation would be well-deserved — she was too sweet and perfect all the time. She needed to be knocked off the pedestal that Margaret and the others put her on.

Hurrying up the front steps of the keep, Laina pinched her cheeks to give them a glow. This was her chance to tell the laird how grateful she was to him. He had been so patient with her. Excitement surged through her as she thought of his face, his piercing eyes, and broad smile. She might just boldly give him a big kiss, she decided!

It was strange that there was no guard on duty, Laina thought. So, taking a deep breath, she hefted open the heavy door just wide enough for her slender body to slip inside. She blinked several times in the darkened interior, then carefully descended the steps down into the hall until she reached the bottom. Candlelight flickered dimly around the room. In the darkness, Laina could barely make out the outlines of the large posts down the center of the room. A muffled sound drew her forward.

"Laird Galloway?" she called out softly. As she rounded the next large post in front of her, her eyes widened and she sucked in her breath. A girl sat bouncing on the laird's lap, her skirt pulled up around her bottom and not a stitch of clothing on from the waist up. The laird's eyes were closed, his teeth gritted together in a tight smile.

Laina sputtered, "Oh...oh my!"

Gavin's eyes sprung open. "Laina! Good lord, what are you doing here?"

Horrified, Laina turned and ran, her face flushing red and her eyes stinging with tears.

"Laina! Stop!" Gavin shouted. Dislodging the half-clothed girl from his lap, he charged toward the door.

Laina held up her long tunic to take the stairs two at a time. Hearing the laird racing up right behind her, she stopped and bent her head. "Oh, m'lord, I am so terribly sorry. I was told you wanted to see me." She kept her gaze fastened to the floor. His clothing appeared to be undone.

"Who told you such a thing?" he asked, adjusting his trousers.

"Audrey."

"Ahh. Seems the lass was playing a cruel trick on you." Gavin reached over and gently tilted Laina's face up to look at him. She tried to look away but he held her eyes with his direct gaze. "I'm sorry," he said. "This was not something you needed to see."

"I'm sorry I intruded m'lord." Laina tried to bow her head but he wouldn't let her.

"It was not your fault," Gavin reassured.

Even in the darkness of the entryway, she could see the gentle way he looked at her.

"You know," he said, "there will be a time for you and I, Laina. I care about you, and I haven't wanted to rush you into anything you weren't ready for. But I have needs I must take care of. You understand, don't you?"

"Yes," she lied. She felt humiliated. She didn't care what his reasons were, she just wanted to get out of the horrible situation she found herself in. What did it matter what she thought, anyway? He was the laird — he could do whatever he wanted.

"If only you knew, lass..." he chuckled, pulling her to him. He hugged her fiercely and planted several kisses on the top of her head. Then, tipping her head back, he captured her lips — gently at first, then more demanding as he thrust his tongue into her mouth. After a moment, he pulled away and laughed roughly. "If only you knew how much I want you."

Laina swallowed hard. Did he want her like the girl she just saw on his lap? Laina bit at her lower lip. She couldn't think straight.

"Soon," he said simply, lifting his hand and stroking her cheek. Then he turned and trotted back down the steps into the great hall.

Laina rushed outside and stood on the front steps trembling. Fortunately, no one was around to see the humiliation on her face. She wanted to throw up. Slowly she made her way back to the kitchen. Margaret and the others had returned. Gillian and Lucy were arguing and no one noticed Laina enter. Strolling over and picking up a tub of dirty dishwater, Laina walked over behind Audrey and dumped it over the girl's wirey red hair.

Audrey let out a piercing scream as the greasy water soaked through her cap and into her curls, and cascaded down her face and onto her clothes. Gillian and Lucy looked over and grimaced. Shrieking and flailing her arms dramatically, Audrey ran from the kitchen.

Margaret arched an eyebrow and looked at Laina with a faint smile. "What was that about?"

"I wanted to make sure she understood me," Laina said tightly.

Chapter Twenty-one

UPON HEARING of the embarrassing incident that Laina experienced with the laird as a result of Audrey's cruel trick, Margaret put Audrey to work emptying rat traps and scrubbing the cellar floor.

"I'll not be having my kitchen staff responsible for intruding on our laird's privacy or putting others in this kitchen in troublesome situations," Margaret warned Audrey, with a severe look that shook the girl as much as if the cook had physically slapped her. "If you ever think to act in such a way again, you will be dismissed from the kitchen for good. Understood?"

"Aye," Audrey said, looking down at her hands.

"I was all ready to dismiss you immediately, do you hear?" Margaret went on. "It is only because of the laird's patient nature that he convinced me to give you another chance."

"He knows?" Audrey screeched in horror. "You talked to him about me?"

"Yes, he knows!" Margaret snapped. "Did you really think your little prank would only reflect poorly on Laina? Not very smart of you, was it?"

Not only was Audrey mortified to think of what Laird Galloway must think of her, but she couldn't stand the thought of having smelly grime on her hands and clothes from the tasks that Margaret had assigned to her. "How long must I do this?"

"Until I say otherwise," Margaret said sharply.

Three days had passed since the unfortunate encounter with the laird. Laina avoided venturing out of the kitchen, claiming that she wasn't feeling well. Margaret sensed that the lass needed one of her long walks to get herself sorted out.

"Laina, we need some more of those wild mushrooms from

the woods. Will you go and get some for tonight's dinner? You can take your time. Thank you, lass." The cook disappeared into one of the storerooms to avoid Laina's questioning gaze. The girl was getting wise to Margaret's clever ways.

Laina walked to the kitchen door and looked out. Storm clouds were visible in the distance. The scent of rain filled the air. She closed her eyes and inhaled deeply. It would, indeed, be wonderful to visit the stone circle. It had been over two weeks. But she must hurry quickly and hope that she was not seen by the laird. She didn't know what she would possibly say if she were to encounter him. Her humiliation had not diminished, nor had the shocking images of he and the girl on his lap that were burned into Laina's mind.

Lured by the crisp air of the storm, Laina dropped her apron aside, and stepped out under the gray sky. The sudden adventure envigorated her, and the desire to reach the stone circle made her forget all else. She didn't even think to grab a cloak.

Bless Margaret for coming up with an excuse for me to go, Laina thought to herself.

She made it down to the lower courtyard and out of the castle gates without speaking to anyone. Breathing a huge sigh of relief, which she seemed to have been holding for days, she walked toward the woods and the stone circle that lay beyond them. The sweet smell of rain touched her nose. She hoped it would pour buckets, as she would like to sit in it for hours.

A distant rumble sounded.

"Yes, yes, I am coming," she murmured.

The wind played with her hair as she walked. All the fears and worries of the last several days blew away with the storm. Laina began to run, like a deer, sprinting across the hills and through the thick stretch of woods. When she reached the stone circle, she kicked off her shoes and released her hair from its braid. She held out her arms and twirled around. Home. She was safe here.

Another rumble sounded. Laina sat down and slid her hands through the cool, soft grass. The damp, earthy smell filled her with comfort. Tipping her head back, to look up at the darkening sky, she slowly closed her eyes, letting out a long, peaceful sigh. This was what made the most sense to her. Not castles and kitchens and soldiers, but sky and earth and wind and stone.

She listened intently for the next sound of thunder. She wanted to feel it vibrate through her. A rolling rumble responded, not far. The thunder continued growing nearer and louder, rumbling and booming until she knew, at any moment, there would be a loud boom right over her head. She waited. Her senses keenly aware.

A silent vibration tremored through the soil and grass — *a sign of rapidly approaching footsteps.* She felt it just before a deep voice shouted her name.

In terror, she spun around, alarm prickling up her back. The fear on her pretty face transformed into a joyous smile.

"Evan!" she screamed. She couldn't stand quick enough before he was wrapping his arms around her and pulling her up in a single movement. He held her against his chest, her feet several inches off the ground.

"They told me you had come in this direction," he explained. "I'm sorry I scared you. I could not wait to see you!" The rush of his words made him sound like an excited boy, rather than the man of twenty-six that he was.

"I am so happy to see you," Laina cried, her voice muffled as she buried her face in his warm neck. She held on tightly, as if he might disappear if she let go. He smelled of leather and the storm. She breathed deeply, letting it fill her. Everything about him felt solid and safe.

He was completely charmed by her reaction. "Let me set you down just for a moment," he chuckled, "so that I may look at you."

Reluctantly releasing her grip, Laina slid down to stand before him.

He stared at her in disbelief. Somehow her beauty surpassed even the memories that he was sure he had embellished in his mind. Her long curtain of shimmering dark hair cascaded around her like an exotic cloak, while her bright, water-colored eyes swallowed him whole.

She gazed up into his happy blue eyes. His hair had turned more golden from the summer sun. His broad, playful smile beamed at her from his handsome face. She wanted to kiss him.

In an instant, his arms were around her again and his mouth was meeting her's in a rush of joy and passion. Large raindrops began to fall and Laina tightened her arms around Evan. He kissed her mouth, and then he kissed the drops of water gathering on her upturned face, before he returned to her mouth and deepened his kiss. Her tongue intertwined with his, and their bodies molded together.

A boom of thunder sounded overhead and the rain came harder, pounding the ground around them. Evan pulled back, holding Laina by her shoulders, and looked into her eyes.

"I've missed you, Laina," he said loudly, over the roar of the downpour. "I've thought about you every day." He smoothed her wet hair back from her face.

"I've missed you too," she admitted. "I was not sure if I'd see you again."

Time seemed to pause as they stood gazing through the doorways of each other's eyes. Something solid existed between them, but neither of them had the words to explain or understand. It seemed bigger than they were, perhaps even bigger than the lives they were born into. Laina broke the spell when she noticed water dripping off of their noses, and she began to laugh.

Evan wiped at his face with both hands, then cocked his head at her with a satisfied look as more water ran off his nose.

Laina pulled her hair to one side and twisted it, wringing out enough water to fill a tankard.

They both burst out laughing, pointlessly mopping at their faces until they were in hysterics and leaning against each other for support.

"We must get back to the castle and get warmed by a fire," Evan reasoned.

Laina felt warm and happy right where she stood, but she would agree to anything Evan suggested.

Taking her hand, Evan led her into the forest. The canopy of trees offered some relief from the rain as the couple darted under it, their rain-soaked clothes clinging to their bodies. The next rumble of thunder signaled that the storm was beginning to move away from them. Evan pulled Laina to him and held her protectively. "Don't be afraid, Laina."

She tried not to laugh. She was not afraid of nature. Looking up at him, one corner of her mouth turned up impishly.

He leaned down and kissed her again. God help him, he wanted to kiss and lick every drop of rain from her body. Damn! He must control his thoughts. She was young and innocent, after all, and she trusted him.

A moan escaped Laina. Evan's lips were so deliciously soft and gentle, yet bold in expressing their desire. Laina gave herself to the moment, slowly sliding her hands up and down Evan's rain-soaked body. He felt so good. She imagined them standing naked together — the storm raging around them. She had no experience in making love with her body, but she made love to his mouth with her lips and tongue.

Evan couldn't restrain himself. He gave in to her gestures

momentarily…kissing, nibbling, and sucking her soft flesh. He wanted all of her. The lass was driving him mad. With a great deal of strength, he finally pulled back, unfocused and breathless. "Laina, I must get you back to the castle. It is not safe to stay here."

"I'm not afraid," Laina assured him. Her eyes were soft, her lips reddened from kisses.

"It's not the thunderstorm I'm worried about," he said, his eyes moving longingly over her beautiful, glistening face and the clothes that clung to her.

"Look," she said excitedly, pointing to the sky, "the storm is almost past."

"So it is," he said, wondering how long it would take for the storm *within* him to pass. He had not expected his visit to present him with such a challenge. What a fool he was. How could he have forgotten the effect she had on him? Well, he would have to get control over himself once and for all, he decided. "Let's get back and put on some dry clothes," he said, grasping her hand and heading through the woods without further discussion.

When they again stepped out of the trees, the storm had moved to the south, leaving a dull gray sky overhead. The pair walked across the rain-soaked hills slowly while Laina brought Evan up-to-date on her interactions with Laird Galloway. She explained that the laird had been very good to her, but that he was usually too busy to spend time with her. Evan was secretly pleased to hear this, since he had hoped that Laina would still be a free lass for his return. He supposed he should have confirmed that detail before kissing her, but her responsiveness had given him as much permission as he needed. Still, he knew, he had no right to wish to keep her for himself. His visit would be temporary.

"And would you like to spend more time with Laird Galloway?" he tried to sound casual.

Laina admitted hesitantly, "Yes. I enjoy his company." Her mind whirled as she thought of the feelings between she and Evan. But she had been over this a thousand times. Evan had a different life. She had no reason to feel guilty. And he needed to be able to hear the truth.

"Of course," Evan said evenly, trying to conceal the jealousy and disappointment he felt. "That's understandable. What woman wouldn't?"

"That's what everyone tells me," Laina said.

Evan's jaw flexed.

"But…" Laina continued, "it feels strange to me too. I come

from such a different world than here." After they'd walked several more steps, she added quietly, "I wish you could stay."

Evan smiled and squeezed her hand reassuringly. God, how he wished he could promise her something of himself, but he knew that was impossible.

They walked quietly, the castle looming up in front of them, each fondly remembering the passionate kisses they had just shared.

Laina finally spoke again. "It must be a joy to do what you love and to know where your path is leading."

Evan laughed. "Well, you've got the first part right. I do love playing music for my living. But I often don't know with much certainty or warning where the path will lead. I only know that I'll be playing music, and that makes the destination not so important."

The soldiers on the wall watched the couple approach. Laina let go of Evan's hand and called out a greeting at the end of the drawbridge. The guards nodded curtly. Evan accompanied Laina all the way to the kitchen, then asked her if she could meet him in the lower courtyard after changing her clothes. She agreed. He gave her a quick, discreet kiss on the top of her head, then returned to his horse in the stable near the front gate, to get his own dry clothes from the saddle bag and locate his companions.

The small riding party gathered together in the lower courtyard. Tall, thin Ian, swung a small pack from his shoulder and began unpacking his instrument. "We've been riding all day. Let's play some music," he announced loud enough for the castlefolk nearby in the courtyard to hear.

Evan, Andrew, and John removed the instruments from their own packs, as well. From around the courtyard, curious faces watched as the musicians tuned and prepared their instruments.

"A handsome group they are," one woman commented to the friend next to her.

"Except for that old crusty one," the woman's friend snickered, pointing to a fifth man in the party. "That one appears to be skilled only in holding a flask."

The flask of whiskey made its way around the group. Andrew took a drink and handed it to Evan, asking, "So, was the lass surprised to see you?"

"She was," Evan said with a twinkle in his eye. "But not as surprised as I was to see that she grows more beautiful with every day."

"Ah, he's smitten!" Ian laughed. "It's not like you, Evan, to become so captivated by a lass."

"Aye," John chuckled, "he's usually in and out so fast, he barely gets to know their name."

Evan ignored the comments and asked, "Have any of you seen Laird Galloway?"

"Nay," Andrew answered. "We advised the guards of our arrival and our plans. They said they would tell the House Steward. Might as well play some music while we wait to see if the laird has any requests of us while we're here."

Laina strolled happily toward the group of musicians, side-stepping rain puddles on the ground, then suddenly screamed. "Oswyn!" She broke into a run toward the old, one-eyed man. He grinned a toothless grin and held out his arms. Laina hugged him fiercely and planted a kiss on both of his cheeks.

"Now, that's what I call a welcome!" Oswyn shouted.

"You are a dear man!" Laina gushed, stepping back and holding her hands to her heart. "How can I ever thank you for the beautiful dress you gave to me at the Mayday Faire?"

"You just did, lass!"

"Such an expensive gift," she gasped, clutching his hand.

Oswyn tipped his head toward Evan, "This young man and I split the cost...and it was the best coin we ever spent. So, don't you worry about a thing, lass."

Laina turned to Evan. "So, you were in on this?"

"Aye. Do I get a *thank you* like he got?"

Laina smiled and blushed. "Later," she said.

The other musicians hooted their approval, drawing more attention from the small crowd of people who were gathering at a respectful distance from the merry group. The prospect of having entertainment was always alluring.

"Here, lass," Oswyn held out the flask of whiskey to Laina. "Warm yourself up!"

"Well..." Laina said, with a mischeivous twinkle in her eye, "all right." She noticed the look of surprise on Evan's face...which turned to amusement. The liquid fire scorched her throat and she let out several ragged coughs. Then she smiled sweetly at the men and they laughed and nodded their approval. "By the way," Laina asked, cocking her head to one side, "why have you arrived two weeks early for the Harvest Festival?"

"Because we'll not be attending the festival, lass," Oswyn answered.

Laina's smile faded and she asked hoarsely, "You won't be

here for the festival?"

"Not this time," Evan answered. "We have been summoned to play at a wedding celebration for the king's brother on the western coast."

"Don't look so sad, lass," Oswyn said. He slapped Evan on the back. "We're here because this young man insisted that we stop at Galloway Castle on our way."

"And," Evan added, "we'll be here for four days, if the laird will let us stay."

"Four days," Laina said softly.

"That's longer than we would have been here for the festival," Oswyn noted. "Now here, have another nip of this whiskey and let's have some music!"

Laina knew she should be delighted. But how would she feel four days from now? She must not think about that, she decided. She must enjoy what she had right now. She reached for the flask.

With a broad sweep of his hand, Ian asked the crowd, "Would anyone be interested in hearing some music?" Cheers went up and the people moved closer. Ian chimed, "Don't mind the puddles as ye stomp yer feet — though the day is bitter, the songs be sweet." Then, after a quick count of three, the musicians launched into a lively tune.

More people quickly arrived in the lower courtyard, lured by the cheerful music being played under a dull sky.

Oswyn motioned to Laina, "Let's dance, lass!"

He stomped his feet and slapped his legs with surprising flexibility for his age. Laina hitched up the length of her tunic, and stepped light and quick to the music, as if she danced on air. The enthusiasm of the odd pair was contagious. Others joined in, laughing as stiff bones and muscles loosened up. When someone wheeled over a barrel of ale, people began filling tankards.

Laina looked across the courtyard just in time to see Laird Galloway standing on the top step that led to the upper courtyard. Dressed all in blue, his arms were folded and he had a slight smile on his face. Within moments, he turned and disappeared. Warmed by the whiskey and Evan's arrival, Laina no longer felt the humiliation of her encounter with the laird a few days earlier. It now seemed to have happened a long time ago.

The kitchen crew arrived in the courtyard, and Laina caught Margaret's eye and grinned, without missing a step. Turning her head from side to side, Laina twirled and kicked, in perfect time to the music.

She was an enchantress, at least, that's what Evan had decided. He couldn't take his eyes off of her. How in God's name was he going to be near her for the next four days without pulling her into his arms and ravishing her the way every part of his body was telling him to? How could he trust himself when he couldn't keep his thoughts under control? He had always prided himself on his clear instincts and solid resolve. Lord help him, because in the presence of this enchanting lass, his instincts had turned murky and his resolve was shot.

Chapter Twenty-two

ℬ❧

"SO, WHAT THE HELL is going on?" Laird Galloway demanded from across the room the moment Evan Prestwick stepped through the large front door and entered the great hall.

Evan descended the steps and strolled over to the fireplace to lean on the back of a large carved chair of dark wood. He met the laird's gaze from several feet away. "What do you mean?"

"Well, to start with, why are you here?"

Evan ignored the laird's rudeness. "Didn't you receive the message announcing our visit? My travelling companions told me they sent word to you through your guards. We are on our way back to Westport. The king has asked us to play for his brother's wedding in Portsmouth next week, and we won't be able to attend the Fall Festival here, as we had hoped."

"Yes, I have heard that," Gavin said, pacing over to stand directly opposite Evan, his arms folded. "What I want to know is why have you really come?"

Evan measured his response carefully. "It was on the way. I thought you welcomed visitors. And I was under the impression that we were friends."

Gavin chuckled sourly. Evan Prestwick was smooth, and he was going to make the laird take an offensive approach.

"All right," Gavin said, "it has been brought to my attention that the moment you arrived you asked the whereabouts of Laina Makgregor, and then you followed after her, only to return some time later holding her hand and looking dishevelled."

"We were caught in a thunderstorm...of course I looked dishevelled," Evan said.

"Dammit Evan!" the laird boomed. "What is your interest in the girl?"

"She and I are friends," Evan said flatly. "Surely you can understand my casual intrigue with her. She is a sweet girl and full of spirit." Evan noted the deepening scowl on Gavin's face, and quickly added, "But you know me, Gavin, I have no time for a woman. My loyalties lie elsewhere." He stared into the flames in the fireplace for a moment, then turned back to Gavin. "Would you deny a lonely musician a few moments of innocent flirting with a captivating lass? Good god, Gavin, *you* of all people..."

It was Gavin's turn to stare into the fireplace. "Did anything happen between the two of you?" he asked gruffly.

"I kissed her," Evan admitted, knowing that the laird wouldn't believe otherwise — and even worse, that the laird wouldn't believe anything else if Evan lied about that. "I stole a kiss, but she remains as innocent as she was before I got here," he said with a disappointed sigh to make his point.

Gavin thought for a moment. "She was willing?"

"I didn't give her any time to think about it," Evan said. "As a matter of fact, she spent a lot of time talking about you." It was the truth — even if not all of it. Evan didn't like misleading his friend, but the laird had no right to ask such questions. Gavin didn't have a claim on the girl, and Evan didn't have to answer to him. So if the laird wanted to play games, Evan would too.

The laird's frown eased upon hearing that the lass had spoken about him. It appeared that the musician had tried to use his charms on the girl, but obviously she preferred the laird over a wandering minstrel. Gavin was pleased. However, he was suddenly aware that he had not spoken to the lass for over a week. Perhaps Laina didn't understand the laird's interest and intentions toward her. Women needed to be reminded of such things often. He would have to move more quickly with her. He couldn't have Laina's head being turned by someone else in his absence.

Evan watched the laird stew over the situation. The musician purposefully avoided asking about Gavin's interest in Laina. It would be best if such details were not discussed between the two men, so that Evan wouldn't be accused later of going against the laird's wishes. He had explained to the laird that he and Laina were friends, and that his visit would be casual and short. That was explanation enough as far as he was concerned, and it should prevent any further backlash. He still had every intention of spending as much time as he could with Laina during his visit. That was, after all, the real reason he had come.

Shifting the subject, Evan said, "I heard about your brother.

I'm sorry."

"The bastard was mad with jeolousy and vengence," Gavin said, sitting down heavily in the chair opposite Evan. "He would have destroyed everything of value to me if he could have, and he came very close. I never suspected it." The laird rubbed his forehead tiredly, revealing how much the experience still affected him.

"Why would you?" Evan reasoned, noticing the shadows under the laird's eyes. "You hadn't seen him for years. How could you guess that he might be intent on destroying you? I think you did all you could to protect your lands. And, thank god, it's over now."

"Yes, thank god," Gavin repeated. "These past many months have been most difficult. I am ready for some amusement."

"I have an idea," Evan suggested, "let's go quail hunting tomorrow."

Gavin shook his head, "Not tomorrow. I have to finish going over the accounts."

"Well then," Evan said, "perhaps one of the other days before I leave. Listen, would you be agreeable to the musicians grabbing a bit of floor space to sleep inside the hall for the length of our visit? It would save us a lot of trouble in setting up camp...and dealing with all these thunderstorms. We can feed ourselves."

"That will be fine," Gavin mumbled.

Evan studied the laird for a moment. "You really ought to get out, Gavin. You look like hell."

Staring into the fire, Gavin smiled briefly.

Eager to get back outside where the mood was lighter, Evan left the hall.

"Ye better watch yerself," Margaret said, walking into the kitchen alongside Laina, upon returning from the small gathering with the musicians in the courtyard.

Laina stopped and stared at Margaret curiously. "Why?"

"I mean ye better not be getting attached to that musician, Evan Prestwick. He will surely leave just as suddenly as he arrived, lass. That's their way, you know."

"I know," Laina said. "I'm not getting attached."

Margaret eyed the girl.

"I cannot deny that I like him," Laina said, playing with a strand of hair dangling against her cheek. "It is easy for us...being friends. I like Laird Galloway too...in a different way." Her mind wandered over the memories she had with them both. Each man with his own qualities. Both were handsome. Both were passionate. Neither seemed to be very available.

"Well ye better be liking the laird for much more than a friend," Margaret responded. "Ye have to use your head about these things and choose what makes sense for your future."

"I am not sure my future is with either one of them," Laina said, shrugging her shoulders. "One prefers the excitement of bedding many women, while the other prefers the excitement of travelling many roads. Honestly, I think I am just a temporary amusement to them both."

"Here's the difference," Margaret said. "Only one of them is capable of giving you the kind of life that most women dream about. That is where your attention should be directed, and ye best not be insulting him by galavanting about with someone else."

"*He*," Laina pointed out hotly without naming him because both women knew who they were talking about, "is much too *busy* for me. I have been right here, waiting...and he has not sent word."

"Well, then," Margaret said, with a finger pressed to her lips thoughtfully, "perhaps you should take matters into your own hands instead of waiting. Remember, our laird is used to women throwing themselves at him. You cannot expect him to chase after you. He has much responsibility to tend to. He has also been through a rough time, lass, have ye forgotten that? No doubt, he could use some cheer."

"What do you think I should do?" Laina asked.

Margaret glanced around the kitchen, her eyes brightening with an idea. "Let's make a special delivery. I will cook up some of me special sugar cakes that the laird likes so much, and you will take them to him."

"Me?" Laina squeaked.

"Well, who else!" Margaret retorted.

"But the last time I saw him in the keep..."

"Listen," Margaret said, pointing her finger, "that will not be the last time you'll see our laird with a lass on his lap, so ye might as well get used to it. He is the laird of this vast territory. We must allow him his indulgences because he takes care of us all. Ye will not find a better laird, nor one more handsome, in all of Scotland!"

Although Laina knew Margaret's loyalty to Laird Galloway was unshakeable, she trusted the cook's instincts. The woman did have Laina's best interests at heart. And it was true, Evan would leave again soon. How could he keep playing with her emotions that way? It was cruel. The men were simply having fun with her. Well, she could play that game too, Laina decided.

Margaret put a hand on the girl's arm. "Our laird is also just a man. Are ye going to be afraid of a man?

"No," Laina answered. "Of course not." She thought of the wonderful evening when she and the laird had shared stories, laughter, and kisses in the beautiful solar room. She had felt close to him that night, nearly forgetting the differences between them. She would like to enjoy his company that way again. "I'll go."

"Good then," Margaret said. "I'll have the cakes ready in a couple of hours."

One of the laird's men stood near the bottom of the steps outside the keep as Laina approached in the fading light of early evening.

Seeing him eye her questioningly, she explained, "I've brought something for the laird."

He nodded, "You can go right in, lass."

Laina trotted up the steps and entered. The laird sat across the room at the large table with one of his men. Laina confidently descended the steps and crossed the length of the great hall by the flickering light of the lanterns. Seeing her approach, the laird flashed a broad smile.

"M'lord," she said respectfully, upon reaching his side.

"Laina," he said warmly. He gestured to the man sitting near him, "you know Symon, my chief officer."

Laina nodded politely. "M'lord, I've brought some sweet cakes for you." She set them on the table. "Margaret and I thought you might be needing some cheering up."

The laird beamed. "Did you? Well, that's most thoughtful."

Laina smiled brightly at him, clasping her hands in front of her comfortably.

"I must say, though" the laird said, "I believe *you* are much sweeter than any sweet cake. Turning to his second in command, he asked, "Wouldn't you agree, Symon?"

"I would, m'lord," Symon answered.

Both men sat looking at Laina, their eyes twinkling with amusement. She knew she had to say something quick to avoid looking simple and weak.

"So, I have succeeded in cheering you up, m'lord?" she said with a flirtatious wink. "Margaret will be pleased with me."

The laird laughed. "You have, indeed, lass. Tell me, did you come only because Margaret asked you to?"

"No, m'lord."

"I am glad to hear that," Gavin said, extending his arm and pulling Laina up against his side. "You do not need an excuse to see me, lass — at least, not anything more than the simple fact that you want to see me."

Pressed closely against him, Laina suddenly remembered the raw power of his body and presence, and the way it made her legs weak. Drawing on her deeper reserves of courage, she said, "I have been hoping to spend more time with you, m'lord."

Gavin's smile stretched across his face. Laina felt tiny in the embrace of his large, muscled arm. She bravely met his gaze. His green eyes burned into her's. Surely he would not kiss her in front of Symon, she hoped.

"I most definitely intend to spend more time with you, Laina," the laird promised in his deep, smooth voice. Raising his hand to her face, he touched her lower lip gently with a fingertip. "Very soon. But right now, lass, we are in the middle of going over the accounts."

Feeling suddenly that she was intruding, Laina pulled away gracefully. "Oh, forgive me for interrupting, m'lord."

"I am most glad for your visit," the laird assured. "You have cheered me for the grueling work I must do."

"Yes, m'lord," she said, backing away and hastening out of the hall. She heard the men chuckle. Laina was not accustomed to feeling dismissed. But what had she expected, she asked herself. The laird couldn't just stop what he was doing and turn his attention to her. Remembering the size and scent of him made her thoughts thicken like fog. His handsome face floated before her — his eyes, penetrating deep into her. She sensed that he had wanted to kiss her. Would things have gone differently if his first officer had not been there? Would he have pulled *her* onto his lap? Or, perhaps, scooped her up and carried her up to his bedroom? She had not given much thought to that beforehand, she realized nervously.

Well, she reassured herself, she had accomplished her mission. She had confidently approached the laird and determined that he still cared about her. Now what?

She thought of Evan. He could not fault her for exploring her options, especially when he could promise her nothing more than an occasional visit. If she had to accept the fact that they could only be friends, then Evan would have to accept it too.

Laina was not sure what role the laird would play in her life either. But the next time he called for her, she would be ready. She would find out *in what way* she was important to him. With a tinge of sadness, Laina realized that was what mattered most to her. She was not as concerned about her future as Margaret was. Laina cared much more about knowing that she was loved and understood, truly and completely, by those she chose to give herself to. Her heart was not meant to be blown about on the wind, until finding the most favorable place to land. No, she would only be able to give her heart to a man who truly treasured her, above all of his other worldly desires. Did such a man exist, she wondered? God help her to know if she met him.

Chapter Twenty-three

ॐ ॐ

EVAN ARRIVED at the kitchen late the next morning, greeted by the smell of fresh-baked bread. At one of the center tables, Margaret filled a willow basket with food while Oswyn hovered at her shoulder, grinning.

"There you go," she said, pushing it at him. "That ought to keep your stomachs from growling."

"Thank you, Cookie," he said, giving her elbow a tweak and passing the basket to Evan.

Evan looked over at Laina, where she sat chopping carrots. "Will you join me for a picnic, lass?" he asked her.

Margaret glared at Oswyn. "I thought you said that food was for a hunting trip for your group."

"Did I say that?" Oswyn dipped his finger into a nearby bowl of batter to distract her. She reached over and smacked his hand.

Laina's gaze jumped from Evan to Margaret, "Well, I…"

The cook jerked her head at the girl, "Oh, go on."

"Are you sure?" Laina asked.

"I'm sure I'm going to beat this old man for playing games with me," Margaret snarled at Oswyn.

He snickered. "Well I couldn't very well tell ye that we wanted to steal one of yer women for the day. Ye would have said no."

Rising and removing her apron, Laina addressed Margaret. "I didn't know anything about this."

"I know," Margaret said, frowning at the broad grin on Oswyn's face. She whacked him again with a wooden spoon.

"I'll have her back before dinner," Evan promised the cook, winking at Laina.

Margaret studied him soberly, then her face relaxed. Indeed, he was well-mannered and seemed honorable enough. It wouldn't hurt for the lass to go and have some fun. Besides, the musician's interest in the girl might just light a fire under their laird.

"All right then," Margaret said, turning back to her work.

Oswyn had sidled over to Laina and was whispering in her ear. She giggled.

"Now what are you up to, old man?" Evan asked with a smirk, his blue eyes twinkling.

"Just telling this lass to take it easy on ye!" Oswyn said loudly.

Laina walked to Evan's side, and the pair crossed the kitchen and stepped out into the bright sunshine. The day was warm and had dried all but a few remaining rain puddles from the day before. Making their way to the stable near the front gate, Evan helped Laina onto his horse then mounted behind her.

A thrill surged through her as she sat on the enormous beast, nestled up against Evan between his legs, and surrounded by his arms as he lightly held the reins. She was glad for all the commotion of visitors arriving at the gate, drawing the attention of the guards and sparing her their questioning looks as the pair rode out. Evan urged his horse into a gallop across the hills to the southwest. Laina giggled from the exhileration of the rush of wind in her face and the powerful movement of the animal beneath her. Evan held her securely, and although she couldn't see his face, she felt he was smiling with her.

Reaching the river, Evan brought the horse to a halt under a massive oak tree, its twisted limbs spreading out broadly, forming a natural canopy. Sunlight filtered through the leaves, casting dancing shapes of light on the grass.

Evan lept down from the horse and held up a hand to assist Laina. Despite the distance she would need to jump to the ground, she bravely threw herself forward as if she had done it a hundred times. She gasped when Evan scooped her from mid-air, into his arms.

He chuckled. "Did you think I would let you take such a risk?"

"I wasn't afraid," Laina assured him.

"I have noticed that about you," he said, setting her down. He handed her the food basket, then untied a blanket that was tethered to the horse.

"How about here?" Laina called out. Slipping off her shoes, she raised the hem of her tunic with her free hand and lightly padded around in the velvety grass.

Evan watched her, noticing the smooth and tender curves of her legs and ankles. Good lord, had he made a mistake in bringing her here, he wondered? It was supposed to be a simple picnic. Sitting on a blanket, talking, eating food — that kind of thing. But here she was, so soft and sweet, tiptoeing around like a wilderness faerie, dappled in sunlight.

"What do you think?" Laina asked.

"Looks perfect," he croaked. Collecting himself, he added firmly, "Let's get this blanket spread out to sit on."

Laina smiled brightly at him, her eyes shining with excitement. Being around Evan made her feel playful. After positioning the blanket on the ground, she danced around it, slowly twirling and kicking up her heels while moving her arms in graceful arcs.

Evan watched her. Despite the serious line of his mouth, his eyes showed amusement. The glowing expression on her face was enchanting. He would like to sit and feast his eyes on her for hours. Although totally in control of her movements, she expressed them with joyful abandon. The sight of her made his blood race. Without meaning to, he groaned loudly.

Laina twirled to a stop and faced him. "Is something wrong?" she asked.

"Yes," he muttered, although he hadn't meant to admit it.

"What is it?" she asked, her brow wrinkling with concern.

He sighed. "I'm going mad at the sight of you."

Laina stared at him, and then burst out laughing. He looked pale and enchanted, indeed. Ah, so this was going to be even more fun, she realized. If Evan thought he could stay detached — picking her up and setting her down like a simple toy — perhaps, she could show him what he was going to miss when he left again. And the best part, she didn't even have to make an effort. Simply being herself was undoing him.

Evan silently scolded himself and turned back to his horse to secure the reins and loose straps. He certainly wasn't off to a very good start in keeping things casual with Laina. Lord, what was wrong with him? He had been with many women before. Where was his self-control? He would have to harden his resolve even more with this one. It was ridiculous to let any lass throw him off balance, no matter how pretty and sweet she might be. He would not allow such weakness in himself.

His face firm and set, he confidently turned away from the horse to join Laina.

Across from him, she stood bent over, digging around in the basket. Her small, round bottom wiggling from side-to-side, pointing right at him.

Good god, Evan thought. Was he kidding himself? Had he known all along what he was setting up? What was he doing putting himself in such a situation with her? Everything she did aroused him. Every inch of him was screaming to know every sweet inch of her. He must, he told himself, remember that his time with her was very short and he did not wish to cause pain to either one of them by complicating their involvement. There simply could not be any expectations between them, and he would not ruin her chances with someone else.

"Laina!" He spoke louder than he had intended.

She stood upright and spun around. "What is it?"

His face was stressed. "I think we should go."

She smiled softly upon realizing the struggle he was already facing. Men were so weak about some things, and they seemed to have trouble relaxing. She waltzed toward him, "Here, take a wee nip," she said, holding up a flask of scotch.

"Where did you get that?" Evan asked.

"A gift from Oswyn for our picnic."

Evan didn't know whether to thank Oswyn or curse him, but he reached eagerly for the flask and swallowed a hearty gulp. A warming sensation slid down into his chest and radiated out into his arms and legs.

Returning to the blanket, Laina plopped down casually. "What is your life like on the road?" she asked, hoping to distract Evan from his concerns.

His face relaxed and he joined her on the blanket. "Well," he began, the smoothness returning to his voice "every day is new and different. We — the other musicians and I — see old friends almost everywhere we go, and the crowds are usually happy we've arrived."

Laina nodded with a look of admiration on her face. "That sounds wonderful."

"It is a good life," Evan acknowledged. "It has drawbacks too, of course. So much travel can be tiresome. We miss the comforts of home especially when one of us or our horses fall ill. And then there's the occasional quibbles we have over the fee or timing for our engagements."

Laina took a sip from the flask and squeezed her eyes shut while it burned her throat. "Do you ever wish you could stay in one place?" she asked hoarsely.

"On rare occasions," Evan answered. "Like now."

"Like now?"

Evan reach over and took her hand, caressing it gently in the large warmth of his own. "I am very fond of you, Laina. Why do you think I came back?" He shook his head slowly and laughed. "But lord, you might be the death of me, lass. It takes every ounce of my strength to remain focused and honorable when I am around you."

"Maybe you try too hard," she suggested softly.

Evan quirked an eyebrow at her.

She realized that she was treading into potentially dangerous new territory, dealing with something beyond her experience. The matters between men and women could be very scarey, she had thought. But being with Evan ignited a flame within her, hot enough to burn away her worries and doubt, it seemed. It felt very freeing, and she was curious to discover more.

"You know I cannot stay," he said gently.

"I know." Her eyes began to glisten just before she closed them and tilted her face up into the sun's rays streaming through the tree branches. "It's a beautiful day," she whispered.

"Aye, it is," Evan agreed solemnly, admiring the gentle slope of her neck, and taking another drink. Then, taking her hand and raising it to his mouth, he kissed her fingertips one at a time. With amusement, he saw her own lips mimic the light kisses. He could not stop himself from leaning forward and meeting her lips with his. God help him. She moaned softly and he pulled her up against him. One after another, their kisses grew passionate and hungry.

Laina's eyelashes sparkled with happy tears. She could not deny her feelings for Evan. Everything she wanted was in this moment. Weaving her hands into his hair, she made love to his mouth with her lips and tongue. Exploring him and letting him explore her.

Evan couldn't think straight. Suddenly things were racing out of control. Gently, he pulled back and stood up. "Laina…"

She stood up, facing him, and shook her head. "Is your sense of honor for you or for me?"

He shook his head, confused. "Both of us."

"Then, as far as this concerns me, I release you. So you have only to deal with yourself."

Good god, what was she saying, he wondered? Was she giving herself to him? The poor girl didn't realize what she was suggesting. She couldn't know. It was up to him to be strong for the both of them. The way she was looking at him was staggering — the clarity and courage in those beautiful eyes, and the turn of her mouth, so sensuous and seductive. Damned right, he wanted her. It was all he could think about.

Their mouths were suddenly meeting again, hot and hungry. Standing on her tiptoes, Laina reached her arms around his neck. The sweet, earthy smell of him lured her to his warm neck, where she kissed and nibbled and stroked him with her tongue.

Evan was tired of thinking. He only knew that he wanted to bring her closer, as close as he could get to her. Suddenly cupping his hands under her bottom, he hoisted her up so that her face was level with his. In his strong embrace, she wrapped her legs around his hips as her tunic slide up to her knees. She moaned softly and let her head fall back to reveal more skin for him to kiss.

His eyes glazed, Evan carried Laina over to the trunk of the massive tree, and placed her back up against it. Keeping his hips forward, he was able to hold her up while freeing his hands.

She smiled at him, her lips red and slightly swollen from kissing him, her eyes soft.

He reverently stroked her face and hair, his gaze loving and protective. Laina's tunic was stretched tightly across her breasts which were practically in his face. He swallowed and closed his eyes. This is very dangerous territory, he warned himself. Laina began wiggling and he opened his eyes. She was tugging upward on her tunic.

"Help me lift this over my head," she said breathlessly.

"No, Laina, we must not," he choked out.

"I just want to be more comfortable. I will still have my chemise on."

Evan looked worried and torn. "I don't know if I can cope with less material between us."

She laughed. "It will be all right."

Working together, they pulled the tunic up over her head without changing her position against the tree.

Evan had a sense of dread, but couldn't seem to stop himself.

"Ah, 'tis much better," Laina said, raising her hands freely toward the sky in celebration.

The lower part of Evan's body had begun its own revelry, which he was trying to ignore. He noticed that Laina's chemise didn't offer a bit of protection. He could clearly see the outline of her breasts and feel their warmth just below his face.

Laina tightened her legs and arms around him and began kissing his warm spicy neck again, while stroking her slender fingers through his silky, golden hair. Being with Evan was delicious, and she wanted to enjoy every drop of him for as long as she could. She would not fight it as he did.

Evan felt like his head was about to explode. Fire raged throughout every part of him, showing no mercy. Lord knows he had come here with the right intentions. But he was just a man, after all.

Laina's chemise fell away from her shoulder, revealing new soft skin. Evan's head dropped to it. She groaned and arched her back — suddenly her breasts popped free of their covering right in front of him.

"Sweet mother of..." Evan choked.

Admitting defeat, he buried his face in the soft mounds before him. He heard Laina's moans and gentle laughter. At some point, his legs must have given way because the couple ended up tumbling into the grass.

Evan opened his eyes to find Laina looking at him...a dazzling expression of contentment on her face. He was stunned, seeing her laying there in the grass, half-naked, so free and happy. It was the most beautiful sight he had ever beheld.

Propping himself up on one elbow alongside her in the grass, his expression turned serious again. He must regain control of himself, he decided. They had not yet gone too far. They could stop right where they were. He had to prevent them both from doing something they might regret later.

Laina chose that moment to move her hand to the enormous bulge in Evan's breeches and touch it gently.

Evan yelled as if he'd been struck by a hot coal, and he rolled onto his back. "You're going to be the death of me, lass."

She giggled shyly.

He smiled painfully and rolled back onto his side to face her. "We must not go any further, Laina. Although how I will be able to think of anything else from now on, I do not know."

"I cannot bear to think that you will be leaving again," Laina admitted sadly.

For a few moments they sat silently, staring into each other's eyes.

"We still have a few days," Evan said finally. "But we must not do anything we will regret later." He gazed at her affectionately. She lay on her back in the grass, her face turned up to the sky. Her long hair tossled across her satin skin, while the sunshine played across the rosy tips of her beautiful full breasts. Lord help him, he would never be able to get these images out of his mind for as long as he lived. He could not deny how much he wanted her. But, most of all, he wanted the best for her, and that was much more than he was able to give her.

Laina didn't want the moment to end. Being with Evan sent ripples of pleasure pulsing through her body unlike anything she had ever experienced. She wanted to see and touch and kiss him from head to toe. She didn't want to worry about whether it was right or wrong. How could anything that felt so good be wrong? She wanted to share everything she could with Evan. But clearly, the man was in pain trying to preserve her honor. She supposed she should make some effort to do the same, although, what difference it really made to her life, she didn't know.

Her thoughts drifted to the laird. What would he think of her if he saw her now? Was she willing to give herself away so easily to a travelling musician who was just passing through? And how was this different from what the laird might want of her? Well, for one thing, she reasoned, Evan Prestwick was doing his damnedest to protect her honor by depriving himself — whereas Laird Galloway could take whatever he wanted, and that was somehow considered honorable, as well. Strange. Perhaps this was to be her life now. Her body given for pleasure or duty. She could try to protect her heart, but still, she was like a seedling sent on the wind to find a place to settle and take root, wherever that might be. The thought sobered her.

"I'm hungry," she said, suddenly rising to retrieve her tunic. "Are you?"

"I don't know," Evan said, "I have lost complete track of my senses." He stood up and smiled stiffly, brushing the grass from his breeches before joining her on the blanket.

They ate quietly, feeling the wind and listening to the birds. The leaves rustled over their heads. A happy, soothing sound. The space and the moment connected them, though they sat apart. They were as one, although neither dared bring attention to it.

Evan was the first to speak again. "I may be able to return after Edmund's wedding. We will be travelling back by here on our way east again."

Laina nodded numbly, lost in her thoughts.

As the pair collected their things and prepared to leave, there was sadness in Laina's eyes.

Evan pulled her into a strong embrace and kissed her forehead. "It will be all right, Laina. Everything will be all right."

Lowrens entered the great hall and approached Laird Galloway at the table. Several piles of paper lay scattered in front of the laird.

The large soldier waited politely for a moment before speaking. "M'lord?

"Yes?" The laird answered without looking up.

"Symon requests that you attend a practice fighting session this afternoon if at all possible. The men are trying some new maneuvers, and he would like your approval." Lowren's face reflected the pride he felt about the news.

"Can't my men determine for themselves if they are making good tactical decisions?"

"Well, yes…"

"Must I continually be interrupted to double-check the decisions of everyone else?"

Lowrens was stunned. The laird had always been interested in what his men were doing. The red-haired man scratched his curly beard. He had known the laird long enough to speak more freely than most.

"Laird, is there a problem? Or something I can do for you?"

"You know what you can do for me?" the laird rumbled, looking up, his eyes seering into the surprised gray eyes that returned his gaze. "You can get my life back for me." His face, hard as stone, scowled at the man standing before him. After a moment, it appeared he was waiting for a response.

"M'lord," Lowrens began, trying to ignore the discomfort he felt from the laird's anger being directed at him, "I realize you have been through a terrible bout of tragedies lately." Seeing the laird's eyes soften a small amount from the acknowledgement, Lowrens continued. "Having your lands attacked for months without any clue as to who the enemy was. Then discovering it was your own brother, and having to kill him." Lowrens watched the laird's head drop slightly. "And that awful woman Elinor of Dunstenshire, causing all kinds of trouble in your castle. It has been a most difficult run of bad luck, and it would wear on even the strongest of leaders, m'lord."

Laird Galloway rubbed his temples, then looked up, his eyes dull.

Lowrens waited quietly.

"Do you know," the laird finally said, "how long it has been since I've been hunting? Or taken a long ride into the countryside? Or had a woman in my bed for longer than one evening? Or," he added, his voice rising again, "had one blessed day without all this damned paperwork?" In a giant sweeping motion, he sent the papers in front of him flying to the floor. He stood and paced heavily to the fireplace, saying nothing more.

Lowrens finally spoke, although feeling that his end of the conversation was weak, but not knowing what else to do for his laird. "Is it more paperwork than usual, laird?"

"Yes, it's more paperwork than usual!" Gavin bellowed, spinning around. "The king has decided he wants a full accounting of every expense and any type of income for the past two years for every territory he oversees. We haven't kept those kind of detailed records. Saw no need. We have tracked what we needed to." Gavin made an effort to relax the rigid line of his shoulders and lower his voice. "If we don't provide the information to his satisfaction, he will determine a penalty that we owe."

Lowrens shook his head angrily. "That is ridiculous. Is there some way I can help, laird?"

"Yes," Gavin grumbled. "Get me drunk."

Lowrens smiled. "I can do that."

"I don't want any more surprise visitors turning my life and castle upside down," the laird raged again.

"Evan Prestwick?" Lowrens suggested.

"He's just a minor pain in the arse at the moment" the laird said. "But I'm ready for him to go too." Gavin walked back to the table and sat down. "I want control over my days and activities again, Lowrens."

"Understood, m'lord."

"I want to stop answering endless requests, and get back to making some of my own! That is supposed to be the way it works." Gavin bent to pick up a few of the papers he had hurled to the floor.

"I'll tell Symon you're busy, m'lord. We'll let you know how the training practice goes." Lowrens backed away slowly, pausing only to make sure his laird wanted nothing further of him.

"That would be good, Lowrens…thank you," the laird mumbled as he glowered at the slightly crumpled paper he held.

Chapter Twenty-four

❧ ❧

"EVAN PRESTWICK, GET UP." The guard nudged Evan's sleeping form with the hard toe of his leather boot.

Evan rolled over and groaned, "What is it?"

"The laird has asked that we speak with you about a matter of great importance. Come with us."

In the darkness of the great hall, lit only by a low-burning torch at the back of the room near the staircase, Evan could just make out the dark outlines of the two guards standing over him. "What is this about?" he asked.

"We will not discuss it here," came the reply. "Come with us now."

Evan rubbed both his eyes at once with one hand, using his thumb and middle finger, then squinted up at the dark figures with his best peeved expression. It was of no use — he couldn't see their faces and measure his affect on them. He rose stiffly and raked his hands through his sleep-tossled hair.

Oswyn and the others remained asleep, snoring softly on their straw mats on the floor. The guards directed Evan out of the keep and across the two courtyards in the dim, pre-dawn light. Dark shapes moved around the perimeter of the large open spaces, going in and out of structures, busy with early-morning tasks, except when they stopped to curiously take notice of two guards accompanying someone across the courtyard.

The three men arrived at the guard tower at the front gate. Evan had a bad feeling. The escorts disappeared, and a tall guard, apparently in charge, frowned and motioned for Evan to sit on a stool just inside the door.

Evan sat — noticing a short guard with small, dull eyes and an over-sized stomach standing nearby — then he met the tall guard's gaze directly and offered his own look of irritation. "Now will someone have the courtesy to tell me why I've been roused from my sleep and told to come here?"

"Are you aware," the guard asked his own question, "that the laird has an interest in miss Laina Makgregor?"

Ah, so this was what it was all about, Evan thought. He had been hoping to avoid something like this. He folded his arms and leaned back casually toward the wall behind him, balancing his stool on two legs. He shrugged his shoulders. "I know Laird Galloway has spoken with her a few times, but I was not aware that his interest was very serious."

The short, round guard stepped forward and hissed at Evan, "Anything of interest to our laird is serious." The little man appeared to be trying to puff up his chest bigger than his belly — a hopeless endeavor.

Evan showed no reaction and played dumb. "What does this have to do with me?"

The tall guard answered. "You and Miss Makgregor have been seen together several times, as well as returning to the castle after spending time alone. The laird wishes to know what occurred between the two of you."

"I've already spoken with him about it," Evan said, casting his eyes to the ceiling with a look of impatience.

"We want you to speak about it again...with us."

"I have not dishonored her if that's what you want to know."

The tall guard paced a few steps across the floor. "Yesterday, the two of you were gone all afternoon."

"Yes," Evan answered.

The guard turned around abruptly when no further explanation was freely offered. "What did you do?" he asked tightly.

"We went on a picnic."

"And?" the guard asked, walking over to face the cocky musician.

Evan smiled at him. "We talked. We are friends."

"I want details Prestwick. Tell me all that happened. What did you talk about? Did you kiss her?"

Evan raised his eyebrows. "I don't see that it is any of your business. Laina is a free lass."

"Oh, is she?" the short guard snarled.

"Yes, I believe she is," Evan said, glaring at the annoying little man.

"It is most certainly our business," the tall guard said,

"precisely because of the laird's interest in the girl. This is *his* castle, she is one of *his* servants, and you are but a guest here."

"Which you may not be much longer," the short guard added.

"As a matter of fact," Evan said, unfolding his arms and rubbing his bristly chin with a heavy sigh, "the Westport Musicians are leaving tomorrow. So, you have nothing to worry about. Can we wrap this up now?"

The tall guard paced across the floor again. "I want to go back to the question of what happened between you and the lass."

"All right, you do that," Evan said, standing, "and I am going back to the keep…"

"Sit down!" the short guard yelled, walking over and poking his finger into Evan's chest while looking up at him.

Evan's face darkened and he raised his own voice. "Listen, I don't have time for this. I have done nothing wrong and you have no right to hold me."

"We have not yet determined that for ourselves," the tall guard said. "You are not going anywhere until you answer our questions to our satisfaction."

In a quick scan of his surroundings, Evan noticed that the short guard had put his hand on the knife on his hip, and two guards standing just inside the door to the next room appeared to be waiting to see if they were needed. Clearly the laird's men felt they could detain and interrogate anyone for anything, and they wouldn't let it go until they felt satisfied.

Remembering his own knife laying with his other belongings back in the keep, Evan let out a sound of disgust and sat down on the stool with a thud. Getting into this kind of trouble was exactly why he preferred to have as few connections with people as possible. They were always overreacting and trying to impose their will on everyone else.

Seeing the musician come to the full realization of his predicament, the tall guard smiled. "Now, during your *friendly picnic*," he continued with a mocking tone, "did you kiss the lass?"

"Yes, I did," Evan answered, knowing — again, as he had known when questioned by the laird earlier — that they wouldn't believe any less.

"And, did you touch her?" the short guard asked, approaching to within a foot of Evan's left knee.

"Well," Evan said, "a kiss usually involves that you make contact."

The short guard's small eyes bulged. "Did you touch her in

any other way?" he screamed, sending a few flecks of spit spraying onto Evan's face.

Evan stood up angrily and addressed the tall guard, "I'm not going to answer any more questions if this idiot can't keep his spit in his mouth."

The tall guard gave a sharp nod. Glowering, the round man stalked away to stand by the opposite wall.

The tall guard repeated, "Did you touch her?"

Evan sighed and turned his head to gaze out through the doorway to the courtyard beyond, which was brightening and growing busier with morning activity. "Aye," he admitted, "I held her in an embrace." Remembering the embrace that her legs had around his hips as he held her up against the tree, while his face fell forward into the soft, wildflower-scented mounds of her breasts, he resisted the urge to smile.

The scent of smoked meat wafted in through the open doorway, causing Evan's stomach to growl. Turning back to the tall guard, he said, "It is normal to embrace a lass when you kiss her."

"Did anything else happen?"

"As much as I would have liked it," Evan said, "no. Her honor is in tact, as I said before. I do not want to ruin Laina's chances for a good life with someone who can remain in one place for her. And unfortunately, that is not the life for me."

The guard's face relaxed. He seemed satisfied with the musician's sad admission. "And what are your intentions now?" he asked.

"I intend to go get some breakfast," Evan answered.

"Don't play games with us," the tall guard flared hotly.

Across the room, the short guard slammed his fist against the wall. "We don't play games!"

Evan laughed sourly, wanting to point out that he thought that's *all* they did. "What do you want from me? I've told you that my friendship with the girl is casual, her honor is in tact, and I'm leaving tomorrow."

The tall guard nodded. "We want to make it clear to you that you have no business here, and you are not to interfere any further in matters that concern the laird. The laird has an interest in the lass, and it is in her best welfare that she be available for such."

"What do you mean it is in her best welfare to be *available*?" Evan asked. "Does the laird not intend to have an honorable relationship with her?"

"That is not your concern," the tall guard answered. "Regardless of the laird's intentions in the matter, the lass will be well taken care of."

"Do you think *you* could provide better for her?" the short guard chuckled, nodding at Evan's presently rumpled appearance. "Or do you desire her for yourself?"

Evan had a desire to punch the short guard in the face. Unfortunately, he knew they were right about Laina being better off at the castle — she would be taken good care of. He hated to think of her being used for the laird's will. But Laina's life must take its own path, just as he had found his own path over the years. He could not go around saving every lass who fell prey to powerful and lusty men. It was just the way of things. Perhaps Gavin would fall in love with her — *how could he not?* — and marry her. At least then she would have more of a place.

The whole trail of thought was making Evan feel sick. He hated every image except the one of her in his own arms. But there was just no sense in fighting the way things were.

The tall guard spoke. "Now, let's go over the rules of conduct for the remainder of your visit."

Evan clenched his fists in his lap and listened while the guard went over the details.

When finished, the guard nodded toward the pit room and said, "You will follow these rules until you leave, or we'll take care of this another way. Do you understand?"

"Aye." Evan stood. "Can I go now?"

"You can go, but we'll be watching you Prestwick."

Evan stalked out of the guard room and across the lower courtyard in the bright morning sun, making his way back up to the keep. Oswyn met him in the upper courtyard.

"Where have ye been?" Oswyn asked, noticing the strained look on Evan's face.

"The laird's guards have been questioning me about my involvement with Laina, and I have been ordered not to interact with her further while we're here."

"Are ye going to follow that order?"

"Hell no."

Oswyn burst out laughing and slapped his own hip.

"Unfortunately," Evan continued, "they have threatened to throw me in the pit if I don't follow their rules."

"Oh," Oswyn turned serious, "that does complicate things just a bit."

The two men stood in silence for a few moments, discreetly eyeing their surroundings.

Oswyn was the first to speak. "I know ye care a great deal for the lass. How about if I create a diversion by throwing meself on the ground in convulsions, while you toss the girl across your horse and ride out of here?" He snickered at the thought.

"Truth is," Evan said sadly, "she *is* better off here than she would be with the kind of life she would have on the road."

Oswyn studied his friend a moment and then shouted, "Have ye gone mad?"

Several people around the courtyard looked up, realized it was Oswyn, and went back to what they were doing.

"Ye don't know what her life is like here," Oswyn said, pointing a crooked finger at Evan. "She has had no other choice! Hell, I've never seen a lass kick up her feet like that one — she has more spirit than the likes of these soggy castlefolk she is surrounded by. She might be drowning in boredom and doesn't even know it because she's simply glad to have survived being murdered!"

Evan nodded with a lump in his throat. The lass had already endured a lot in her short life. He remembered his own early years, when he had made the decision to avoid serving those with money or following in the unimaginative footsteps of others. Although it had been a hard path to take, nothing was of greater value than freedom, and Evan had never looked back. He knew in his heart it was what suited him best. Perhaps it suited Laina too.

"But how can I know what's best for her?" Evan said.

"Ask her." Oswyn answered simply.

"When?"

"When I create me diversion!" Oswyn chuckled. "In the meantime, we better get our horses packed-up. I'm thinking we'll be leaving today, one way or another."

Chapter Twenty-five

෨)෬

JUST AFTER BREAKFAST, a soldier arrived at the kitchen with a summons for Laina. He waited until she stepped outside the door, to relay the message privately. "The laird asks that you come at once. He will meet you in the solar."

Feeling nervous, Laina followed the soldier. The grass still wet from rains the night before, licked at her shoes and ankles. The last time she had been inside the keep, she had been delivering sugar cakes to the laird. She was confident then — even flirted openly with him. Although too busy to pull himself away from his duties, he had seemed pleased by her visit.

Perhaps he had time for her now. Unfortunately, she felt none of the confidence of her prior visit. She had layed awake half the night trying to make sense of the situation she found herself in. Despite the easy connection that she and Evan seemed to have, he was continually intent on holding her at arm's length — more committed to following his code of honor than his heart. He was clearly unable, perhaps even unwilling, to be in her life with any consistency. Laird Galloway had openly welcomed and encouraged her interest in him. He offered more stability for her as well. But he, too, seemed to have other priorities much of the time.

It's not that she needed someone's undivided attention, for that was not the case at all. She simply was not sure that either of these men were interested in her for more than what she aroused in them. They, both, stirred feelings deep within her. Yet, both waited until it was most convenient for them to make time for her. It was not in her nature to wait to see what other people might do. If Evan and the laird did not already see or value the spirit that pulsed strongly within her, she was not going to spend effort trying to convince them. Perhaps both men were self-indulgent fools and she was better off having nothing to do with either one of them.

The soldier sprinted up the steps of the keep and opened the door for Laina. "I've been told that you know how to find the solar," he said.

"Yes, thank you," she answered, stepping through the door. It closed behind her with a thud, blowing a heavy puff of air against her back.

The hall was empty and quiet except for the clatter of dishes as two girls cleared the table of the morning meal. The smell of tallow in the lanterns mixed with the smell of leftover food. Laina descended the steps into the hall. The serving girls looked up, then exchanged a look between themselves and went back to work.

Feeling odd and out-of-place, Laina walked stiffly across the room to the staircase, her chin firm and her eyes focused straight ahead. It did not matter what the girls thought of her, she told herself. They had no understanding of her interactions with the laird. She had no secrets and nothing to be ashamed of.

Ascending the steps, she followed the hallway along the back of the keep, then climbed the second, smaller staircase that led up to the solar. The door of the solar stood ajar. Laina swallowed and pushed it open slowly. Squinting her eyes against the bright sunlight flooding in through the large windows, she stepped inside. The laird was not there.

She had forgotten how beautiful the room was. The large windows framed the green rolling landscape below, as well as the brilliant expanse of blue sky above. The room felt welcoming and comfortable. Laina's breathing softened and slowed.

Noticing a book with an engraved leather cover on the table, she approached and ran her finger over the pebble-like surface, then traced the curved sunken marks that she knew were lettering. Treasures such as this were the privilege of the wealthy, she thought to herself. How wonderful it must be to have such fine things. Her finger poised along the edge of the cover, Laina guessed that the laird would not be upset if she were to look inside — else he would have stored the book away. And since she could not read, she was not really prying.

Carefully opening the cover, she began slowly turning the light brown pages marked with beautiful writing. Turning more pages, she gasped when she came upon enchanting, colorful drawings, done in great detail.

"Beautiful, aren't they?" Gavin asked from the doorway.

"Oh yes," Laina stammered, looking up. "I've never seen

anything like it."

He stood towering in the doorway, dressed simply in black breeches and an emerald green shirt that matched his eyes.

"The book is for you," he said, smiling.

"For me?"

"Yes, I want you to have it." He walked toward her.

The height of him sent excitement through her body. The sudden realization of her situation — being alone again with Laird Galloway, himself —unnerved her.

"It's a very special book, Laina, crafted by one of the king's best artists. It tells the story of the long siege of Barnaby Castle."

"M'lord, it is such a fine gift..." she hesitated, "but I do not feel worthy of it. I cannot even read."

He gave a confident nod to show that he had already considered that. "I thought we could start spending some evenings in front of the fire, while I read the book to you. Now that my mission of rebuilding the villages is well underway, my life can start returning to normal here at the castle, and I would like us to spend more time together."

"You would?" she asked, her voice barely above a whisper.

"Also," he said, looking back down at the table and picking up a shiny piece of cloth beside the book, "I want you to have this. It is a scarf made of silk. It has come all the way from Asia." He laid it in her hand.

The dark purple scarf had small designs of golden thread woven into it. Laina lifted the elegant fabric up to her cheek and closed her eyes, smiling at the feel of it against her skin.

Gavin chuckled. It gave him great pleasure to see her reaction to the gifts. He liked the way she openly showed her delight. He longed to see more of it.

Laina slowly opened her eyes and saw the laird watching her, his gaze soft with affection. Perhaps she had misjudged him, she considered. She had been impatient and doubtful of his true feelings for her, while he had simply been doing all of the important duties a laird must do. He did not need to win her with expensive gifts...or any gifts at all, and yet he chose to give them to her. The laird had been her champion over and over again — giving her a home, tracking down her father's murderer and putting the terrible man to death, even though it was the laird's own brother. And now, Laird Galloway stood before her expressing an interest to spend more time with her. A sudden image of her picnic with Evan flashed through her mind and Laina felt ashamed.

Unlike Evan, the laird was making it clear that he wanted her in his life.

"Forgive me, m'lord," she said, laying the scarf gently beside the book. "I'm so overwhelmed by your generous gifts, I've lost my tongue. Thank you. I will treasure them always."

"I want you to know how much I care for you, Laina," Gavin said. He walked back to close the door, then motioned for her to join him on the floor pillows in front of the windows.

Settling herself as gracefully as possible atop the slick satin and velvet cushions, Laina leaned on one arm, with her feet to the side of her. The laird sat down facing her, with one knee up, and his other leg crossed in front of him — his knee touching her's.

"I want to tell you," he began, casually toying with his beard, "why I have not called for you until now."

His intent gaze penetrated her. Laina bravely met his eyes.

"In part," he said, "it is due to the business I must attend to on a daily basis. You understand that, don't you?"

"Yes," she answered, licking her lower lip nervously as she considered their positions of closeness.

"It was also," he continued, "due to my concern that I not rush you into anything."

Laina wasn't sure what he meant, so she waited for him to say more.

Gavin took her hand, small and slender against his own, and rubbed it softly. She could feel his strength, even in his fingers, and yet his touch was gentle.

"I find you very pleasing, Laina. I have wanted to see more of you. But I wanted to wait until you were ready." He raised her hand to his lips and kissed it slowly and tenderly, watching her reaction. Then he smiled warmly. "Are you ready?"

She swallowed. "Ready?"

Lifting his other hand, he lightly stroked her smooth, reddening cheek with the backs of his fingers. "Would you like to start spending more time with me, and see what becomes of it?"

Being so close to him, her thoughts suddenly scattered. The way his gaze held her, made her feel that she was already his. That might not be such a bad thing, she considered dimly. She felt the heat from his hands where they touched her, while she noticed the alluring curve of his lips, and the silky texture of his neatly trimmed beard. Her body buzzed with the kind of excited energy that precedes a thunderstorm.

It was all happening so fast. Then again, what was she waiting for? Evan would be leaving tomorrow. Laird Galloway wanted her in his life. He had already proven that he would do everything he could to protect her and care for her. It really didn't make any sense to wait on Evan to visit the castle whenever he could manage it. The thought of his departure stabbed at her heart.

"Yes, m'lord." She heard the words slip from her mouth. "I want to spend more time with you."

Beaming, Gavin pulled her to him and embraced her against his broad chest. "I will take good care of you, lass. Do you trust me?"

"Yes, m'lord." It was the truth. Despite his overpowering presence and all that he excited in her, she felt safe with him. Relaxing against his firmness, she turned her head to gaze out the windows a few feet away from where they sat. With her left cheek pressed flat againt his chest, she could feel the strong thumping of his heart. Looking out across the Galloway lands that stretched as far as she could see, Laina marvelled at how it had come to be that she was receiving the laird's interest. She, a leatherworker's daughter. And, an orphan at that. She would not kid herself, though. She knew there were other women in the laird's life as well. The laird was not to be her's. But it appeared that she was *his*. She wondered if Evan would be jealous. Damn him! He had no right to blame her.

"What are you thinking about?" Gavin's deep voice vibrated through his chest. Gently holding her back from his chest so he could look into her eyes.

"Being here with you," she said.

Leaning down, he captured her lips in a kiss. His lips were soft and warm, gently pressing and plying. The smell of him was clean and masculine. Laina responded to him, her mind whirling.

In one moment he was kissing her tenderly, and in the next moment he parted her lips with a powerful thrust of his tongue. Laina involuntarily lurched backward onto the pillows, gasping for air, her face flushed.

Gavin chuckled with a look of surprise. "Have you grown afraid of me in my absence?"

Feeling childish and foolish, Laina smiled weakly. "I'm sorry, m'lord. You surprised me."

"Well then," he said, playfully moving forward on his hands and knees to straddle her body, "I will go very slowly so you won't be surprised." Noticing the look of fear on her face, he added softly, "Have you already forgotten the passionate kisses we shared on previous occasions?"

"No, m'lord."

He lifted her hand and slowly planted kisses there, after each word that he spoke, "Perhaps... m'lady... I need... to... refresh... your... memory."

Laina giggled.

"The trick, you see," he said, continuing to plant kisses up the length of her arm, "is not... to spend... too much time... thinking about it." Reaching her shoulder, he lowered himself onto his elbows on either side of her and captured her mouth again in a searing kiss. His tongue explored boldly and possessively, over and over.

His soft beard rubbed her face, and his hands threaded into her hair on both sides of her head. She whimpered softly from the power of him.

He moaned in response. Slipping his arms underneath her, he quickly rolled over onto his back, so that she was on top of him. Laina held onto him tightly, not sure what he might do next. He flashed a dazzling smile at her, his eyes electrified with desire.

Suddenly embarrassed by her position of laying on top of him, Laina pushed herself up from his chest, too late realizing that she was now sitting quite unladylike on the massive mound of his manhood. The size of it was shocking. Her eyes grew large with surprise.

The laird burst out laughing, then desire flooded back into his expression. Grasping her slender hips with his large hands, he gritted his teeth and playfully growled like a beast. "Oh lass, how I've waited for this," he said breathlessly.

Laina opened her mouth, but no sound came. Not only was he holding her against *it*, but he was grinding her down onto *it*. She had to do something. In another clumsy attempt to rise off of him despite his powerful hold on her, Laina lost her balance and fell forward onto his chest once more. His hands immediately moved to her backside, holding her even more firmly while he gently squeezed her buttocks. His breath was coming harder and faster.

Not wanting to create another humiliating incident between herself and the laird, Laina's mind raced as she tried to think how things had come to this. She had simply agreed that she wanted to spend more time with him. She had not realized what he may have meant by that. Things were moving much too fast for her, but she must not offend him again.

He began nibbling hungrily on her neck, his breath hot and

moist. Her arms were useless, pinned by his. The massive size of his body made all of her movements pointless. She could sense his desire growing like the thundering approach of horses. And just as quickly, panic arose within her.

His hands on her backside kneaded and explored, while her frontside was grinding against his massive hardness, with only a few layers of cloth between them. She wondered if there was any part of her that he would not lay claim to this day? Terror bolted through her.

"M'lord!"

The panic in her voice jolted the laird out of his own thoughts.

"M'lord," she repeated, tears of humiliation gathering in her eyes, "I can't do this now."

Gavin sat up, taking her with him. "Laina, you are making too big a deal out of this. I can make you feel things you've never felt before."

"You already have, m'lord."

He laughed.

As Laina moved to get off of the laird's lap, her hand accidently came down on his engorged crotch. She jerked her hand as if it had been burned, and quickly scrambled away from him.

The laird's face turned dark. "Lass, I am growing tired of waiting for your fear to wane. I asked you if you were ready, and if this was something you wanted. Are you playing games with me? Is it your desire to be forced? For I can surely play that game."

"No, m'lord," she said shakily. "I am not playing games. I am truly sorry that I am not responding in the way that I should. This is all just so sudden...after I had come to believe that you were not interested in me."

The laird considered her silently for several moments, his face slowly softening. "I see. Forgive me, lass. You are right. You had not heard from me for some time, and now I am suddenly unleashing all the desire I have been storing up for you."

A few hot tears trickled slowly down Laina's cheeks.

The laird rubbed his beard. "How about if you take a day to absorb what we have talked about," he said. "Then I would like you to join me tomorrow and we will get beyond this. All right?"

Ashamed, she stood quickly. "Thank you, m'lord."

The laird laid back on the pillows, putting his hands behind his head. "Tomorrow, then."

Wiping her face, Laina hurried from the room and the keep, going out the side entrance to avoid the stares of some of the laird's soldiers sitting in the great hall. Once outside, she turned and pressed her forehead against the cold stone wall and broke into sobs, her slender body heaving from a deep sorrow she couldn't explain. Is this what her life was to be, she wondered? Was she being childish to resist it? When she tried to reason it out, her thoughts swam in circles. It's as if her own mind was not her own anymore.

Drying her face with the hem of her tunic, she turned away from the wall just as Evan came around the corner of the keep. Upon seeing her, he ran forward.

"Laina, what has happened?"

She glared at him. "The laird," she said stiffly, "he...wants me."

"I know," Evan said, wrapping his arms protectively around her.

She pulled away. "Why would you care?"

"What do you mean?" Evan looked confused. "Of course I care."

She gave an indifferent sniff and looked away from him.

"Laina, I need to talk with you," Evan said. "Can you meet me in the garden shed in a few minutes?"

She looked at him, surprised, her annoyance fading. "The garden shed?"

"Yes. Don't let anyone see you." He looked over his shoulder. "I'll be right back."

"Where are you going?" she asked.

"I have to take care of something. Wait for me there." He gave her a quick kiss on the forehead, and then sprinted back toward the courtyard.

Chapter Twenty-six

ဢℛ

LAINA DISCREETLY MADE HER WAY to the garden behind the keep and slipped inside the tiny wood shed in the back corner. Moving aside a few baskets on the floor with her foot, she made room for herself...and for Evan when he arrived. Light filtered in through the cracks between the boards of the roughly-made building, casting lines of light across the curved blades and wedge-shaped tools leaning against the walls. Laina heard shouts in the distance.

A few minutes later, the crooked-hanging door to the shed opened and Evan entered, ducking under the low doorframe.

"What's going on?" Laina asked.

"Oswyn is creating a diversion for us," Evan answered.

"A diversion?"

"Yes. He is acting like he is having a seizure in the courtyard. It's a very effective distraction. He is quite good at it. But he can only keep it up for so long, so we must talk quickly." Evan took Laina's hands in his.

"Why does there need to be a diversion for us to talk?" she asked, confused.

"Because I have been ordered by the laird's guards to stay away from you until I leave." Evan waited for her to grasp that detail, and then continued.

"Laina, I want you to come with us when we leave. I must be honest and tell you that life on the road is hard — dangerous at times. It is the life I must lead and I cannot settle down anywhere right now, nor can I promise what the future might hold for you and I. But I know this...I cannot bear the thought of leaving you again." He paused, his throat tightening and his eyes growing glassy. "Do you think you could be happy coming with me?"

Her mouth fell open and she stared at Evan in disbelief.

From her expression, he could not tell what she thought. He realized she may very well have lost trust in him. He had given her so many mixed messages. The poor girl had been tossled around by men. He, himself, pushing her away for days. And now, all he could think of was how badly he wanted her in his life. How he couldn't stand the thought of leaving without her. It would serve him right if she decided to stay at the castle.

"I've spoken with the other musicians," he added. "They welcome the idea of you joining us. Your dancing would be a perfect paring with our performances." He squeezed her hands encouragingly. "You can try it out, Laina, and always come back here if you change your mind."

Until this moment, he had not considered the pain he would feel if she declined. He searched her eyes for an answer, his gut twisting.

Her head began moving...bobbing slowly. "Yes," she said. "Yes, I would like to go with you."

Evan nearly let out a shout of joy from their hiding place, but caught himself. He took a deep breath and tried to stay focused. "Are you sure? What about leaving Margaret and everyone you know here?"

"It will be sad," Laina said. "But I do not feel that I belong here, Evan. I never have."

He embraced and kissed her tenderly, revealing more about the depth of his feelings than he could say.

She responded, letting him capture her breath. Her affection for him surged effortlessly to the surface. It was the kind of reaction that Laird Galloway had wanted from her a short time before. Her head still spinning from the day's events, Laina knew that she could not be sure that either man could give her his heart. There was only one thing to do amidst all the confusion: make her choice based on the path that made the most sense for her, regardless of the men. That's how she decided to leave the castle and go with Evan. Now she could only hope it was the right choice.

Their kiss ended and Evan stood up to his full height. "There is not much time for your goodbyes," he said. "We are packed and ready to go. There could be much trouble if we are caught."

"I must say goodbye to Margaret," Laina said.

Evan nodded.

"I feel bad leaving without giving Laird Galloway an explanation," she said. "He has done so much for me."

"You can send him a letter once we reach our next destination," Evan urged.

"Where's that?" Laina asked, feeling the excitement of the new adventure in her life.

"Westport, my home — at least, as much of a home as a travelling man can have. Have you ever seen the sea, Laina?"

"No."

"There is a place I want to take you," he said. "Atop a cliff and overlooking the ocean as far as you can see, there is a giant stone circle. I've heard it is the site of many important gatherings." He smiled in response to the brightening in her eyes.

There were no longer any sounds coming from the courtyard.

"We have to hurry," Evan said. "You must go talk with Margaret now, and collect your things in a small bag."

Laina's eyes filled with tears.

"Are you sure you want to do this?" Evan asked.

"I am sure."

"All right then. Oswyn will come for you shortly at the kitchen — as soon as he recovers from his seizure." Evan laughed and squeezed her hands once more, then raced out the door.

Laina waited for a few moments before leaving the shed and hurrying to the kitchen.

Fortunately, Margaret was the only one there.

When the cook looked up, Laina could see that the older woman knew what was going on. Margaret rushed over and embraced Laina with tears in her eyes.

"Oh, lass...I knew you would agree to go. I trust you are making the best decision for yourself. But I am going to miss you terribly."

"How did you hear?" Laina asked, stepping back and wiping at her own eyes.

"Oswyn told me. He wanted to make sure that you had the best chance of leaving if that was what you chose, so I have your things already packed up to go." Margaret pointed toward a small leather bag leaning against the leg of one of the work tables.

"You have been so kind to me," Laina said.

Margaret stiffened her shoulders and set her jaw. "Has been

good for both of us, lass. Now 'tis important for you to keep your head on for what you must do."

Laina wiped her cheeks once more. "Is it too risky to say goodbye to the others?" she asked, already knowing the answer.

"There is no time, and no one can be trusted," Margaret said. "I sent the girls off to pick berries."

"Will you please tell everyone how much I have appreciated..."

"I will tell them."

"And Laird Galloway," Laina added.

"I will talk with him," Margaret reassured. "Don't you worry. He can take care of himself. He always has."

Laina was glad that she had left the book and scarf behind in the laird's solar. It wouldn't have been right to take the gifts and leave.

"I will send him a letter when I can find someone to write it for me," Laina said.

"That would be good," Margaret agreed.

They both looked up to see Oswyn standing at the door, still red-faced from his choking performance.

"I'm feeling much better now," he said with a grin. "Are you coming, lass?"

"I am."

"Then grab ye bag and come out behind the building with me. I've got some costuming for you."

As Margaret and Laina followed him, Oswyn proudly revealed the rest of the clever plan that had been his idea.

"Ye see, earlier, three of our musician's took a short ride out of the castle on *two* of our horses. The guards didn't seem to take notice of the double-riders on one of the horses going out, and only one rider on that horse when it returned. Andrew was dropped off down by the river. That means we've got an empty horse within the castle walls for you to leave on, lass."

Margaret laughed. "You're brilliant! No one will question that five in your party arrived, and five are leaving."

Oswyn grinned. "Aye. We'll pad up the lass a bit with some clothing and a hooded cloak, and then put her on a horse."

"I have not ridden a horse much by myself," Laina said nervously.

"Just hang on lassie! Once we get outside and down to the river, Andrew will take back his horse, and you'll ride with Evan. You just have to get through the castle gates!"

Reaching into a cloth bag he had stuffed behind the building, Oswyn handed some of Andrew's clothing, including a pair of brown breeches, to Laina. "Andrew is the smallest in our group," he explained. Then he turned his back to give Laina privacy to change clothes behind a pile of crates while he told Margaret the plans for the group's journey. They would ride hard to reach Westport, not risking a night of camping with the lass. "We're low on supplies," Oswyn explained. "Will be better to get stocked up and add some items for her comfort and safety before we introduce her to living on the road."

"You've got to bring her back to visit every once in awhile, you know," Margaret demanded.

"We will, cookie."

"I'm ready," Laina said. Oswyn turned around and snickered upon seeing the lass. The baggy breeches were pulled up over her chest so they wouldn't drag on the ground, but the oversized tunic concealed that fact. The wide belt around Laina's waist had to be looped around several times and tied, to avoid falling off her hips. Oswyn picked up the thin green tunic she'd removed. "Excuse me, lassie," he said, stuffing it down into the front of Andrew's tunic that she wore. The belt at her waist held it in place. Laina and Margaret laughed at the new shape her body took on.

"Here, pull these on over your shoes," Oswyn said, handing her a pair of men's boots.

Laina did as he said, then playfully patted her fake belly, making Margaret laugh.

"I've saved the best for last," Oswyn said. Reaching into the bag, he pulled out a shaggy dark mat of hair with a small fake beard attached. "Made it meself," he boasted, fingering the leather ties for attaching it.

"Where did you get that?" Margaret said, grimacing.

"I spent some time in the animal pens this morning, gathering materials together," He tipped his head proudly. "I work with the theater company, you know. I know how to do these things."

"Yes, I know," Margaret said, chuckling at the sight of Laina as Oswyn attached the animal fur onto her head.

Laina scratched her face and tried to ignore the sour, musky smell of the fur.

Oswyn wrapped Margaret's brown cloak around the lass. "Margaret says ye can keep this," he announced.

"It never did fit me quite right," Margaret explained, "and you'll be needing one."

Over the brown cloak, Oswyn swirled a second dark gray cloak, and pulled the large hood up to conceal her face.

Margaret gasped. The bulky disguise was very effective. She and Laina exchanged a quick hug one last time.

"We'll see each other again, lassie," Margaret assured. "Now take good care of yourself."

Her heart racing, Laina followed at a distance behind Oswyn across the courtyard, since he had brought so much attention to himself earlier. He hobbled along in his usual way, waving at people who asked if he was feeling better.

In the lower courtyard, Evan was seated on his black stallion, looking anxious, alongside Ian and John. When Evan saw Laina in her hooded disguise, relief washed over his face and he gave her a small smile. Then, with a firm tone of voice, he called out, "Hurry up Oswyn and Andrew. Clearly we're not welcome here, so let's be on our way." He glared toward the guard tower in the distance.

The brown mare to be Laina's was cleverly positioned next to a straw bale, enabling her to scramble up easily when no one was looking.

Although there were a fair number of people about, no one seemed to be paying much mind to the small group, other than a guard near the gates who looked over occasionally.

Evan nudged his horse over near Laina's to ensure that she was seated securely.

"Sit up very tall, keep your face down, and don't kick your horse," Evan instructed. "And most important, no matter what you may hear, stay with Ian — there on the white horse — and do not look back."

Laina's horse fidgeted. "Evan..." Laina said nervously.

"Don't worry, everything is going to be fine," he answered, gazing directly into her clear eyes, that peered out from the furry wig Oswyn had created. "And when I get you outside of this castle," Evan said quietly, "no one, besides you, can stop me from kissing you as often as I want!"

Under her beard and cloak, Laina flushed with warmth.

The musicians waited briefly to time their exit along with the largest crowd of people entering and exiting the castle. As the small group on horseback approached the gates, two guards on the wall and three below eyed them carefully.

Laina's horse became restless.

"Hey!" one of the guards shouted.

At that, Oswyn jerked sideways and fell off of his horse. Evan stayed with him, while the other riders continued on. The guards turned their attention to watch Oswyn thrash around and then struggle to get to his feet with much gagging and moaning.

"Are you sure he is well enough to travel?" one of the guards called over. "He had a terrible spell in the upper courtyard a short time ago."

"He's just an old, senseless man; he'll be fine," Evan assured, enjoying the opportunity to embellish his description of his old friend. He knew he would pay for it later. "Don't worry," Evan added gruffly to the guard, "we're taking our leave as quickly as possible, as you requested."

The guards nodded their approval and gloated amongst themselves at their power over the visitors. The laird would be pleased with them.

By the time Evan and Oswyn were through the gates, the three other riders were well on their way to the river. Evan continued to ride slowly beside the ailing rider, as the guards watched them go. Oswyn pulled out his flask of scotch and took a drink.

"I should be performing, rather than just making costumes," Oswyn snickered.

"I'm surprised you don't hurt yourself when you thrash around like that."

"I do! That's what the scotch is for."

Laina had dismounted and was waiting with the others by the river when Evan and Oswyn came riding up.

Pointing at Laina, Andrew yelled at Oswyn, "Is that what you think I look like?"

Laina stood grinning from behind the bristly beard, her fake stomach shifted unnaturally to the left.

"Of course, not," Oswyn answered. "She looks a lot better than you do."

Everyone laughed.

Evan lept from his horse and scooped Laina up into his arms. Slipping the wig and beard from her head, he gave her a kiss. "You can change back into your own clothes for the rest of the ride," he said.

"What if the laird's men come in pursuit?" Andrew asked.

"If the laird's men come in pursuit," Evan said, setting Laina back on the ground, "they'll know much more than any disguise can save us from.

While the men discussed their route, Laina retreated behind a group of bushes and changed into her own clothing. As soon as

Andrew's extra clothing was again stowed in the horse packs, Evan set Laina upon his horse and then swung up behind her.

"Home, to Westport, as fast as we can go!" he said.

The group turned their horses in unison. In the brief moment before his horse bolted, Evan leaned down and moved his lips lightly against Laina's ear. "You have my heart, lass."

Chapter Twenty-seven

ഌൢ

EVAN'S ARMS HELD LAINA securely in front of him as his black stallion galloped powerfully across the sun-dappled landscape. Silky ribbons of Laina's hair worked their way loose from her braid and teased the lower half of Evan's face. Despite a faint musky odor from the animal wig disguise she had been forced to wear while leaving the castle, Evan could still smell the scent of sweet herbs from her hair and skin. Her slim, soft body molded perfectly against him. The movement of her between his legs made him grow hard. They still had a nine-hour ride ahead of them, and Evan was sure it would be the longest ride of his life. If they had been travelling alone, and not on the run from Galloway Castle to avoid trouble, perhaps he would have found a hidden glen and laid her down on a soft blanket of earth, and...

"Do you think Laird Galloway will be angry?" Laina asked, turning her head to the side so Evan could hear her.

"We are free to come and go as we please," Evan answered. "If he is angry, I am sure he will get over it when he thinks it through. He is not inclined to tie himself to anyone."

"Still, it seems rude that I did not say goodbye to him," Laina said.

"You didn't have much choice," Evan reminded. "The laird put a lot of pressure on you. He will realize that it was he who scared you away. He will not blame you. I can assure you, it's not the first time a lass has run away from him, although I will admit, it is rare."

"Everyone told me that I should not pass up such an opportunity — being favored by the laird."

"And yet, you did," Evan said, smiling with the knowledge that she had chosen to come with him instead.

"Yes."

"Did I lead you astray?" Evan asked.

"You led me *away*," Laina replied, then added softly, "and I wanted you to."

"Even though you don't know where you're being led?" he teased softly in return.

"It doesn't matter," she said. "For the first time since my father died, I feel alive again. I much prefer the unknown than simply moving through each day waiting to see what happens to me."

Evan gave her a small, affectionate squeeze.

"I am grateful for everything Laird Galloway did for me," Laina said.

"Of course," Evan acknowledged. "He is a generous man."

"He was very good to me."

Evan leaned down and whispered in her ear, "And I will be too."

Laina giggled and tipped her head back against his chest. The castle had been her home for many months. She had not known what would become of her or what was expected of her. She only knew she didn't seem to fit there, and she doubted she ever would. Now she sat atop a horse, riding for Evan's home. How quickly things could change from one day to the next.

In truth, she really did not know much about Evan Prestwick. She only knew how comfortable and safe she felt with him. Strange, considering she had thought him so rude and uninteresting when they'd first met in her village. Since then, she had come to appreciate his character. Although arrogant at times, he was never cruel. Intelligent and independent, he knew who he was and what he wanted. Being honorable seemed of great importance to him, at least when it came to his involvement with her. He was strikingly handsome too, she thought with a devilish smile, and his kisses were as sweet and smooth as warm honey.

Feeling Evan's firm body pushed up against her's, Laina remembered her encounter with the laird that morning. She had been sitting on top of his engorged crotch. The memory brought a rush of embarrassment to Laina all over again. Relaxing in the safety of Evan's embrace, she wondered how engorged Evan might get for her. That mysterious mound…warm and hard.

"Are you thinking about me?" Evan asked.

Laina jumped. Thank goodness Evan could not see the guilty blush rising to her face. "Yes," she answered in a small voice.

"I'm thinking about you too," he said.

"You are?" She wondered what images of her might be dancing through his head.

"U-hmm…" he muttered. "I was thinking about the first time I met you. I thought you looked like a graceful elf in your baggy clothing. Then when I saw you at the Mayday Faire, I thought you looked like an angel in your stained apron. But when I saw you in one of Oswyn's beautiful gowns, you were a vision beyond words."

"How about when you saw me wearing Oswyn's beastie beard?" Laina teased.

Evan let out a hearty laugh. "Aye, you just keep surprising me, lass."

Laina bit her lip lightly. Yes, he would be surprised if he knew what she had been thinking about him. There he was cherishing his memories of her, while she was imagining him naked. It was shameful. When had she become such a naughty little tart, she wondered? It must have been all that talk in the castle kitchen, she decided. Those girls talked of little else.

"We can stop the horses and take a break anytime you'd like," Evan suggested.

"Oh, I'm fine," Laina said quickly. She did not want to face him now. She needed time to get her passions under control. The rules for her life were changing. Until now, most of her choices had been directed by other people. Now, she was truly free to do whatever she wanted. That freedom, combined with the way Evan stirred her, was unnerving. She must keep her head and not make foolish decisions she would regret.

The rhythmic movement of the horse was comforting. When Laina again heard voices, she opened her eyes and realized she had fallen asleep. The landscape had grown dark and the small group was slowing.

"We'll take a short break here," Evan said, bringing his horse to a stop beside a group of trees.

"Where are we?" Laina asked.

"About three hours from home," he answered.

Ian pulled dried meat and bread from his pack and passed it around. John shared water from a crescent moon-shaped bag of leather. After everyone had put a bit in their stomachs and taken care of their private needs, the group was back on the road. Exhausted from all the excitement of her day, Laina slept the rest of the way. The next time she opened her eyes, they were approaching the edge of a darkened village. A few glowing lanterns swung in the salty-scented wind.

Sensing that she had awoken, Evan said softly, "We're home."

Oswyn came up alongside. "I'll see ye two tomorrow," he said, with a tired wave.

The other musicians mumbled their goodbyes, as well, and Evan turned his horse down a narrow lane containing a few small stone cottages.

"What's that sound?" Laina asked, noticing a muffled roar.

"The sea," Evan answered. "I'll show you tomorrow."

Stopping his horse in front of a small stone cottage, he jumped down, then lifted Laina down.

Her legs shakey from the long ride, Laina let Evan lead her into the cottage and then waited while he lit two lanterns.

"I've got to take the horse over to the stable and get him fed and watered," he said, handing her a lantern. "There's a biffy around back if you need it."

"Thank you," she said, looking around nervously.

"I'll be right back," he said, giving her a reassuring smile.

After visiting the biffy, Laina returned to the cottage and waited for Evan. The cottage was simple but comfortable. A table and two chairs were arranged near the front of the room. A bench covered with a tapestry sat by the hearth to the left. In the right back corner of the room, a mattress covered with fur was laid on a wood platform. Along the right wall, an assortment of musical instruments, books, and chests, all neatly organized under two shuttered windows. Two more shuttered windows hung on either side of the door.

The door swung open and Evan stepped inside. With a heavy sigh, he dropped their packs on a bench by the door. Then, digging in his own pack, he pulled out a bundle of bread, cheese, and dried meat wrapped in cloth. "Are you hungry?" he asked, holding it out to Laina.

"A little," she said, taking it and moving to the table to slice some of the cheese with her knife.

Evan walked to the hearth and got a fire going, using logs from a small pile of wood in the corner. When the flames filled the room with light, he turned around to face Laina. She smiled at him, while tugging on a piece of dried meat with her teeth. Joining her, Evan tore into some of the meat himself. The two stood looking at each other, their eyes lit with excitement, despite their exhaustion. Laina suddenly walked toward her pack by the door and pulled out a small bottle of whiskey.

Evan laughed. "Oswyn sure does keep you supplied!"

"He says it's good for everything," Laina answered.

"I'm sure he does," Evan said.

"He said it warms ye when you're cold, and strengthens ye when you're weak, and gives ye courage when you're afraid." She imitated Oswyn's manner of speech.

Evan laughed and reached for her, pulling her up against him. He looked into her eyes. "Are you afraid...coming here with me?"

"No," she whispered, tipping her face up to his.

He lowered his head to meet her lips. The kiss was tender. He would not force himself on her as Laird Galloway had done. And he would not get drunk and forget himself as he had almost done on their recent picnic.

He savored the softness of her lips a moment longer, then stood upright. "I am glad you are here with me, Laina. I have no expectations of what is to be between us — I want you to know that. I want you to be happy and free."

She looked up at him brightly. "I know. That is why I feel safe with you."

"I won't deny," Evan's tone deepened as he turned toward the hearth, "that I have very strong feelings for you." He took the tapestry from the bench and spread it out on the floor in front of the fire. He stared into the flames, keeping his back to Laina. He did not want to overwhelm her, but clearly he would not have suggested she come with him if he didn't care deeply for her. He had never met any women that he would consider doing such a thing with.

Still holding the bottle of whiskey, Laina walked over beside him and popped out the cork. "I care very much for you too, Evan." She tipped the whiskey bottle and took a sip, then waited for the fire to die down in her throat. "But I understand that you have a life that you love, and I do not want to disrupt it. I have no expectations either." She would not admit, at least not now, that she had hopes of something more with Evan. She didn't understand it fully herself, so it was best, perhaps, not to speak of it yet.

She handed the bottle to Evan. He took it and set it on the table behind him without taking a drink.

"Laina," he said, taking her right hand and pulling her to sit on the tapestry on the floor with him, "I think you know that I do not want to dishonor you in any way. It's just that...", he searched for the right words to say, "I have a very hard time..." He looked into her eyes — beautiful, untouched mountain pools that he wanted to dive into.

"Yes?" she said.

"I have a very hard time controlling myself when I'm around you."

She burst out laughing, holding her stomach with her free hand as if it were almost too funny to bear.

Evan smiled, embarrassed. "It's the truth." He had expected her to take it as seriously as he did. For the last few days, he had shown considerable restraint to protect her honor, despite the overwhelming desire to take her every five minutes. Her playful antics had proven most challenging for him, and yet, he had held fairly steady, at least more than any man should be expected to. Didn't she understand how difficult it was for him? Didn't she realize he was doing it for her? He didn't know how much longer he could hold up under such pressure.

Laina had never seen him look so vulnerable. It was endearing. She looked down at her hand in his. His hands were strong and well-shaped, his fingers long and gentle. She raise one of his hands slowly and planted a soft kiss in his palm. "I trust you," she said, smiling up at him.

"Laina," Evan said gruffly, pulling his hand away, "this is the kind of thing that you cannot do."

"What?" she asked bewildered.

"Acting sweet and seductive."

"I'm not acting."

Evan's voice rose. "If you had any idea what it takes for me to restrain myself..."

Her face showed amusement. She knew she probably shouldn't taunt him, but his struggle made it so fun. "How must you restrain yourself?"

"You don't want to ask that," he said, looking away.

"Well I just did, so I suppose I do," she countered.

"Laina..."

"Just tell me," she urged, leaning forward and poking him.

He knew she was playing with him, and she was winning. But the foolish girl didn't realize where it might lead. Perhaps he could scare her a little — make her realize how dangerous the situation was.

"All right," he said, turning back to face her. "You want to know what I'd like to do?" He flashed her an evil grin.

"Uh, yes?" she said quietly, suddenly feeling that she had poked at the bear too long.

"First of all," he said, "I'd like to remove all of your clothes with my teeth..."

"Oh, I see!" Laina said, shifting uncomfortably. "Well..."

"And then I would like to..."

"I get the picture!" she said loudly, standing up and walking to the table, where she crammed a big chunk of bread into her mouth.

It was Evan's turn to laugh. "I'm just getting started. Don't you want to hear more?"

"Noh, Ih thinck nawt..." Laina mumbled with her mouth full.

Chuckling, Evan held out his hand to her. "Come here and sit down with me. I promise I won't bite, although, now you know I'd like to."

Laina returned to his side, wiping the crumbs from her mouth.

"Maybe we just need to keep your mouth full of bread," Evan suggested, "and we won't get into trouble."

Putting his arm around her, they sat facing the fire and leaned into each other, listening to the snapping of the hot, glowing logs. Sometime during the evening they laid down — Laina in front and Evan close behind, his arm still encircling her — and fell asleep.

Just after dark, Gavin stormed into Galloway Castle's guard house. "Where the hell is she?"

Lowrens stepped forward. "M'lord, no one saw her leave." Just moments before, the large soldier had arrived at the guard house to warn the men that the laird had become aware that Laina Makgregor was missing.

"We were watching all who passed through the gate," explained the chief soldier in charge. "We had the usual flow of villagers going in and out. Around midday, the Westport musicians left. Other than one brief incident with the old one in their group, nothing out of the ordinary took place today."

"What kind of incident?" the laird asked hotly.

The man smirked at the memory. "The drunkard fell off his horse in some sort of spasm. Flopped all over the ground like some sort of fish. Evan Prestwick helped the old fool get back up and they left."

"A distraction," the laird growled.

"I assure you, m'lord, our attention did not waver," the man defended.

"Where were the other men of their party during this?" Gavin asked.

"They rode on ahead."

"Of course," Gavin said, nodding.

"M'lord, we saw only men ride out. The girl was not with them."

"Well, she's not here." The laird folded his arms and scowled. "And she has not gone on one of her walks, correct?"

"She has not passed through the gates today," the man acknowledged.

"I think it's more fitting to say that you've not *seen* her pass through the gates today," the laird corrected the man.

The guard shifted his weight uncomfortably and swallowed nervously.

"They must have smuggled her out somehow," Gavin said.

"Would the musicians take her against her will?" Lowrens asked. "That hardly seems in their character."

"I don't know," Gavin grumbled, wondering if his earlier advances toward Laina had anything to do with her disappearance. He had been rather forceful with the girl, telling her she had only one more day to lose her shyness with him. "I just know that Evan Prestwick was interested in the girl. He may have convinced her to go with him."

"Perhaps the cook knows something?" Lowrens suggested.

"I stopped by the kitchen before I came here," the laird said. "Margaret was not there, and I got little information from those wide-eyed girls. They said only that Laina had left earlier in the day and they didn't know where she went, or anything else about it."

Gavin pointed at the men and then at the ground at his feet. "I want her back here! I want Evan Prestwick back here too. God help him if he has something to do with this. He has been testing our friendship lately, and I will no longer show him special consideration. I want..."

Noticing a young messenger boy waiting nervously at his side, the laird looked down at him. The dark-haired boy fidgeted and wiped his nose.

"What is it?" Gavin snapped.

"M'lord, the castle cook is waiting in the keep to speak with you."

The laird raised his voice to his men, "Find them both, whether they are together or apart." Then he turned and strode quickly back toward the keep.

Margaret was waiting in the great hall, sitting on a bench along one wall. The laird came through the door and descended the steps quickly. The older woman stood, her face drawn tightly.

"Margaret," he said, with a curt nod, approaching her. "What do you know of Laina's disappearance?"

"She has gone m'lord," Margaret answered.

"Where?"

"I don't know exactly," the cook hedged.

"Dammit, Margaret, you *do* know!" the laird roared.

"M'lord, the lass was not happy here."

"What do you mean? Why not?"

"She was overwhelmed by what might be expected of her. She came from a village, you know. Their ways were different. Freer, perhaps, to make their own decisions."

"Was she overwhelmed by me?" the laird asked.

"Well, of course, m'lord! What woman wouldn't be?"

"She left with Evan Prestwick, didn't she?" the laird demanded.

"M'lord, I…"

"Dammit, Margaret, tell me!"

"Yes, m'lord. She did. But it was her choice."

"She is young and doesn't know what is best for her own good," Gavin bellowed. There is no comparison between the life I can give her and the pathetic scraps she will have to live on with an unreliable musician. She is in danger being on the road. Why did you let her go?"

Margaret was not afraid of the laird's rage. She shrugged her shoulders and snorted. "'Tis not up to me to control the girl's movements. We don't own her."

Margaret's logic annoyed him. Gavin knew only what he wanted and that was all the logic he needed to guide him. It was in the girl's best interest, whether she realized it yet or not.

"Where did they go?" he asked again.

Margaret set her mouth firmly, while she returned the laird's intense gaze.

"Evan's home?" the laird suggested. "Westport?"

Something flickered in Margaret's expression.

"Of course," he hissed, turning to leave.

"M'lord," Margaret called out. "Ye won't win the lass by strong-arming her. She's a gentle one. Follows her heart."

The laird had already sprinted back up the steps. "Her heart will belong to me," he answered just before the door slammed behind him.

Chapter Twenty-eight

ഔ൫ Cൠ

EVAN WOKE LAINA just before dawn. "I have something to show you," he said, kissing her lightly on the forehead. Leading her outside into the darkness, they silently mounted his horse like ghosts, their cloaks pulled snugly around them to ward off the chilly fog. The village lay quiet except for the roar of the sea at its western edge. Heading south, they rode half-an-hour to a stretch of dark jagged cliffs bordering the ocean. Evan directed his horse along a narrow winding path through the rugged landscape, then slowed as they came over the last rise.

Laina took in her breath. A circle of immense, white pillars stood in front of them, glowing softly in the breaking dawn. Laina had no memory of Evan's horse coming to a stop, or of Evan lifting her down. Nor did she notice the vast stretch of blue ocean becoming visible in the day's first light, and stretching all the way to the western horizon. Something within her pulsed strongly, like a heartbeat more powerful than her own, pulling her forward to the stones.

Evan watched her enter the circle then stand motionless with her palms open and her face tilted upward, eyes closed. Margaret's brown woolen cloak whipped around Laina's slender form, flapping wildly in the sharp ocean wind. Yet, the lass looked peaceful among the stones, like she belonged.

There were mysteries, Evan knew, that he had not yet discovered about the lass. An unusual wisdom flowed in her veins, as if she were guided by something much larger than herself. It intrigued him greatly, although…he had to admit…the sight of her made it difficult for him to think of little else than covering her with kisses and every other part of him.

She looked so small standing among the giant rocks. He

longed to stand beside her and hold her protectively. He swallowed and blinked the dampness from his eyes. Good god, his feelings for her were becoming too overwhelming to deny. He loved her. And that would surely change almost everything in his life. It was a realization that he would have resisted fiercely just two weeks earlier. Indeed, he had done everything he could to go about his life normally after meeting her. He gave a small laugh under his breath. His resistance had never had a chance of succeeding. She belonged with him, and he belonged with her.

He stood at the edge of the circle, his eyes soft with quiet acceptance, willing to wait and remain there for her, as long as she needed.

Laina's heart pumped in her chest in rhythm to a larger pounding heartbeat vibrating her entire body. She stood brave and firm as tingling sensations began travelling up through her feet and out through her head. Although startling, it felt oddly familiar and safe. The separation between herself and the stones vanished. She was one with them, existing throughout time. Solid, strong, always reaching up to the endless sky. And yet, suddenly, she was one with the sky and the stars too. Stretching far beyond what she had imagined her own origins to be. Merging with it all, she floated peacefully, feeling the completeness. No questions. No worries. No separation.

She suddenly gasped aloud, as if rising from a deep body of water and taking in breath for the first time. A calm knowing settled over her. She was here, in this life, to experience all that she could, and to love. She felt the truth of it fill her completely, as a sparkling fountain would saturate a dry clay jug. Her heartbeat slowed and the pounding in her ears stopped. Noticing the fresh ocean wind caressing her face and the excited call of the seabirds, she smiled and turned.

Evan returned her smile as she faced him, her face radiant.

"Thank you," she said, walking back to his side, and noticing with surprise for the first time, the enormous expanse of sea that sparkled in the sunshine. How long had she been inside the stone circle, she wondered, looking up into the sky at the position of the sun. Enchanted by Evan's thoughtfulness in bringing her to such a place and waiting patiently for her, she flung her arms around him and looked up into his eyes affectionately as he embraced her in return. His fair hair and handsome face glowed in the golden light of the day. He looked different somehow. Peaceful and content.

The roar of the waves far below seemed to call out to the pair.

They turned their gaze toward the shimmering ocean and the birds riding the currents of air effortlessly above. Standing with their arms around each other, the world looked new. All that had come before seemed meant to lead them to this moment. Now things felt as if they were finally in place.

The sun was overhead as Evan led Laina back to his stallion, and they continued their journey on horseback down a long steep trail that led to the base of the cliff. Laina took in long, deep breaths, wanting to fully experience every moment. Reaching the bottom of the path, the thunderous ocean waves roared and hissed as the couple dismounted.

It was as if she stood at the edge of a dragon's lair, the mist of the beast's breath moistening her face, Laina mused. Following Evan's example, she removed her shoes, and walked with him across the sand to the water's edge.

She giggled as the water lapped at her feet. Closing her eyes, she listened to the song of the sea and licked the salty mist from her lips. When her eyes opened again, they sparkled like the ocean waves in the golden sunlight. She turned to Evan, sliding her hands up around his neck and pulling him gently to her, then kissed him with the raw power she felt surging through her. She didn't care if she were boldly tempting him again. Threading her fingers into his sea-dampened hair, her lips and tongue merged with his — salty and wet.

He embraced her tightly and returned the kiss with his own fierce passion. Plunging his tongue into her hot, sweet mouth, he desperately yearned to plunge another part of his body deep inside of her, and to hear her cry out in pleasure.

Her body, moist from sea spray, molded against him, her breasts pressed softly against his chest. He couldn't think straight. He wanted her more than anything he had ever wanted in his life. It wasn't just lust. It was something else — something he couldn't name. A driving need to connect with her as completely as possible. He had never felt it with anyone before. He only knew that all of his rules and hesitations were being pulled away from him by the tide, leaving him stripped of all but his raw desire.

Laina kissed him feverishly, caressing him with her hands. She wanted to be closer to him. She wanted to experience all of him.

Evan stepped back, his eyes glazed. Taking her hand, he led her silently across the sand away from the waves. His horse, following as the pair walked along the cliff face.

Her own eyes unfocused, Laina followed as if in a dream,

feeling the warmth and softness of his hand. Evan appeared to be looking for something.

He stopped when he found a small alcove. He pulled Laina into the private space and held her face tenderly in his hands. Shielded from the sea spray, he kissed her again, deeply. Then, his voice ragged, he said, "Laina, I don't want to stop…"

"You don't have to," she answered.

He gazed into her eyes, seeking any last bit of logic that might help guide him, but he saw only a path leading forward. He would resist no more, he decided, his hands moving affectionately over the gentle curves of her body.

She responded to his touch, her moans inviting him to explore further. Molding to him, she moved with him, her own hands discovering the power and firmness of him. A strange tingling between her legs began to taunt her. With a sudden step back, she pulled her tunic up over her head. In a few more movements, she had cast all of her clothing to the side.

Evan stood stunned. His eyes soft, expressing a longing as deep as his soul.

She stood before him, her body so perfect. Full, firm breasts with rosey tips begged for his lips. A small, slim waist and flat stomach, pleaded for his hands to hold her. And the patch of dark hair just above her long, shapely legs…cried out for him to be inside of her.

Watching her long mane of hair whip wildly around her like some sort of goddess from the sea, Evan removed his own clothes without taking his eyes off of her. He could no longer fight it. He would not even try.

Laina watched him, feasting on every part of his strong, lean body that was revealed. And when he removed his breeches, she gasped at the long, smooth penis, rigid with desire.

Evan gave her a moment to take him all in, then pulled her to him, their bodies meeting with an intimacy that they could never go back from.

"Are you sure this is what you want?" he whispered breathlessly.

One corner of her mouth curled up. "Are my clothes on the ground not proof enough for you?"

Quickly spreading his cloak onto the sand, he pulled her down with him. He covered her with kisses, stroking her with his hands and the full length of his body. Gentle, yet hungry, the strength and need of him excited Laina. Her hands explored every inch of him, as her mouth met with his again and again. She loved the way his hands felt on her. She loved everything about him. She wanted him to possess her.

He took his time, letting her learn his body as he learned her's. She touched him eagerly, lovingly — her eyes filled with desire. When at last he slipped between her legs and slowly entered her, gently pushing through the last veil of resistance and filling her so completely with himself, she cried out like a wild animal and clutched at him. Their bodies moved together, rhythmically as one. Gradually, his pace quickened, driving into her again and again, like the pounding surf just beyond their hiding place.

Laina held onto him tightly, his strong arms rigid, his face rapturously intense. Their breath came fast together, their eyes locked in a shared realization of the door they were passing through. Nothing would ever be the same.

Screaming out together, their bodies exploded with thunderous sensations that rippled through every part of them. Over and over the ecstatic waves came, crashing into one another...until at last, a calm settled over them, and they lay transformed in each other's arms.

It was late in the afternoon when the pair rode in quiet contentment back to the village and arrived at Evan's cottage.

"I need to meet with Oswyn at the tavern to discuss our trip plans for tomorrow," Evan said.

"Tomorrow?" Laina asked dreamily, stepping across the threshold into Evan's cottage.

"Yes. We all leave for the wedding in Portsmouth tomorrow morn. Oswyn and I need to sort out some of the details. It won't take long," he said, reaching for her hand, holding it to his lips, and kissing it. "Why don't you come over to the tavern in half-an-hour? It's just two lanes over, toward the sea."

"All right," she answered. She watched him go, then dug through her small pack of clothes to pull out her nicer, blue tunic and a fresh chemise. As she changed clothes, her mind wandered lazily over all the events in recent days. She thought of Laird Galloway. Picturing his easy smile and handsome face, she could hear his laughter, and still feel the awe of his powerful presence.

She had been genuinely intrigued with him, despite the unexplainable longing she had felt for Evan. Now she was sure. She had made the right decision to come with Evan. She loved him, and she felt happier than she'd ever been.

After brushing and rebraiding her hair, Laina started a fresh fire in the hearth and laid her clothes out on a bench to dry. Strolling over to the tavern, she revelled in the beauty of the small coastal village, glowing in the sun and constantly echoing with the cry of the seabirds. The buildings and lanes were tidy and windswept. Collections of driftwood and large shells adorned many of the stone structures. It was not hard to find the tavern. Laughter and voices rang out from the small stone building with the blue door. A sign hanging from a post over the door swung in the breeze, with a picture of a bird on it. Laina could not read the writing.

Stepping just inside, she nodded shyly at the people sitting nearest the door who looked up at her with interest. She blinked as her eyes adjusted to the dim light. Several tables sat spaced throughout the room — people had gathered at the three tables nearest the door, which offered the most light coming in through the partially opened shutters. Behind a wood counter lined with tankards and surrounded by kegs, a sun-darkened man with leathery skin eyed Laina without expression.

From the back of the room, in the shadows, more voices and laughter could be heard. Laina smiled at the sound of Oswyn's grizzled voice. Weaving around tables and chairs, she crossed the floor towards the voices, her eyes finally focusing in the dim light. The Westport musicians sat around a long square table, a single wall lantern casting them in a soft yellow glow. Laina stopped cold. Evan sat at one end of the table with a red-haired woman on his lap, her arms around his neck.

Laina's mouth dropped open just as the woman leaned forward and planted a big kiss on Evan's lips.

As if burned by a hot cooking pot, Laina screamed. All heads turned to look at her, including Evan's.

"Laina!" He quickly moved the woman off of him and stood.

Her face filled with confusion, Laina sputtered, "How...could you..." Her eyes became glassy, and her voice rose, "We just..."

"Ah, have I caused some trouble?" the red-haired woman asked with a playful grin.

"Laina..." Evan said, moving toward her.

"I trusted you..." Laina hissed, backing away, her eyes

darkening.

"As well you should," he replied. "Let me explain."

"There is no explanation," she snapped, then whirled around just out of his grasp and ran back across the room and out the front of the tavern. Several chuckles rose up as the tavern's customers watched the scene unfold.

"He's in trouble..." someone announced.

Evan rushed out after Laina, catching up with her outside. "Laina, this isn't what you think."

She spun around, her face twisted with pain and betrayal. "You are no different than any other man, Evan Prestwick. In fact, you're worse! Because you hide who you are. At least with Laird Galloway, I knew who he was. I don't know you at all!"

"Laina, listen..." he pleaded, trying to pull her into his arms.

She jerked free, and ran in the direction of his cottage.

Evan rubbed his jaw as if he'd been hit. It pained him deeply to hurt her.

"Did I mess things up?" a voice purred beside him.

"Dammit, Sienna!" He glared at the red-haired woman.

"I didn't know," she said, apologetically.

"You didn't give me a chance to tell you!" Evan fumed. "This girl is really special to me."

"Do you want me to help patch it up? I can explain to her."

"No. I doubt she'll listen to you. That could make it worse."

"I'm sorry, Evan. I was just so glad to see you. You've been gone for weeks."

"I know. You're right. I shouldn't blame you. I must finish talking with Oswyn before he leaves, and then I'll explain things to Laina." He turned and walked back inside the tavern, met by laughter and cheers.

Laina ran all the way back to Evan's cottage, tears blurring the outlines of the narrow lanes and small buildings. Rushing inside, she leaned forward onto the table and broke into sobs. How could she have been so mistaken about Evan? Had everything been a lie between them? Had he been playing with her from the beginning? Suddenly, she stood up and angrily wiped the tears from her eyes.

Rushing to the bench by the hearth, she grabbed her loose, damp clothes and stuffed them into her pack. She would go to the stables and find someone who could give her a ride...anywhere else. Evan had been trying to keep his distance from her — perhaps he had known he could not be faithful to one woman. Maybe he had tried to protect her. Perhaps it was she who had fooled herself into believing what she wanted to about him.

A heavy knock at the door caused her to jump. Was Evan playing more games with her? Opening it angrily, her eyes widened in surprise.

"Laird Galloway!"

Seeing her tear-stained face, Gavin stepped inside and pulled her into his arms protectively. "Lass!" he rumbled, "What's wrong?"

Even if she could have found the words to express the confusion and torture she felt, the laird was squeezing the breath out of her.

"Has Evan dishonored you? Where is he? I'll kill him!"

"No, m'lord..."

"Did he bring you here against your will?"

"No, m'lord...I wanted to come."

The laird released her and gazed gently into her eyes as he held one of her hands. "Why Laina? I thought we were enjoying getting to know each other."

"Yes, m'lord," she said sadly, noticing the sincerity in his sparkling green eyes. "I'm sorry. I was just so overwhelmed. Life at the castle was very different than what I've known." Fighting back new tears, she added, "I felt safe with Evan. He was my friend."

"Then what has he done to make you cry?"

"He has a woman here," she said, her lips quivering with anger.

"Well, of course he does!" the laird roared, his handsome face darkening. "He's on the road all the time, you know. He has women everywhere."

Laina burst into tears again.

"Lass, don't cry," the laird said, softening his tone. "You don't need him. Come back to the castle with me. You have people there who care about you. Margaret misses you terribly. And I care about you, Laina." He motioned to one of his men at the door, and then handed a small linen bag to Laina. "Look, I have brought you the gifts I gave to you. You left them behind."

"M'lord, I'm so sorry that I left the way I did. I wanted to say goodbye to you."

"I wouldn't have let you say goodbye," Gavin said firmly, shaking his head. "Evan knew that."

"It was a very difficult choice for me to make, m'lord."

"I am sorry I pushed you too fast and scared you," Gavin said gently. "We can go slower. I want you to come back with me."

One of the laird's soldiers spoke from the doorway, "M'lord, Evan Prestwick is approaching."

The laird turned around to step outside. "Damn him to Hell. I'll kill him and make this easy."

"No!" Laina screamed, grabbing onto the laird's solid, muscled arm. "He has done nothing wrong, m'lord. It is I who had faulty expectations."

Evan strode up to the doorway glaring at the guards and addressed the laird. "What the hell is going on here?"

Gavin jerked his arm away from Laina and slammed his fist into Evan's face.

"No! Stop!" Laina screamed.

Despite a trickle of blood flowing from Evan's nose, he recovered quickly and reached for his knife. The laird's soldiers drew their swords in unison, making a metal singing sound.

"You have no claim here, Gavin!" Evan shouted.

"The hell, I don't! You were made well aware of my interest in this lass," the laird roared.

"Please," Laina screamed, "stop this!"

Evan laughed with a sneer. "You have an interest in *every* lass, Gavin!"

"That is none of your affair," the laird roared. "And the way I see it, you have no right to speak against enjoying a bounty of women, so why don't I cut out your tongue right now?"

Laina looked around the room for something that she could use to create a distraction.

"If you lay a hand on either Laina or myself again," Evan threatened, wiping his bloody nose on his sleeve, "you might as well kill me because I won't stop until I kill you."

"That suits me just fine," the laird said.

A loud clanging noise sounded, crashing over and over, causing everyone to turn and look inside the cottage to determine the sound of the racket. Laina stood on the table banging a large pot with a metal spoon. Her fierce facial expression made Evan smile.

"What is wrong with you men?" she screamed. "I am not a possession. I never have been and never will be. If you want to fight over something you can never possess, go ahead. But I am LEAVING!" She jumped down off the table and dramatically grabbed her bag of clothes and stormed up to the door, but had to stop because the laird was blocking her exit. She looked up into his blazing green eyes. There was a hint of amusement in them.

"You don't own me," she said quietly.

"I know," he answered. "But I want to take care of you, Laina. You are clearly not being taken care of here."

Evan slipped his knife back into its sheath and stepped up to the doorway at Gavin's back. The laird's guards stood ready. "I intend to take very good care of her," Evan said hotly. "This was all a misunderstanding, Gavin, which I am most anxious to set straight." Looking around the laird's hulking form at Laina, he offered her a pleading look.

The laird turned around to face him. The two men completely filled the doorway, standing just inches apart. "I think she has had enough of your reckless lifestyle, Evan. I'm taking her back with me to the safety of Galloway Castle."

"I think it should be up to Laina, don't you?" Evan challenged. "And if you are so sure that this is the right thing to do, you won't mind if she and I have a few moments alone to speak. You respect her enough to give her that, don't you?"

Gavin turned to consider Laina.

She looked back and forth between the two men. The laird's face was still red with rage. Evan's face reflected sincerity, although she couldn't imagine how he could explain this away. But she could give him a chance to say what he wanted before she left, she decided. She looked to the laird and said stiffly, "I will be fine."

The laird turned and glared at Evan, then stepped outside.

Evan entered and shut the door. He spoke quickly and earnestly, knowing that he didn't have much time. "Laina, nothing has changed between us, I assure you. What you saw in the tavern was not what it looked like. Sienna and I have been friends for the past two years. And, yes, on an occasional cold night now and then, we have shared a bed." He saw Laina stiffen, but continued. "I do *not* love her, Laina. I love you. I love you so much I can hardly think straight. I want you with me. I've never felt like this about anyone." He looked down briefly as if gathering the right words, and then looked back into her eyes. "I want you with me for the rest of my life."

Laina hadn't expected this. Her eyes moved over his worried face, as she considered him carefully. In truth, she wanted to believe him.

"When Sienna saw me," he continued, "she rushed over and plopped down on my lap before I had a chance to tell her that things have changed for me. It's the kind of greeting she has always given me, and she did not mean to cause any trouble. I am so sorry that this hurt you — and even more, that it caused you to doubt me. I have been true in everything I've told you, Laina."

Standing close to him, Laina could feel the strength of his love for her. He was telling the truth. Quietly, she stepped forward and put her arms around him, burying her face in his chest.

He wrapped his arms around her and held her tight. He swallowed and fought back his own tears.

In a muffled voice, Laina admitted, "I told you I didn't have any expectations, Evan. I'm sorry. I did not mean to intrude on your life. That was part of our deal, wasn't it?"

"I don't think there ever was a deal," he chuckled tiredly. "The moment I asked you to come with me, I knew my life would change. I chose it. I think there has always been more between us than we could admit. The important thing is that we are together because we want to be."

A knock on the door interrupted the tender moment. Evan reached over with one arm and opened the door, "Yes?"

"Are you done?" Gavin growled.

"No!" Evan snapped.

The laird looked at Laina, her face still buried in Evan's chest.

"Listen, Gavin," Evan said, "I truly care about Laina. I have from the day I met her. You've known me long enough to know that I've never said this about anyone in my life."

"Well I care about her too, and why would she choose you over me?" Gavin scoffed. "I can offer her a way of life far beyond anything you can ever give her."

"It's more than the way of life," Evan said. "There are things worth much more between us."

Evan was talking nonsense — perhaps to impress the girl — and Gavin hated the way Laina was embracing him. "Is this what you want, lass?" he demanded.

She looked up and nodded. "Yes, m'lord."

Gavin scowled and rubbed his forehead. He could easily win this fight and take what he wanted, but it wouldn't be good for his reputation. Was he turning into a damned fool to be so obssessed with one woman, he wondered? He noticed the way she looked at Evan. It made him want to vomit. But, he had to admit, the lass was right in that she hadn't settled into the castle as well as other people did. She was a different sort.

"Well, if he doesn't treat you well," Gavin said, "you always have a home at Galloway Castle."

"Thank you, m'lord."

Gavin glared at Evan one last time for good measure, then turned to leave with his soldiers. "Let's drop in on the tavern before we go," he growled.

Evan shut the door and kissed Laina's forehead and cheeks. "As I was saying," he continued, "we are together because we want to be. It's not because you were wanting to escape the castle...or I was having lusty thoughts about you...or anything else."

"You were having lusty thoughts about me?" Laina asked, with a small grin.

"A few," he said, leaning down to plant a quick kiss on her lips. "You are the only one I want," he whispered.

"You're the only one I want too," she whispered in response.

For the first time in his life, Evan's path had come into complete view all at once. He did not need to wait to see how things worked out. He just knew which way to go. "When we get back from attending the wedding of the King's brother," he said, looking into Laina's sparkling eyes, "I would like for us to plan our own wedding."

A smile spread across Laina's lips, her face glowing from within as it had earlier that week during their picnic by the river, when she had laid joyfully revealed in the sunshine, so innocently open to him.

"Will you marry me, Laina?"

"Yes."

Chapter Twenty-nine

৯১৩୯ୠ

LAIRD GALLOWAY TIPPED HIS CHAIR BACK and sat, arms crossed, scowling at the ceiling in the White Gull Tavern. His soldiers knew better than to try to keep him company, which is why they took up positions around the room at other tables.

Gavin didn't know if he was more angry that a wandering musician with little wealth had captured the heart of the lass that he, himself, favored, or more angry at himself for being so taken with her. There were hundreds of women passing in front of him all the time, after all. He must be getting old and a bit daft to get so attached.

"What'll ye have?" a sultry voice asked at his shoulder.

He looked up into the attractive face of a rather stunning woman, actually, with hair the color of fire falling just below her shoulders, and bright green eyes. Her full red lips stretched into a smile, wrinkling the small mole near the right side of her mouth.

"Something strong, perhaps?" she suggested with a knowing chuckle.

"Whiskey," he answered, staring a hole through her.

She disappeared briefly, then returned with a glass of the tavern's finest whiskey.

The laird watched her movements. She was confident and had the look of someone with intelligence. She looked at him as though she could see below the surface. Far prettier than most of the tavern wenches he had known too. She had all her teeth, and they were white and straight. Her hair was a bit wild — looking as though she hadn't troubled to brush it after being out in the wind — but it rather suited her.

Of course, she must have noticed that he was a laird, but she didn't seem impressed or intimidated by him. That intrigued Gavin immensely.

"You'll get over it you know," she said.

"What?"

"Whatever it is you're brewing on. Things come and things go. That's the way it is." She crossed her arms and smiled at him. "And I wager you always come out on top."

"Is that so?" he said in a husky voice. "What if I don't want to be on top?"

She tilted her head back and laughed, then strolled away.

The laird watched her and smiled as he sat forward and took a drink. The whiskey warmed him and calmed his thoughts. It was only a matter of time, he reasoned, before Laina would tire of Evan's life on the road. And then she would be anxious to return to the safety and comfort of Galloway Castle. Gavin would welcome her. She would be more seasoned and ready for him. Perhaps it was for the best. In the meantime, there would be more than enough women to warm Gavin's bed.

The fire-haired woman hesitated as she passed by his table. "Have you got all you need?" she asked.

"No," he answered, "but I suppose I have enough."

She smiled at him and cocked her head. He was a handsome devil. She'd heard someone say he was Laird Galloway. Very wealthy from the looks of him. But he looked sad and tired.

He smirked. "Have you got me all figured out?"

"I'm still working on it," she boasted, reaching to wipe off a table next to him.

"What would you like to know?" he asked.

She turned to consider him further.

He winked.

Placing her hands on her hips, she swayed playfully. "Well, for starters...what brings Laird Galloway to Westport?"

"A wild goose chase," he answered sourly, taking another drink from his glass.

"Hmm," she said, puckering her lips. "Well then, what's a handsome, rich devil like you chasing a goose around for?"

He laughed and smiled broadly at her. "I don't know," he said. "It makes no sense. I guess we all lose our heads from time to time."

"Isn't that the truth!" she said.

"So, you know my name, how about telling me your's?" Gavin leaned back in his chair, giving her a full look at his strong, masculine body.

"Sienna Wardwyn," she said smoothly, concealing the excited quiver that rose up within her upon the sight and manner of him.

"You're a fiesty lass, Sienna," the laird teased.

"Ah, 'tis only my mouth. It's necessary you know — working in a tavern. If I showed my soft side, I wouldn't have a chance."

The laird snickered. "You have a soft side, do you?"

Sienna rolled her eyes at his suggestive meaning. "Yes, of course. I was raised a good girl. But I've had to fend for myself. You learn what you need to." She nodded for emphasis. "And you don't let anyone know who you really are." She walked to another table to wait on a new customer who had arrived.

"Pity," Gavin muttered. He suddenly felt worse. The tavern wench seemed more in control of her emotions and passions than he was. She had found a way to keep it simple, or so she said. Just keep to herself. She could be lying, but Gavin didn't think so. She appeared to be the kind of person who said what she really thought.

A loud smacking sound was followed by a scream. "You bitch!"

Sienna stormed away from the red-faced man sitting at the table she had just walked over to. A hand print started to appear on his left cheek.

The thin, sun-darkened man that owned the tavern, intercepted Sienna. "What the hell do you think you're doing?" he demanded.

"He grabbed a handful of me," she answered hotly. "You know how I feel about that."

"This is the third time this month you've slapped a customer!" the tavern owner accused.

"Well it's the third time this month someone has grabbed me," Sienna hissed.

Everyone in the tavern was watching the confrontation. The red-faced man at the table rubbed his cheek.

"This is part of your job, Sienna. It doesn't hurt you to let the men have a little fun."

"It is NOT part of my job, you bastard, and how the hell do you know what hurts me?"

Gavin smiled.

"You're fired!" the tavern owner yelled.

"You're an idiot!" Sienna yelled back, before disappearing into a back room.

Gavin laughed out loud, and tipped his drink to finish it. Throwing a coin on the table, he stood up. His soldiers immediately finished their drinks, and stood up as well. At that moment, Sienna reappeared, carrying a small leather bag. From the look on her face, she was clearly wasting no time in leaving.

Gavin reached out and touched her arm lightly as she passed. "Sienna, may I speak with you outside?"

She looked back at him with a slicing gaze, and saw the cool green of his eyes. "Yes, of course," she said, before hurrying on across the room and out the door.

Gavin signaled for his soldiers to wait, then strolled out after her. Several paces away from the building, she stopped and turned around to face him, her hands fisted, but her voice calm.

"Just like I said, things come and things go," she said. She blew a strand of hair out of her face and laughed dryly.

Gavin approached her, towering above her head. "You left very quickly. Doesn't he owe you wages for the time you've worked?"

"He won't give it to me. He still owes me for last week."

"What are you going to do?"

"I don't know." She rubbed the back of her neck and looked toward the watercolor haze of the sea.

The laird stood quietly with her for a moment. Then, clearing his throat, he said, "Well, you could come to Galloway with me. The village has a tavern. For someone with your skills, we could surely find reasonable work."

Sienna turned back and studied him. "Why would you make such an offer to me?"

He couldn't tell if she was suspicious or simply curious. "I like your spirit," he answered. "You seem honest and intelligent."

She raised a finely-shaped eyebrow and licked her lips thoughtfully. "Laird Galloway is offering *me* a job?"

The laird smiled. "He is."

"Will I be serving men who try to grab a feel of me?"

"Most definitely."

"May I slap them?"

"Absolutely."

After another thoughtful glance in the direction of the ocean she spoke again. "Well, I suppose I can give it a try."

Chapter Thirty

IN THE FULL MOON'S LIGHT, the towering white stones glowed brightly against the clear night sky. Their giant forms seemed alive, waiting and watching for those who could hear their message — a message that revealed secrets of power and knowledge.

The moon watched them, and they gazed back. Tall swaying grasses laughed, and the stones chuckled in response. The wind whispered, and the stones responded in deep booming voices. Their wisdom reached beyond the mortal world, to something greater.

Gathered at the base of the stones, mortal hearts thumped with excitement, and the stones pulsed their own thunderous rhythm in return. No separation, except for those who refused to see beyond physical form.

A group of hooded figures dressed in white stood inside the circle of stones, forming a ring, while a small group of onlookers watched from outside.

"What are they doing mama?" a young girl asked, tugging at her mother's sleeve.

"Shhh, we must be quiet," the fair-haired woman answered, putting a finger to her lips.

"But what are they doing?" the girl insisted.

"I don't know yet," her mother whispered. "Be still and let me see."

The summer solstice had returned to the land and it was a special time for the southern territories. Villagers across the land were celebrating their good fortunes. The devastated villages of the previous year had been rebuilt and were thriving with Laird Galloway's generosity and assistance. New trade routes and alliances were bringing new wealth and security to the Galloway territory. The wedding of the king's brother, Edmund, had been a very successful affair, bringing much generosity from the king, himself. It was a time of bounty and gladness.

But there was something more to this ceremony. The woman watched the figures in the circle as her daughter clung to her skirt.

A tall hooded form stood in the center of the stones. An odd, very large hump on his shoulders, caused his head to bend forward. He held up a goblet and spoke in a deep, low voice. The wind muffled the sounds, so that the onlookers could not make out his words. He turned to the four directions, as the others in the circle chanted softly. When he turned in the direction of the onlookers, the woman could see that he was very old.

Turning away again, he placed the chalice on the low stone platform in the center of the circle. Then, one by one, the other hooded figures stepped forward and placed herbs and plants as offerings on the stone.

"They're celebrating life..." the mother whispered to her daughter. "The old one, in the center, appears to be the leader."

After all the offerings had been given, the tall hunched man turned to a smaller figure in the circle and extended his hand. The smaller figure stepped forward, white robe rippling in the wind. A strange jingling sound filled the air, as if hundreds of bells were ringing.

"Do you hear that, Missy?" the mother nervously asked her little girl.

"Hear what, Mama?"

The mother looked around at the people gathered nearby, to see if they seemed to hear the sound. No one was reacting. A tall, handsome man standing off to the left, however, was smiling broadly, his blonde hair reflecting the moonlight.

The mother returned her gaze to the circle, and relaxed as the jingling sound faded. The smaller hooded figure in the center of the circle suddenly made a joyful sound...laughter. With slender hands, the figure reached up and pushed back her hood. The moonlight illuminated Laina's radiant face. Her dark hair fell forward from the confines of the hood, and cascaded down over her shoulders to her waist. Raising her arms to the sky, she chanted softly with the elder man in the center.

From his place near the back of the onlooker's group, Evan's eyes softened at the sight of her, and at the brief glint of moonlight that reflected off the gold band on her finger.

"Who is that?" the little girl asked, watching Laina intently.

"I don't know," her mother said, "but it appears that the

offerings are for her."

Standing inside the circle, Laina's dark hair danced magically around her in the wind. With her arms raised, and her face turned to the sky, she breathed deeply of the clear night air. Her rippling robe suddenly blew back and open, revealing a shimmering white dress beneath, flowing down and over her belly — as full and round as the moon, itself.

THE END

ℰ♋

About the author:

Having enjoyed an award-winning career in writing for technology companies, Sycamore Wilde is now exploring her passion for writing medieval romance. Intrigued with medieval life for many years, Ms. Wilde is using this setting as the backdrop for creating adventurous, fun, spicy tales with twists that aim to keep the story lively and delight the reader with the unfolding. Sycamore Wilde lives in the woods with her dwarf goats, chickens, dogs, and cats. She also hosts a small medieval gathering twice a year.

10814790R00133

Made in the USA
Charleston, SC
06 January 2012